# HATE TURNS TO LOVE

*And then he was leaning toward her, close, closer, until his lips touched hers, soft at first, feather-light, his breath fanning her face. She moved toward him, and pressed her hands against his chest. He tasted the salt of her tears, traced her lips with his tongue. It only made him want more. She was strength and softness, light and dark. He reached for her, eased her against his body. More.*

# A FAMILY AFFAIR

## Mary Campisi

Jocelyn Hollow Romance

*A Family Affair* by Mary Campisi

© 2006 Mary Campisi
Published by Jocelyn Hollow Romance

For information on Jocelyn Hollow Romance books,
call 615/256-8484.

ISBN 1-933725-52-4


Design by Armour&Armour
armour-armour.com

First Edition 2006
1 2 3 4 5 6 7 8 9 10

To my children,
Danielle, Nicole, and Alexis,
and my stepchildren, T.J. and Laura—
for all you are today and
all you will become . . .

# Prologue

H E SAT IN THE dark, staring at the slit of moon illuminating the small of her back. She was asleep, the slow, methodical rise and fall of the chenille spread taking her dreams away from him, safe, protected, while he hung caught between sleep and wakefulness, dark and light, too afraid to close his eyes lest he miss these last few hours with her. It was always like this, the dread mixing with the longing, pulling at him, shredding his sanity.

Perhaps, this month, he'd find the strength, merge past with present. He fell back against the soft cushion of the wing-backed chair, closed his eyes. Perhaps this month....

# 1

CHRISTINE BLACKSWORTH scanned THE jagged red and black lines on the computer screen, one crossing over the other, peaking, sliding back, inching forward again. She glanced at her watch. It would take at least fifteen minutes to run comparisons, ten more to analyze them, and another five to make recommendations. If she started right now, she'd be done in half an hour ... the twenty-minute drive would put her at her parents' house around 7:25 P.M. Twenty-five minutes late for her father's welcome home dinner.

Unacceptable. Her mother planned these gatherings with such precision that walking in even ten minutes late would upset the entire evening, not to mention what it would do to Gloria Blacksworth's emotional state. Christine rubbed the back of her neck. Twenty-seven should be old enough to just pick up the phone and tell her mother she'd be late, or not be there at all. She'd tried that once a year and a half ago when she and Connor opted for the theater instead of a family dinner. What a disaster that had been.

It was time to go. She dimmed the computer screen, gathered up her papers, and placed them in a folder to the side of her desk. Uncle Harry was probably already there, draining his first scotch and antagonizing her mother. They tolerated one another for her father's sake. He insisted that Harry attend, though after the initial pleasantries and somewhere part way through dinner, the conversation usually turned to business, which left Uncle Harry and her mother staring at their wine glasses. Christine promised herself every month that she would try harder to include them, perhaps inquire about Uncle Harry's latest golf game, or her mother's garden club meeting—anything to avoid business, at least until coffee was served. But the pulse of the Dow was in her blood, surging up and down; the need to connect with her father emerging past *hello* and *isn't this Veal Oscar fabulous?*

She understood the necessity of her father's monthly trips to the Catskills. The success of any great executive was down-time, and Charles Blacksworth, CEO of Blacksworth and Company Investments, had found his own piece of Nirvana seven hundred miles from Chicago in a tiny cabin just outside the Catskill Mountains.

And he deserved it.


"DIDN'T ANYONE EVER teach you that overwork is one of the great sins, Chrissie girl? Especially on a Sunday?"

Christine tipped her glass of chardonnay at her uncle, smiled. "I think it was you, Uncle Harry."

He let out a loud laugh, downed the rest of his scotch. "No, girl, I would have said *work* on any day is a sin." He winked and headed toward the liquor cabinet. He was a handsome man, tall, tan from hours on the back nine and frequent jaunts to Bermuda or St. Croix with his latest intrigue. Just shy of fifty, he was more fit than many of the men Christine knew, perhaps from the daily trips to the gym or perhaps because Uncle Harry *worked* at staying in shape and it was the only type of *work* he engaged in.

While other men were carving out their careers, striving for betterment in wealth, recognition, and fatter portfolios, Uncle Harry closeted himself in his office on the sixteenth floor practicing his putt, reading *Golf Digest*, and managing one solitary account, his own.

Christine saw the way other people watched him when he came to her office, their eyes moving over him, taking in the Armani suit, the silk tie, the

Italian loafers, and then discarding him as though he were the morning courier come to pick up FedEx packages. They laughed at the crude, off-color jokes he told them every morning at the coffee station and then moved past him, to their offices, to their work.

"I'm getting worried about your father," her mother said, picking up a linen napkin, folding it just so, setting it back down. "He should have been here by now." She moved to another napkin, picked it up.

"Maybe his plane was delayed. You know how flying on the east coast is in January: one minute you're boarding the plane, thinking about getting home in time to watch your favorite TV show, and the next, you're stuck in your seat for two hours while they de-ice."

"It isn't raining or snowing outside."

Christine shrugged as she watched her mother pinch a droopy leaf from a poinsettia. "He'll be here, Mother."

"He'll be here, Gloria," Uncle Harry said, swirling the ice in his drink. "Do you think he'd miss an opportunity to get back here to his lovely wife?"

She didn't answer, merely pinched another leaf and then another. She looked beautiful tonight in her beige dress, but then she always looked beautiful, so tiny and delicate, like a porcelain doll that's been constructed with the utmost care. Christine had always felt awkward next to her, graceless, like a colt that can't quite find its legs. Even now, as a grown woman, attractive in her own right, she couldn't match the ethereal beauty of her mother.

"I say we start without Charlie," Uncle Harry said, his deep voice filling the room. "Damn sorry luck if he misses out on the lamb."

Christine glanced at her mother, who was picking at specks of glitter that had fallen from the petals of the red poinsettia onto the white linen tablecloth. "Mother? What do you think? It's almost seven-thirty. I could try his cell phone again."

Gloria pressed her forefinger against the cloth, her gaze on the glitter stuck to her skin. "If we don't eat now, the lamb will be ruined," she said, her lips tight, the muscles around her mouth strained. Then, in a low voice, "He knows dinner's at seven . . . he knows."

The highlight of her week had been to create the perfect meal in the perfect atmosphere, only to find out that the guest of honor had not arrived. It was amazing enough that her mother still carried on this ritual for him, after all these years of marriage, or that he took great pains to accommodate her wish: to be where he said he'd be, when he said he'd be there, at least most of the time. Several of Christine's friends had parents who were alone, whether by choice or divine intervention, and even those who still shared a name didn't often share a bed or a relationship.

"Sit, sit," her mother said in a loud, bright voice. "Harry, pour the wine, will you?"

He eyed her a moment, opened his mouth to speak, closed it. "Wine for three, coming up." He picked up a glass and poured.

"He'll be here, Mother. You know he will."

"I know that, Christine." She picked up her wine glass and took a healthy swallow. Her face flushed to a pale rose. "Would you please tell Greta to serve the salad?" There was something sad and disappointed tucked away under the smile, beneath the serene calmness of her poised exterior as she spoke.

"Sure." Christine headed for the kitchen and the radicchio salad. Next month would be different; she'd make sure her father showed up an hour early with a dozen red roses and a bottle of Chanel No. 5.

That would make her mother smile, make her forget all about tonight.


HOW MANY TIMES DID he have to tell her that he didn't like all this crap in his salad? Iceberg lettuce, that was it, with tomato, cucumber, and a little bit of red onion. Period. Was it that damn hard to remember? So what if iceberg had no "nutritional value," if the real nutrients were in the darker greens, like romaine or Boston, or this radicchio shit? He didn't like the stuff, didn't like the looks of it, the feel of it, the taste of it. If he were a goddamn rabbit, then he'd eat it, but he wasn't. Harry pushed a raspberry to the side of his plate. And what was with fruit stuck in the middle of a salad? Who the hell thought of that? Armand, at The Presidio, was the only one who didn't try to get fancy, who didn't put mesculin mix or dandelions, or raspberries, in his salad, for chrissake.

Gloria was so hopped up she probably didn't know what she was telling Greta to put in the salad. Next she'd be sprinkling Crown Royal on top. And he didn't buy that bullshit about her constant pain. She'd fallen off that damn horse sixteen years ago, and, broken back or not, she should have enough dope and booze running through her veins to make her numb.

Harry laid down his fork, took a drink. He'd need two more scotches just to block out the pathetic look on her face. So what if Charlie was late? Maybe he was holed up in some hotel room banging some young piece of ass and forgot about the time. He almost laughed aloud. That would really make Gloria cry.

But Charlie was too straight for that kind of behavior. That was Harry's style. Given the opportunity, he'd be the one shacked up in a hotel room, screwing some young piece of ass, wife or not.

And that's why there wasn't a wife, why there would never be a wife.

Just thinking about screwing made him hard. Bridgett was only a phone call away: six feet, blonde, blue-eyed. Twenty-three, great tongue. *Shit.* Why was he sitting here with a hard-on when he could be banging Bridgett?

He knew why. Christine and Charlie. They counted on him being here for this circus for one night every month, and he wasn't going to disappoint them, even if he had to put up with Gloria.

One night a month. No one ever depended on him for anything, not his work, not his women, not even his cleaning lady who demanded he pay her at the beginning of the month because he kept forgetting the weekly checks. Maybe they thought him incapable, uncooperative, or merely uninterested.

And maybe they were right.

The phone rang in the background. It was probably Charlie, trying to pave the way for his late entrance. Good old diplomatic Charlie.

"That might be Dad." Christine half-rose from her chair.

"Sit down," Harry waved a hand at her, stood. "I'll go see." He grabbed his drink, let out a small laugh. "I have to warn him to put his boots on before he comes in here, or your mother's tears will ruin his shoes."

He swung open the kitchen door, and Greta held out the phone to him. She was a pretty thing, close to forty, divorced, two kids. He'd thought about banging her when he first met her a year ago, unwinding that long, blonde bun and wrapping it around his fist while he pumped into her, but he'd quickly dismissed the idea—too much baggage, and he liked her, which didn't make for a quick, mindless screw.

"Mr. Blacksworth, it's a man, for Christine," Greta said.

He laughed, momentarily distracted by Greta's accent. He liked the way she said his name, all throaty and ruffled, like she'd just crawled out of bed, naked, of course.

"Mr. Blacksworth. It's a man—"

"I know, I heard. So? Christine's twenty-seven years old, she can talk to men."

Greta shook her head, the thick bun swaying from side to side, making him think of hips and sex. "He says it's about Mr. Blacksworth."

That jolted him. "I'll take it." He snatched the phone from her hand. "This is Harry Blacksworth. You're calling about my brother?"

There was a second's hesitation, then a deep voice filled the line. "There's been an accident . . . your brother—"

"What kind of accident? Is he all right? Where is he?"

The other man went on, "... was driving on the back roads, and it was snowing ... hard ... Jesus, I'm sorry."

"What?" Harry gripped the phone. "What the fuck happened?"

"Uncle Harry?" Christine stood inside the kitchen door. "What's the matter? Is it Dad?"

Harry covered the receiver with his hand. "It's for me. You go back and keep your mother occupied, Chrissie. I'll be there in a minute." She hesitated, then turned and left.

"Hold on," Harry said into the receiver. He went out the back door, down the steps, and onto the patio, mindless of the cold. "Now tell me where the fuck my brother is."

"There was an accident."

"Jesus, I already heard that."

"His car hit a guardrail and flipped over an embankment."

*Jesus God.* Harry's head started pounding, splitting down the middle.

"It took three hours to get him out ..."

"Where ..." Harry tried to push the rest of the words out, stalled, tried again, "where is he?"

"He's dead."

The words burst into his head, sucked out the oxygen, making him dizzy and nauseated. "Who the *fuck* are you?" Harry sank into a patio chair, gulped in clumps of cold air. "And where's my brother?"

There was a long pause on the other end of the line, so long that for a second he thought the man might have hung up. "He's dead. He was driving on Sentinel Road in Magdalena when he lost control of his car, hit a guardrail, and flipped over an embankment."

"It can't be." A speck of hope crept into his soul. "Magdalena's almost a hundred miles from Charlie's cabin. You've got the wrong guy."

"It's him. I know . . . knew Charles Blacksworth." The man paused. "I'll make the arrangements to have him sent back as soon as possible."

The salad pushed its way up Harry's throat. How could it be Charlie? Charlie was too careful, too exact; he didn't make mistakes, especially not the kind that got him killed. This asshole was wrong. Charlie would be here any minute, just a little late, flight delay.

"I'm sorry."

"It's not Charlie."

"Your brother's dead."

How could he sound so certain? "Where is he? Where's this person who's supposed to be Charlie? What hospital?" He had to see for himself.

"Don't come. I'll take care of everything. It'll be easier on everybody if I just handle it."

*"Who the fuck are you?"*

"Nate Desantro. My mother was with your brother when he died."

The puke came then, green bits of salad and Chardonnay spewing on his trousers, his Italian loafers, the snow at his feet and two yards beyond. The heaving and gasping covered him in sweat as new snow fell, and his stomach clenched in exhaustive spasms, purging until there was nothing left but emptiness.

# 2

SIX DAYS HAD PASSED since Uncle Harry changed their lives. *Dear God, he's dead.* The rest of the night unfolded in an underwater blur, eyes open, mouths moving but not speaking, hearing nothing. Her mother fell forward, clasping her hands against her forehead, a flower wilting inch by incredible inch. Uncle Harry talked and drank, talked and drank, but it was hard to concentrate on what he said; the underwater currents blocked everything, sound, sight, feeling, certainly understanding.

Christine remembered little of that night other than the smear of life and loss pulling her under, sinking her soul, and the sight of her mother crumpled in a chair with Uncle Harry and his glass of Johnny Walker Red. *A man called*, he'd said, . . . *from the hospital. Charlie was in an accident, his car flipped . . . nothing anyone could do. They're sending him home.*

Sixty seconds and a handful of sentences was all it took to change their lives in horrible, drastic ways they could never have imagined. Her father had taken this trip for years, even in snowstorms gusting ice and hail, and always, always came back. She'd never expected to kiss him goodbye one afternoon seven months shy of his fifty-ninth birthday and never see him again.

A tiny speck of hope still clung to the possibility that the man in the accident wasn't her father, that by some grand, bizarre confusion, it was another man, maybe a thief who'd stolen her father's wallet, knocked him unconscious, and left him along a deserted road, then took his car, too.

But when the funeral director contacted them to say the body had arrived, she went with Uncle Harry, praying for a mistake, a miracle, anything. But even at the entrance of the room, some thirty feet away, she recognized the straight nose, the silver-gray hair, the high cheekbones.

Her father was dead.

Her mother refused to see him that first day, spent most of her time sequestered in the master bedroom, coming out only once when Doctor Leone brought over a bottle of pills for her. Valium. *Your mother will need these*, he'd said. *This is going to be very difficult for her*. He was right, of course. She'd depended on her husband to keep life even, and her daily dose of Vicodin to keep her arthritic back under control.

*Now what?* Christine rubbed her temples, trying to ease the dull ache in her head. She could step in, take care of money matters and the daily inconveniences that always seemed to overwhelm and upset her mother. But what about the rest?

No one could replace Charles Blacksworth.

He was the one person she could count on for honesty and direction. Hadn't she carried the sealed letter from Wharton around in her briefcase four days, waiting for his return so he could share the joy or torment of its contents? Wasn't he the one who helped her shop for a condo and then fought the real estate company when it tried to renegotiate the terms?

And how could she ever forget the day he promoted her to vice president? They'd been eating chicken burritos at El Charro's when he reached in his pocket and pulled out a single key, the one to the large corner office next to his. The reception six days later was a lavish, formal affair, with two roomfuls of colleagues and friends in attendance, but it could not compare to the afternoon in the corner booth of that dark Mexican restaurant.

*I'm so proud of you, Christine.*

*Thanks, Dad. That means a lot to me.*

*You remind me of myself at your age.*

*I'm only doing what you taught me.*

*And you do it very well.*

*I'm going after Granddad's pocket watch next.*

*It's only a watch, Christine.*

*We both know that's not true, Dad. It's so much more than a watch.*

*And it's caused more harm than good in this family. I'd just as soon toss it out.*

*In that case, I'll take it now.*

*Your grandfather meant well, but he rewarded the wrong things. I earned it because I practically lived at the office. Is that what you want?*

*I want to be the best, Dad, like you.*

*You are the best, Christine, right now, just the way you are, and no father could ever be prouder than I am of you.*

And now he was gone, and she was sitting across from Thurman Jacobs's gigantic cherry desk with Uncle Harry squeezed into a Queen Anne wing chair next to her. Thurman Jacobs had gone to M.I.T. with her father, then on to Georgetown before joining his father at Jacobs and Jacobs, one of the most prestigious law firms in Chicago. The firm handled all of the legal issues for Blacksworth and Company, and Thurman himself took care of her father's personal matters, including his will.

It was the matter of the will that brought them to see Thurman this afternoon. She'd hoped to hold off at least another week before dealing with the business side of her father's death. Who cared how many stocks and bonds he'd had, how many unit trusts, the value of his investment property? *Who cared?* None of it would bring him back; most of it would just be a brutal reminder of his death. *Death.* A horrible word. But Uncle Harry had insisted. *It's best to get it over quickly, deal with it straight up.* It was an odd piece of advice from someone like Uncle Harry.

She'd come, though, to appease him and immerse herself in the emotionless distribution of assets, anything to stop thinking about her father's face, pale and wax-like against the satin lining of the ebony coffin.

Thurman Jacobs entered through a side door, his tall, lean frame slightly stooped, like a sapling whose trunk isn't sturdy enough to hold it erect. His gray suit hung from his shoulders, the excess material drooping at the sides. He was bald on top with a trim edge of dusty brown rimming the sides and back of his skull. The round wire frames he wore made his nose seem a bit too long, his face too narrow, and that, coupled with his gangly, bent stature, gave him an Ichabod Crane appearance. At fifty-eight, he looked a full ten years older, yet when he spoke, the rich timbre of his voice blurred the outward visage, and the listener forgot about the awkward homeliness encasing the man, forgot the stooped shoulders, the too-long nose, forgot everything but the pure eloquence spilling from Thurman Jacobs's thin lips.

"Christine, Harry." He held out his hands to them from across his desk, bony hands traced with thin blue veins. "Thank you for coming so quickly." He eased his hands away, took a seat behind the massive cherry desk, and opened a black portfolio. "Christine, your father and I went back a good many years"—he bestowed a sympathetic smile on her—"since our days at M.I.T. I wasn't just his attorney, I was his friend." He cleared his throat, and, when he spoke again, the richness of his voice filled the room. "Which makes this whole situation that much more difficult."

"Thank you, Thurman. I know my father held you in very high regard."

"Yes," he nodded, rubbing his right eye under his spectacles, "and I him. We had an understanding, Charles and I, one that went well beyond business." He flipped open the black portfolio, pulled out a thick document, leafed through several pages. He rubbed his eye again, coughed, shifted in his chair. "Christine, I wish there was some way to say this, some way to prepare you ..."

"Thurman, she's a big girl. Just say it." Harry reached over, grabbed her hand.

Thurman Jacobs cleared his throat again, tugged at his shirt collar, his skinny neck inching out like a chicken. "The estate's been apportioned into an equitable distribution: one part, including assets, real and otherwise, to you, one part to your mother," he paused, "and one part to a third party."

"A third party? Who, Thurman? M.I.T.?"

"No, it wasn't M.I.T." His voice turned quiet, unfamiliar.

"What then? Or who? Maybe it's you, Uncle Harry."

"It isn't Harry." Thurman's strong voice deflated, the air spilling out in one long, slow whoosh.

Uncle Harry squeezed her hand tight, but his gaze remained on Thurman. "Just tell us, so we can be done and get the hell out of here."

Thurman's thin lips moved with effort. "One part has been left to a Ms. Lily Desantro."

The words were out, forming a complete sentence, and yet they made no sense. Who was Lily Desantro? Christine didn't even know anyone named Lily. The pressure from Uncle Harry's fingers dug into her flesh. She stared at their hands, locked together; her nails pressed into his tanned skin, leaving small, red moons on the back of his hand.

"Jesus," Uncle Harry swore under his breath, "What the hell was he thinking?"

Christine dragged her eyes from Uncle Harry's

marked skin to the man behind the desk. "Thurman? Who's Lily Desantro?"

Thurman Jacobs was a man possessed of great eloquence, the one chosen by colleagues and corporations to represent, to present, to speak, about matters great and small, at conventions and rotary club dinners. And yet now he sat staring at Christine, speechless, his bony fingers rubbing the sides of his protruding temples.

"Thurman?"

"Lily Desantro." The name fell out between half-closed lips as though he struggled between duty to tell, loyalty not to.

"I don't . . . understand."

"Do you have an address?" This from Uncle Harry.

Thurman Jacobs picked up a pen, scribbled something on a piece of paper, and held it out. Harry snatched it from him. "Thanks." Then he stood up, still clutching Christine's hand. "Come on, kid, let's go."


THE WHOLE WORLD WAS one great big screw-up. Harry sat in the lounge at the Ritz, waiting for Christine to come out of the restroom. He'd decided to bring her here for a drink before he told her the truth. Actually, he was the one who needed the drink, several, to give him the guts to carry it out.

Why couldn't people just be who they were, womanizers, drinkers, liars, manipulators, instead of pretending around it all, hiding the secrets like dirty laundry stuffed under a bed, and then dying, so the grieving got whammed with two losses, the flesh and blood bodies and the images they *thought* they knew.

Charlie should have told him he had something on the side. Harry would have understood; Gloria was a pathetic piece of flesh and bone, a real martyr, served up super-size. How much pain and self-pity should a man have to take? Charlie should've gotten rid of her years ago. So what if she was Christine's mother? No woman would've pulled that clinging crap on Harry. He'd never get married. Marriage was nothing but a primitive form of torture, women strapping their hands around a guy's balls and yanking. Move too far to the left, *yank*, one extra step to the right, *yank*. Breathe too hard, *yank*, not hard enough, *yank*, breathe at all, *yank, yank, yank!*

So, what was he going to tell Christine? He didn't like being left to clean up messes; he wasn't good at them. Creating the mess, now that was his specialty; trash it and duck out, move on to the next catastrophe. Nobody ever expected him to stay around, and certainly not to figure a way out of something like this. Hell, no. But Christine was the one decent human being in this screwed-up world. Should he lie and buy a little time, maybe make her think this Desantro woman was some do-gooder out to save the world or some other bullshit?

"Uncle Harry?" Christine slid into the booth beside him. "Are you all right?"

"Just thinking." He eyed the drinks on the table. "I must be thinking way too hard if I didn't see the waitress bring these drinks." He let out a halfhearted laugh, picked up his scotch, and swallowed.

Christine sipped at her wine. "Uncle Harry, what's going on?"

"It's tough, Chrissie." He stared at the scotch in his glass. Three more of these should do it, mellow him out enough to get the words out.

"Uncle Harry, who's Lily Desantro?"

Harry polished off his drink and set it down. "The first time I heard the Desantro name was the night your father died. The phone call." *Shit*, he did not want to do this. "Remember that? There was a man on the phone, he was the one who told me about Charlie, said he hit a guard rail and flipped over." He didn't mention the part about its taking three hours to pry Charlie from the car. "Anyway, this guy said not to come, he'd have the body sent home. I asked him who the hell he was, and that's when he told me about the woman, said she was in the car with Charlie." He paused, pinched the bridge of his nose. "She was his mother."

"Is she alive?"

Harry shrugged. "I don't know. I guess so. He didn't say she died, but I didn't ask."

"So, this woman, what exactly was she to Dad?"

This was the part he'd wanted to avoid, the uncertain, almost fearful look on her face, speckled with the tiniest glimmer of knowing. People played games with themselves all the time, asked questions for answers they already knew deep in their gut, yet couldn't admit, or didn't want to admit. He saw it every day, with his married friends who bought their wives bracelets and two-carat rings stuffed with diamonds and rubies. All signs of romance, love, affection, devotion, whatever in the hell you wanted to call it, and yet, it wasn't that at all, it was duty, and ninety-eight percent of the women had picked out the piece, designed it, ordered it, and *then* told their husbands where to pick it up. *Happy fucking Anniversary.* These same men followed every piece of ass, every short skirt, tight shirt, screwing them with their eyes, sometimes with their dicks, but if you asked any one of them if they loved their wives, they'd say of course, not even a second's hesitation, which always told Harry they were lying and they knew it. That was the knowing part. They knew whatever love they'd felt in the marriage had been reduced to trips to Tiffany's and their Gold Card, and if they had found something on the side, they knew, too, that it would stay right there, on the side, because they weren't giving up their homes, their country club memberships, their right to see their kids every night, their 401(k)s . . . their life. They weren't giving up their life, and yet none of them realized they'd already done just that.

It was pretty sad that he could see this when none of the others could. His women were the same way, all thinking they'd change him, love him so much that he'd want a wife, a family, a child . . . an SUV, for chrissakes. And then came the mothering. That's when they had to go.

And now Christine was staring at him, not wanting to believe what her gut must be telling her. *Shit.* He reached for another scotch, swallowed, let the burn fill his throat, consume his lungs.

"You know, this is really hard, Chrissie, especially for me."

"That's why I'm asking you, Uncle Harry. You're the only one who'll tell me the truth."

She was relying on him for the truth. Now that was just damn sad. "If I were a betting man, and I've been known to be that in my lifetime," he said, covering her hands with his own, "I'd say your father was . . . involved with this Lily Desantro."

"You mean an affair?"

*Christ.* "Looks that way. Charlie loved you, Chrissie. This has nothing to do with you."

"And my mother?" Her voice wobbled. "Did he love her?"

"I'm not the one to ask; you know that."

"Is that where he was going every month? To see *her*?"

*Jesus.* "I don't know."

"Well, I'm going to find out."

"Chrissie, let it go. It's over. Charlie's dead. Finding out isn't going to bring him back."

"I need to know."

"Sometimes it's better not to know. Nothing can change what is or what happened, and digging around in the past is only going to make you miserable."

Her eyes were bright, shiny. "I don't care. I have to know."

Harry shook his head, reached for his drink. "Remember Pandora's Box? This is the same thing. Don't open it."

"How can you expect me to forget what you just told me?"

"I said she *probably* was."

She threw him a disgusted look. "Uncle Harry, I'm not twelve years old. I know that she was his mistress."

Harry shrugged, took another drink.

"And knowing that changes everything."

"It doesn't change the fact that he loved you."

"But everything he told me, about honor and integrity, was it all a lie?"

"Of course not."

"And this woman, who was she? What kind of woman could make him leave his family to be with her?" She didn't wait for him to answer. "I can't live my life with this lie. I have to find out."

"So what do you plan to do, just pack up and take off on an excursion? Close up shop? Charlie wouldn't like that."

"Phil's a perfectly capable CEO. He'll be fine with me leaving for a week or two. Besides, no one expects me back in the office so soon after the funeral."

"And your mother?" This would send Gloria over the edge. She'd be popping those Vicodin like Sweet Tarts.

"This would kill her."

"She doesn't have to find out."

"She *can't* find out." She rubbed her temples. "She just can't."

"Relax. She won't."

"Uncle Harry, you have to help me. We'll say I went to clean out Dad's place in the Catskills, which is part true, and I'm taking care of a business deal he started up there, which is also part true."

"What business deal?"

"A few months ago, he told me he put up the

collateral for some machine shop. I guess the guy was having a tough time making his payments, and Dad was going to help him out, set up some alternate financing or something, and he wanted me to get involved. I could check that out while I'm up there."

"Chrissie, we don't even know if this Desantro woman is still alive. She could've been killed with your father." Jesus, why couldn't she just let it go? The most she could hope to gain was a piece of the truth and that would end up haunting her for the rest of her life. He should know; thirty-two years ago he'd begged for the truth, and it had almost destroyed him.

"I have to know. Don't you see that, Uncle Harry?"

The damn, sad fact was that he did see. He knew exactly how she felt, how she needed to search out the truth so she could understand the pieces of her life that no longer made sense.

"I think you're making a mistake."

"I have to know."

"And if what you find out is worse than not knowing? Then what?" He felt it all rushing back, the words, the lies, the pain. "Then you've got a face, a voice that will haunt you for the rest of your life, Chrissie. It could fuckin' destroy you."

"I know. But if I'm going to end up hating the

man I loved most in the world, then I want everything about that woman, her face, her voice, the color of her fingernails, embedded in my brain, so every time I think of my father, every time I wonder why I can't forgive him, I'll think of her, and I'll know I have a *reason* to hate him."

# 3

"SO WHY, EXACTLY, ARE you going away?"
Christine folded another sweater, a tan cashmere, zip in the back, and placed it in the open suitcase on her bed. "Connor, I told you. I'm going to the
Catskills to close up my father's place." She turned
away so he wouldn't see her face, not that Connor
had ever been able to detect anything she hadn't
wanted him to. When she'd called him the night her
father died and he offered to come over, she told him
no, it was late, and he had to get up early; he'd left it
at that, hadn't insisted on coming, or better, hadn't
just showed up on her doorstep, pulled her into his
arms, and held her the way she'd needed him to.

"I don't get it," he said, crossing his arms under
his head and stretching his long body on the bed. "I
guess I just don't get this whole trip thing. Why'd he
go there every month, anyway?"

*To see Lily Desantro, that's why.* "It was his way of
relaxing, I guess." She pulled another sweater from

her drawer, black angora, tiny pearls. "An escape from the pressure of his job." *An escape to another woman.*

"Couldn't he just go to the health club? Or play a round of golf?"

"I don't know, Connor. I don't know why he had to go there. He just did."

"Okay, don't get all testy." He smiled at her, white on white against his tanned skin. "Just trying to figure it out, that's all." Connor James Pendleton, age thirty-two, fourth generation graduate of Princeton and heir to Pendleton Securities, Inc. The Pendletons believed in the stock market, Ivy League educations, and first class. Christine and Connor had been together almost two years, had sunbathed side by side in Hawaii, snorkled in Cancun, skied in Aspen, and taken the Concorde to London—twice. With Connor, it was only the best, always: the hotels, the restaurants, the theaters, the people. The only part that lacked was their relationship. It was third-rate, maybe less, and no matter how she tried to dress it up, with pearls or diamonds or a package deal to Trinidad, it was still just that, third-rate.

Being with Connor was like investing in blue chip stocks; they might be a safe bet and look good in a portfolio, but they'd never give you the ride a tech stock would. Weeks could pass without making love, and it didn't seem to bother him; in fact, he didn't seem to notice. But then, neither did she. That wasn't exactly true; she *did* notice, it just didn't bother her. *How sad was that?* Some days, she'd catch herself listening to her assistant, Elena, talk to her husband about inconsequential things like what would he like for dinner, and could he pick their daughter up at daycare. It wasn't what Elena said, but how she said it, soft, caring. Christine had tried that once with Connor, called him for no reason just to chat and tell him she was thinking about him. He'd put her on hold, just for a minute so he could talk to Tokyo, and five minutes later Bette, his secretary, came on the line and told her Connor would be tied up longer than expected, "closing a deal, you know," and then asked if there was a message. There was no message, none that he would understand, anyway.

People expected them to get married—her mother, Connor's parents, everyone who saw them together. *You make a beautiful couple,* her mother had told her. *You with your fair skin and black hair and Connor with his classic good looks, everyone notices the two of you.* Connor's father was more straightforward: *Great gene pool, can't wait to see the kids.* Her own father had been polite with Connor but there'd been no "join our family" sentiment in his words or his behavior and certainly no references to extending the family with Connor's gene pool.

"Christine? Are you listening? Do you think you'll be back on the twenty-third? I have to go to New York, and I thought you might want to go with me, do a little business, take in a show."

"I don't know." Perhaps, deep down, her father's lack of acceptance had kept her from committing to Connor.

"I know how you love the city." He paused, smiled at her. "Besides, I'm meeting with Niles Furband, and I was hoping you could work your magic on him again."

"All I did was talk to the man, for heaven's sake."

"That's just it, Christine. You talked to the *man*. Nobody talks to Niles Furband, the man. They talk to Niles Furband, CEO of Glen Systems, or Niles Furband, heir to the Furband fortune, or Niles Furband, chairman of the board of St. Catherine's Hospital. They ask his opinion on variable loans in the current market and leveraged buy-outs, or how many zeros they can add to whatever donation they're seeking. Or, and Jesus, this is so lame, the names of his kids, as if they cared."

"I cared."

"That's my point. You cared. The rest of them are just blowing smoke."

She tucked several pairs of underwear into the side pocket of her suitcase. "Like you, maybe? Bring me along so you seem more credible when you hold out *your* hand?"

He did have the good grace to turn a very dull shade of red. "I've got a good deal for him. It's not bullshit."

"Are you asking me to go to New York to spend time with you, or are you asking me to go to set up a deal for you?"

"I want to be with you." He sat up, reached for her hand, stroked her thumb. "You love New York. I just thought," he paused, squeezed the soft flesh of her palm, "... this could be a huge deal. You have no idea how big." The stroking started up again, then the white smile. "Just think about it, okay?"

"I'll see." She stood there—the touch of his fingers on her skin, the steady movement brushing back and forth, slow, methodical—and felt nothing.

CHRISTINE LOADED THE BMW the next morning at 6:15 A.M. and began the long haul to the cabin in the Catskills. Snow pelted the windshield in thick, wet chunks as she maneuvered through the dark, untamed landscape before her. How many more miles until she reached his cabin? His other home. Was this where he took *her*? Was this where they shared a glass of wine, a meal ... a bed?

Images rolled over her, seeping from her brain

into every part of her body, organ, tissue, cell. What did she look like? Young? Oh, God, please not someone Christine's own age, or worse, younger. Older? How much older? How had they met? Did she know he had a wife and daughter? *Another life that had nothing to do with her?*

The guessing drove her mad. She'd know soon enough, and then she'd probably wish she didn't, because once she saw with her own eyes, heard with her own ears, the image and the sound would imbed itself in her memory, and nothing, no amount of denial or drugs or therapy would erase it. But still, she had to know.

She'd spent hours trying to imagine the confrontation. Faces, inflections in speech, odd little nuances, even something as unassuming as educational background or socio-economic condition could help determine what should be said, and how. Yet all she knew about this woman was her name.

Hadn't her father ever thought about what might happen if his family found out? Had he been so consumed with love, desire, *lust*, that it hadn't occurred to him, or if it had, was the longing so overpowering that he discarded the needs of his family? She hated this faceless woman. As for her father, his lies had turned her whole life on its axis, and it would take time to sort out truth from lie, love from hate.

She stopped only twice during the trip, once to refuel and grab a bag of pretzels and a Coke, and the second time to use the restroom and buy a large, black coffee. Hours and miles fell behind her in a white haze of nameless highway, her brain consumed with her destination, filled with both anxiety and dread. By early afternoon she'd reached the New York state line, and, when dusk seeped down from the mountains, she knew she was in the Catskills. The cabin was located on the outskirts, in Tristan, a tiny dot on the map, smaller than the head of a straight pin, and if she'd calculated correctly, about eighty miles from Magdalena, Lily Desantro's home.

The road that led to the cabin was little more than a single lane, covered with snow and dipping off at the edges, no guard rails or posts to guide or protect. What if she slid off to the right, over the embankment, rolled the car? No one would find her for days. She gripped the wheel tighter, inched toward the middle of the road. There were trees all around, thick, ominous, pushing her along the slick road, forcing the BMW through a vortex of dense brush and overhang.

She slowed to a crawl. The snow had started again, huge, wet splotches beating the windshield. Christine rounded another bend, spotted a mailbox off to the right, draped in white. The driveway lay tucked between a copse of evergreens, and she passed by it, then had to back up to find the turn-off. The cabin stood straight ahead, a small log structure surrounded by evergreens and thick-waisted, naked trees whose coverings had long since fallen. Snow lay in pure, scalloped drifts along the perimeter of the cabin, edging its way to the front door.

Christine shifted the car into park, fished the key to the cabin from her coat pocket, and stepped outside. She left the headlights on to carve a path through the gray of dusk that enveloped her.

She fumbled with the key, forced it into the lock; the door opened with a slight push, then a grudging creak. She stepped inside, reached for a light, and flipped it on. There was a couch done in blue and cream plaid; a chair, navy blue, a rocker, matching blue and cream plaid cushion, worn and slightly faded; and a small coffee table. A single hurricane lamp rested on the coffee table alongside a ceramic ashtray. This would be the living room. The kitchen snaked to the right, a tiny oblong packed along the edges with a gas stove, a white refrigerator, a stainless steel sink and countertop, a single wicker chair, and a set of four TV trays with sailboats on the front.

There were two doors past the short half-hallway that butted up to the kitchen. She opened one, flipped on the light, and found a double-faucet sink, dingy white with rust around the silver fixtures, a white commode, and a porcelain tub with claw feet and a plug dangling on a chain that had been wrapped around the cold fixture. A cracked bar of soap sat in a white plastic tray. No toothbrush, no shaving cream, no sign that anyone had been here a week ago.

She turned away and opened the door on the opposite end of the hall. This was the bedroom. She stood in the semidarkness, staring at the bed. It was a double, covered with a light chenille spread, no accent pillows or fancy afghans draped at the foot like her mother preferred. Was this *the* bed? Christine turned away and closed the door.

She worked her way back to the living room, sat in the rocking chair, coat still on. He'd come here every month for years, and yet the place looked unused. Where were the copies of the *Wall Street Journal, Forbes,* James Michener's *The Centennial,* a gift she'd given him at Christmas? Hadn't he told her he was taking it with him on his next trip? Where was *anything* that hinted a body moved about within these walls, lived a life, even if it were only four days a month?

The answer was sitting there, around the ring of rust in the bathroom sink, on the coffee table filmed with a fine layer of dust, in the shininess of the navy ceramic ashtray.

He'd told them all a great, fantastic story of the rejuvenating powers found in this cabin hundreds of miles away from everything, where he could think. It had all seemed so noble then, inconvenient, yes, but noble. How many other lies had he told? Tomorrow she'd have her answers.

She didn't know how long she sat in the rocking chair, coat on, hands clenched together, staring into the blue emptiness of the ashtray perched on the edge of the coffee table. Eventually, she got up, went to the refrigerator, and found it empty except for a box of Arm & Hammer Baking Soda. She quietly closed the door and made her way to the bedroom, kicked off her shoes and lay down on the left side of the bed, the side her father always slept on. She didn't pull down the chenille spread, not even to rest her head on the pillow. And then exhaustion took over, and she slept.

MAGDALENA WAS EXACTLY seventy-eight miles from Tristan. Christine woke up to the pre-dawn sounds of birds and some other unnamed wood creatures. Her back was stiff, her legs sore, her head pounding. And she was starving. Food wasn't something she thought about much, not the way her mother did, arranging and presenting it with such dignity. Christine preferred ordering out or microwave-ready, the faster the better, easy cleanup, better yet.

She rolled off the bed, stared at the chenille spread, crumpled from sleep. The questions wouldn't stop, not until she found the one woman who held the answers, and then there might be hundreds more. She stripped off her coat, took a quick rinse in the porcelain tub, scrubbed her face, her teeth, pulled a comb through her thick hair, and put on the same jeans she'd worn the day before. She reached into her suitcase and grabbed the first shirt she found, a black turtleneck. Ten minutes later she was on the road, stopping only at a 7-Eleven to grab a large coffee and a sweet roll.

She entered the outskirts of Magdalena seventy-eight miles later and began to wonder if she should've taken a bit more time preparing for this meeting. Perhaps she should've worn her pearls, a business suit, flipped her hair in a chignon. In business, the aura of inapproachability had served her well, gained access into board-rooms, earned invitations and introductions. Her personal life hadn't reaped the same benefits; not that it had suffered, but it hadn't thrived. Aside from Connor, who was a family friend, many men thought her too standoffish. She wasn't, not really; it was more a cloak she donned to protect herself from overexposure, like sunscreen, a way to avoid the undesirable effects of undesirable people, men in particular.

Since the moment she heard Lily Desantro's name, she'd thought of the second when she'd see the woman and a name and a face would merge, one breathing life into the other to form a person, a memory, a past where all supposition would fade into features and voice and realness.

Christine followed the road to the edge of town, to the address on the back of the business card Thurman Jacobs had given her. Eleven sixty-seven Artisdale Street. The houses on this street were older, larger, more dignified, with scattered roof peaks; high, shuttered windows; and grand porches. They spoke of memories, family, and tradition, some with sturdy pillars along the front porch, others boasting wide steps and wider walkways. She was drawn to one halfway down that had pillars *and* walkways, crisp white with black shutters, an expanse of windows spreading up and out, covering first and second stories. The number above the door read 1167 Artisdale.

She parked the BMW and shut off the engine. Holly bushes filled the front beds, scatterings of evergreens clustered in between. To the right, blocking the tan house next door, stood a copse of pine trees, draped in white. Two wind chimes, one a Christmas tree painted bright red and green, the other a snowman plastered in white, hung from the porch, dangling rhythms of sound and sequence.

She should have sketched brief pointers for this meeting, a flow chart of sorts, similar to what she did when she analyzed stocks. Her stomach clenched, bits of sweet roll rising to the middle of her throat. What was there to analyze? Her father had kept a mistress named Lily Desantro at 1167 Artisdale, and this was most likely where he'd come during his monthly trips, not the cabin in Tristan with its ringed sink and empty refrigerator.

Maybe Uncle Harry had the right idea after all: never settle for one, just plow through them like a tractor in a field of hay, one after the other, multiple, meaningless relationships.

She took a deep breath and opened the car door.

# 4

NATE DESANTRO THOUGHT about ignoring the doorbell, and would have if he'd thought his mother wouldn't try to get out of bed and answer it herself. Why couldn't everybody just leave them alone, *mind their own business*, not his family's?

He couldn't count the number of people who'd been here since the accident, well-wishers offering fresh baked rolls, wedding soup, baked ham with pineapple and cloves. What about peace and quiet? Did any of those do-gooders ever think about offering *that*? His mother needed rest, not a crowd of people hovering over her. He'd kicked them all out last night. Lily hadn't liked that.

In another week or so he'd be able to get back to his own place, back to seclusion, where the loudest noise at night was a flip between a screech owl and a log crackling on the fire. Just the way he liked it. The majority of the human species was nothing but an annoying intrusion on his state of mind, and other than the times when he *had* to interact with them, he preferred to be alone. Of course, family didn't fit into that category, just everyone else. His mother said he was afraid to open up after what happened three years ago. She was wrong; he didn't care about Patrice anymore, didn't even think about her, not since the day the sheriff delivered the divorce papers. Nate heard she was remarried to some bank president in Palm Springs, drove a Lexus now. Probably silver; she'd always had a fondness for silver.

The doorbell rang again, twice, rapid staccato. "Hold on, hold on." Damn intrusive busy bodies. He reached the front door, preparing the same speech he told all the well-wishers. *She's fine ... needs her rest ... she'll be in touch when she's up to it.* She'd be furious if she had an inkling that he was blowing off people like Father Reisanski and Judge Tommichelli, but hell, did she have to be best friends with half the town?

He opened the door.

*It was her.*

"Hello. I'm looking for ..."

Her voice was softer than he'd imagined, more breathy....

"... this is a bit awkward ..."

Her eyes were bluer than her picture....

"Lily Desantro. Is she here?"

That brought him around fast. "Who are you?"

Stupid question, but damn if he'd let on he knew who she was.

She hesitated, a split-second extra air exchange. "Christine Blacksworth. I'm ... are you Nate Desantro?"

He said nothing. Let her squirm.

"Is Lily here?"

"No."

"May I come in?" She tried to look around him, into the house, into their lives.

He blocked the door. "I don't think that's a good idea."

"You ... you know who I am, don't you?"

He stared at her, refusing to acknowledge the man or his daughter as hatred seeped through him, brought back the days, months, years, his mother spent alone, four fucking days a month for fourteen years.

"You called my mother's house ... about my father."

Her voice wobbled. *Good, feel it, Christine Blacksworth, feel what I've felt for the past fourteen years every time I saw your father's bathrobe hanging in my mother's closet, saw his razor in her bathroom, his glasses on her nightstand. Let it strangle you ...*

"I have to speak with your mother." The words were firmer, partly congealed.

"She's not available."

"Can't you work with me so we can get this over with?"

"No, I can't."

"Do you think I wanted to come here? Do you think I would be standing here if there'd been any other way?"

"I don't know, would you? Maybe come to see for yourself?"

"This is just as hard on me as it is on you." Her voice dipped, faltered. "At least you knew. I had no idea. All this time, and I had no idea."

He almost felt sorry for her, but years of living with Charles Blacksworth's comings and goings wiped any pity from his soul. "You think so; you think we're in the same boat, *Christine*? What do you think it's like to see a man coming out of your mother's bedroom in the morning, one who's not her husband? And then the bastard leaves her, every month, goes back to his rich family in Chicago, his prestigious job, his three-piece suits. And he does it year after year after year, and she cries when he leaves, every goddamn time."

She looked away, pinched the bridge of her nose.

"You think you had it worse? You don't fucking have a clue." He gripped the door handle, forced himself to stay still when every cell in his body wanted to jerk her head up, make her acknowledge his words, feel his hatred. "Go home, Christine Blacksworth. You're fourteen years too late."

GLORIA ACCEPTED THE fluted glass bubbling with Dom Perignon, smiled at the young man dressed in black who hadn't left her side all night, Jeremy something or other, investment banker. He couldn't be more than twenty-eight, a year older than Christine, and yet she hadn't missed the way his dark eyes took in her pale-blue gown, moved from the swell of breast to shoulder, settled on the smooth, tanned skin of her neck. Men had looked at her that way her entire life, from the time she was fourteen and discovered that if she smiled wide and long, dropped her voice a few decibels, and *glanced* instead of stared at other boys, she would gain not only their attention, but their admiration. What a ridiculous game it all was, one she'd never succumbed to, preferring intellect to sexuality. But then she'd met Charles.

She sipped her champagne, tried to concentrate on what the young man was saying.

"Have you ever heard Bocelli?" Jeremy something or other was saying. "I saw him in New York. He's exquisite, not Pavarotti, but still quite good."

"And blind."

"Incredible, isn't it?" He took her comment as

interest, moved closer, his breath fanning her ear. "I'd love to take you. We could have dinner at The Presidio first. Next Saturday."

She took a step away, met his dark eyes, sparkling with one too many Dom Perignons. "I don't think so, but thank you for the invitation."

He flattened a hand over his chest. "You wound me, beautiful maiden. Please reconsider."

*Oh, Charles, how could you have left me to deal with this?* "I could be your mother."

"But you're not." He took her hand, stroked his fingers up her arm.

"I just buried my husband two weeks ago." *Was there no respect for the grieving process?*

"I know." He nodded, his handsome face solemn. "All the more reason."

"Indeed." She shrugged his hand off, stepped away. "All the more reason." Gloria lifted her glass, saluted him, and turned away.

She almost hadn't come tonight, not after last year's debacle. The West Mount Memorial Banquet had always been Charles's love; he was one of the original organizers, a major contributor and a staunch supporter of the hospital's research facilities. But this love blinded him, too. When last year's president asked Charles to double his annual pledge, *to help fund research for cancers like your sister's,* Charles readily agreed.

Tonight they were honoring him and had invited Gloria to accept an award in memory of her late husband. How could she refuse such a request? So, she'd chosen a pale-blue Chanel and a clasp of diamonds for the occasion, the muted coolness of color and stone giving her a controlled, untouchable presence, elegant but not overstated, determined in a mask of subtlety but still appropriate for her newly widowed state—her life without Charles.

She worked her way past the fringes of the ballroom to a tiny sitting area papered in heavy cream. There was a smattering of ornate chairs, cherry, she thought, done in burgundy and cream stripes set up in a half-circle around an oval glass table. And in the center of the table sat a huge spray of red roses, more than two dozen, maybe three, spilling out of a gold vase, tufts of baby's breath tucked in between.

Her gaze followed a petal that had fallen on the slick surface of glass and landed on the edge of a bright-blue ashtray. Gloria walked up to the table, studied the ashtray, shiny, clean, unused. She hesitated, fingers hovering over the single petal, its red brilliance not diminished by its solitary state. So much beauty, so much promise.... She brushed it away in one quick motion, mindless of where it landed, her concentration fixed solely on the gleam of the blue ashtray. Then she flipped open her bag, pulled out the black case decorated with needlepoint roses, and tapped out a Salem Light. Her fingers shook as she lit it, drew it to her mouth, and placed it between her lips.

"Now, this is a sight."

Gloria swung around, pulled the cigarette behind her back. "What are you doing here?"

Harry Blacksworth saluted her with his drink. "I was invited."

"As though you cared about contributing to anyone's charity but your own."

He ignored her. "I saw you with that young boy a few minutes ago."

She took another puff on her cigarette, held it, blew out a thin cloud of smoke. "Since when did it become a crime to engage in casual conversation?"

"Don't embarrass yourself, Gloria." He emptied his glass and added, "And don't humiliate Charlie's memory."

She stubbed out the cigarette in the center of the blue ashtray, grinding the butt to a third of its size. "You have nerve, Harry Blacksworth," she said in a low voice, moving her lips just enough to push the words out for his ears alone. "You've disgraced this family for years, and now you have the nerve to question *my* actions?"

"You're Charles Blacksworth's widow. Act like it."

"I intend to."

"See that you do." He turned away from her

then, before she could tell him that he was the real disgrace no one had ever wanted to acknowledge, especially Charles. She wanted to scream at him, so loud that the entire room would turn and stare at Harry. *You! Yes, you, you're the disgrace!*

But of course, she couldn't because he was already gone, and even if he weren't, she wouldn't. And he knew that.

NATE DESANTRO WAS NOT going to stop her from tracking down Lily. He might think he had a four-teen-year edge, but she'd been competing in a man's world long enough to know how to fight, and win.

When the sign for Magdalena shriveled to a dot in her rearview mirror, Christine opened her mouth and pulled in puffs of cold air, greedy to clear her mind. She should've been the one flinging accusa-tions back there, making demands, not him. But he'd been vicious, the hatred pulsing in the cords of his neck, spreading to his throat, spilling out of his mouth. He'd hated her father.

*. . . fourteen years too late.*

*Fourteen years?*

She would've been thirteen years old. . . .

She drove on, mindless of the new snow falling heavily around her, white, pure, forgiving. What had life been like fourteen years before? She tried to remember, tried to pull it back through the haze of work-filled days at Blacksworth and Company, four years of college, Senior Prom, farther still to family trips in Vail, Palm Springs, even middle school. But she could only snag scraps of memories, a half-formed picture of a girl in braces with pigtails, a blue spruce brilliant with lights and ornaments, a black dog named Jesse.

Fourteen years of goodbyes, promises to be home for Sunday dinner, returning with smiles and sharp embraces, and all the while, going to *her*. How had she not known? How had she looked into her father's eyes, listened to his words, and not been able to see the truth?

*Did he really love me? And Mother, what about her?*

They were his family, but had he really loved them, or merely felt duty toward them, obligation, as one does to an old pair of tennis shoes, scuffed and ripping at the seams, which should be tossed out on garbage day but somehow never make it there, instead get relegated as something else, garden shoes, lawn mowing shoes, anything to avoid being discarded completely. Maybe that's what he'd done, relegated them to something else, a lower position, in order to avoid the costly, damaging choice of permanent separation.

She thought of all the days he'd been with Lily

Desantro, all the years he'd let his real family believe he was somewhere else. Her father was the only one she'd ever truly counted on, the standard for everyone else in her life: friends, boyfriends, business associates, even, and she hated to admit this, her mother. Had it all been a grand lie?

Christine drove the remainder of the trip replaying the conversation with Nate Desantro. Part of her wanted to go back to Chicago, forget about the cabin and Magdalena and, most of all, Lily Desantro. The other part worried that the woman would not be so easily forgotten. What if she showed up in Chicago asking for Gloria Blacksworth?

Her mother would never be able to handle this. The thought of the two women face to face gave Christine renewed strength to drive back to Magdalena in the morning, confront Nate Desantro again if she must, though she hoped Lily would answer the door. Then Christine could tell her about the will, the enormous amount of money that would be hers, uncontested, and all she had to do was forget she'd ever heard the Blacksworth name.

It was early afternoon when she reached the cabin. She'd stopped off at Henry's Market, a small grocery store that wasn't much larger than a 7-Eleven, and picked up a quart of skim milk, four raspberry yogurts, a box of Multi-Grain Cheerios, a bag of red licorice, and a small bottle of Palmolive dish detergent. She'd almost asked the wrinkled man at the counter if he knew Charles Blacksworth. *You probably saw him about once a month,* she'd wanted to say. *He came to stay in the cabin up the road. Of course, you'd remember him if you saw him . . . medium build, silver hair . . . distinguished . . . very polite.*

What if they were all mistaken, what if he really had been living in the cabin and only visited the woman once in a while? The shopkeeper would recognize him, wouldn't he? She could find out, give herself hope that maybe he hadn't lied about everything. But in the end, she'd said nothing.

# 5

HARRY ANSWERED THE phone on the second ring. "Hullo?"

"Uncle Harry? I'm sorry. Were you asleep?"

"Chrissie." He glanced at the woman lying in the middle of the bed, full breasts pointed skyward. "No," he reached for his robe, "of course not."

"I went to Magdalena today."

Harry stuffed one arm into his silk robe, then the other, letting the belt hang loose, exposing his nakedness. What time was it anyway? He glanced at the clock on the nightstand. Seven-thirty p.m. He needed a drink, and he needed to take a piss.

"Did you see her?" He closed the bedroom door, kept his voice low.

"No. I saw her son, though."

"Hard ass. What'd he have to say?"

"That . . . that . . ."

"Tell me, Chrissie. What happened?" He poured himself a double scotch, neat, carried the glass and the bottle to the burgundy leather recliner, sat down.

"Fourteen years, Uncle Harry. Fourteen years."

"What? What's fourteen years?"

"How long they were ... together." Pause. "How long he was seeing her, Uncle Harry. Fourteen *years*."

"Jesus." He took a healthy swallow of scotch. *"Jesus."*

"All this time, all these years, and he's been with *her.*"

Fourteen years? Harry took another drink, drained his glass. "Desantro could be lying. We never heard the name before two weeks ago. This could all be a scheme to get more money; maybe the woman blackmailed him into leaving her a wad of cash so you and your mother wouldn't find out, and Charlie just figured he'd live long enough to change the will later. Shit, I don't know. None of this makes any sense, but I'd believe the mother and son were trying to blackmail your father before I'd believe he was," he almost said "fucking the bitch" but reworked it to "in a relationship with that woman for fourteen years."

"Really?"

There was hope in her voice, clinging to one last shred of possibility, and he could not disappoint her, so he said, "I do, Chrissie. I think maybe they both set him up."

"I'm going back tomorrow." She sounded more like the old Chrissie now. "I don't care if I have to sit outside of that house all day; I'm going to talk to Lily Desantro."

"This isn't something you should do alone, kid. Let me come, too; it could get nasty. I can leave first thing in the morning."

"I need to handle this alone. But thank you."

"I don't know if that's such a good idea. This isn't a boardroom; it's real life, and having me there might even out the playing field."

"I'll be okay. Right now, I need you to keep an eye on Mom. I wouldn't ask you if there was anyone else, but can you please do this?"

He thought of Gloria crumpled over in her chair, whimpering the night she found out about Charlie. So much damn self-pity, too much for his patience. "I'll keep an eye on her."

"Thank you, Uncle Harry. I've always known I could count on you."

They hung up after that, Christine sounding renewed; Harry had given her that even when he knew it might all be a big smoke job. But how could Charlie have been screwing the woman for fourteen years and never aroused suspicion? People left trails, somehow, somewhere; they always left trails.

He owed Christine and Charlie, and he would do right by them. The last time he'd tried to do something honorable, his old man had pulled out his wallet and simply taken care of the situation.

That was thirty-one years ago, and he'd hated him ever since.


IT WAS LATE MORNING when Christine pulled up outside the Desantro home. She'd waited a few hours before leaving the cabin, hoping Nate Desantro might not be there. He must have a job, other commitments that would pull him from the house.

She locked the car and crossed the street, sloshing through the thick mix of snow and dirt. Brown sugar, that's what it reminded her of, as she kicked it with the toe of her boot, watched it fly in chunks around her. She climbed the steps of the white house, listening to the faint tinkle of snowman and Christmas tree chimes in front of her.

The door opened before she had a chance to ring the bell. A woman stood in the entrance way, tall, lean, in a bulky wheat sweatshirt and jeans. She wore sandals on her feet, and her toes were long, slender, void of polish. Her hair, a spray of black mixed with gray, was tied back from her face. Tiny clusters of gray and brown stone dangled from her ears on golden wires. Christine took it all in—legs, feet, hair, ears, even hands that were rough and cracked, with long fingers and blunt nails, these too without polish. And then she looked at the woman's face. It was tanned with tiny lines fishing out from her eyes and around her mouth, perhaps from years of laughter, or perhaps not. Her nose was narrow with delicate nostrils, lips thin, cheekbones high, skin pulled tight, free of makeup and blemishes. There was an ethereal quality about her that made Christine want to examine each detail to determine where the line of physical beauty ended and the intangible factors began.

"Christine."

She had a soft, low voice, soothing, even. Christine sucked up these details before lifting her gaze to the woman's eyes. They were hazel, clear, like the mist off a fresh mountain spring.

"I need to talk to you." After days of rehearsing, she was suddenly speechless.

"Yes. Come in."

The interior of the living room boasted an eclectic gathering of color and fabric that in some bizarre manner both calmed and aroused the senses. The walls were pale blue with large oil paintings hanging from them. One was a field of wildflowers, the canvas covered in brilliant splashes of red, yellow, green, and orange. Another was a house in a snow storm, the same long, broad brush strokes trailing through the snow. The third painting held the identical strokes, but it stood out from the others. Done in blue and black hues, it was of a child curled up in a blanket asleep, long black hair brushed part-way over her face.

There were pots of flowers, dried and fresh, scattered in bowls and vases, and a Boston fern hanging from a hook in the ceiling, its leafy fronds stretching to touch the tip of a rocking chair. The furniture consisted of a rocker, two side chairs, and a love seat, all old but comfortable-looking in matching shades of faded burgundy, navy, and cream florals. The floor was a dark, bare wood, oak maybe, with an area rug, woven in shades of black, burgundy, green, and tan. A wind chime hung in the far corner, this one in the shape of a sunflower. There were baskets stuffed with magazines, *Forbes* sitting on top. Christine tore her gaze away, moved to a chair, and sat down. Four small bowls rested on the coffee table in front of her, each carved from different wood, each a different style. They were smooth and glossy, the fine grains of the individual wood woven throughout. One was filled with rose petals, another, lavender, the third, pine cones, and the last, holly leaves.

A phonograph rested against one wall.

Lily Desantro followed her gaze. "Archaic, isn't it?" A faint smile pulled across her thin lips. "Oh, but it plays a lovely sound. Charlie and I used to—" Her words froze mid-sentence.

Christine pictured them gliding across the wooden floor, smiling, laughing. He'd never danced with her mother.

"Christine—"

"Is it true that you and my father were having an affair for fourteen years?"

"We . . . were involved, yes." She ran a hand through her long hair, braided in the back. "It was very complicated."

"You mean because my father was married?"

"Yes, there was that. No matter what happened between your father and me, he loved you, Christine. He always loved you."

"How do you know? Did he tell you? Did you talk about me?"

The woman reached for the chain around her neck, fingered it. It was then that Christine noticed the small gold cross. "I'm so sorry."

"For what? That the man I admired most in the world was a liar and a cheat?"

"I'm sorry we've caused you pain, but I'm not sorry I loved your father." She straightened, pressed her fingers over the cross. "I can never be sorry for that."

"I want you to forget you ever heard the Blacksworth name." It was time to deal with her and get out.

"I want my memories just as much as you do,

Christine," she said. "Charlie's a part of me; he'll always be a part of me."

"He left you a large sum of money in his will. I'll see that it's disbursed as soon as possible, no point of contest, no complications," she met the woman's gaze, "as long as you don't contact us. Ever."

"I'm not interested in Charlie's money." She sighed, shook her head. "It's never been about the money."

"Well, maybe he thought it was." How could she pretend she had a right to those memories, a right to a life that belonged to his family?

Lily Desantro eased back in her chair and steepled her fingers under her chin. "Charlie said you could be a tough one, that you hid your real emotions under your suit jacket."

"You don't know anything about me. And I don't want to know anything about you. I'm here to do a job, and then I'm going back to Chicago, and I'm going to forget I ever heard the name Lily Desantro."

"Lily?" The woman's face turned white beneath her tan. "What does she have to do with this?" Her fingers grabbed at the cross, squeezed.

"What are you talking about?"

"Lily. You know about her?"

"What? *You're* Lily. Aren't you?"

"Hardly." Nate Desantro stood in the doorway, a tall mountain of a man in a red flannel shirt. "You couldn't leave it alone, could you? You couldn't just go back to your rich little world and leave it alone." He took a step toward her and stopped. "Lily Desantro is my half sister. She's yours, too."

# 6

CHRISTINE WAS MORE beautiful than her pictures, with her glossy black hair and fair skin. Miriam could see Charlie in her, the straight nose, the movement of full lips, the blue eyes, even the way she folded her arms over her chest and tipped her head to the left as though trying to assimilate words she couldn't or didn't want to understand.

*Dear God,* Miriam hadn't wanted this. And Nathan, standing in the doorway like an avenging angel, had just spoken the words that would change all of their lives. There was no going back now, no pretending around it. The truth had spilled from his lips, infiltrated Christine's lungs, spread through her body, settled in her brain.

"I . . . don't understand."

Of course she didn't, but in reality she did, though not on a conscious level, at least not yet. That would come later, when facts and feelings meshed together to form a new truth, unwelcome, yet necessary. People made statements daily that bought them time while they tried to absorb words, replace old beliefs with new discoveries, all the time hoping in the subconscious realm for life to return to its previous state.

"Christine," Miriam spoke softly, leaning toward the young woman, who was now clasping her hands together, fingers pressed into flesh, knuckles white. "I'm so sorry you had to find out this way."

"A sister?"

"Seems like you're not an only child after all."

"Nathan. Please." He shrugged, folded his arms across his chest, and leaned against the doorway.

Christine stared at him, then turned to Miriam. With the exception of the white knuckles and the tiny skip in her breath, a person would never know she'd just been told she had an illegitimate sister. "How old is she?"

"Mom—" Nathan tried to stop her.

"Thirteen."

Perhaps Christine hadn't expected this answer; perhaps she'd thought the child would be much younger, a few years at most, a recent indiscretion, not one spanning more than a decade, almost half of Christine's life.

"What's her full name?"

"Lily Eleanor..." Miriam hesitated, added, "Desantro."

"My aunt's name was Eleanor." She stared at one of Miriam's bowls, curly maple filled with lavender. Her voice slipped, "She died when I was thirteen."

"I know."

"That's when he went to the cabin." Her voice dipped lower, as though she were chronicling events, not for them, but for herself, trying to fill in dates, gaps, trying so hard to make sense of the situation. "He said he needed to get away."

"He loved your Aunt Ellie very much."

"Where is she? Where's Lily?"

"She isn't here." Nathan stepped into the room, filling it up with his voice and his presence. He was much taller than his father had been, broader, more muscular. "Lily isn't your concern."

"My father left her a third of his estate." Now she sounded more like the young executive Charlie had earmarked as his successor. "I think I have a right to know the person who's being given this very generous gift."

"We don't want your money. We just want you to leave us alone, go back to Chicago, and forget you ever heard our name."

"My father willed Lily a huge sum of money. It's my job to see that it's disbursed. And to make sure there aren't any loose ends."

"In other words, to pay off the Desantros to keep quiet."

"No."

But Miriam saw the way her gaze broke away from Nathan's cold stare for the briefest of seconds, before turning back to him. His words might be coarse, but they were true.

"No? Really? You came out of the generosity of your heart, to do right by my mother and sister?"

"I came to do what needed to be done."

"That I believe."

There was hatred in his voice. He had always held such animosity toward Charlie, made horrible vindictive accusations against him that had destroyed any chance of a relationship between the two men. He'd spent years comparing Charlie to his own father, disregarding one, eulogizing the other. If he only knew.

And yet Nathan let a soft side of himself spill over into his feelings for Lily as he became brother, friend, protector. It was all three of these that fought now to keep safe whom he deemed the only truly good person in the world.

"I have a right to see her."

"Right? You want to talk about *rights*? Your father didn't think about my mother's *rights* or Lily's rights when he left them every month, did he? He didn't care about Lily's right to have her father there on Christmas morning to watch her open gifts, or her right to have him in the audience with all of the other fathers while she and her class put on their annual Easter special. And what about the right to carry her father's name, didn't she deserve that?"

"I—"

"Do not talk to me about rights." His breathing came hard, fast. "I have stood by and watched my mother give up every right she ever possessed, and whether she did so willingly or not is not the fucking point. Your father was the reason, and he should have been man enough to make a choice."

"Nathan, please. Stop." A sharp pain throbbed along the right side of Miriam's temple, a full-blown migraine threatening to explode. She massaged the pounding with two fingers, all the while keeping her eyes on Charlie's daughter.

When Christine spoke, she directed her words at Miriam. "All I want to do is disburse the money and gain your assurance you won't contact my family."

Miriam nodded, the sharpness of the headache piercing her brain. She would not be offended that Christine might think her capable of such duplicity. After all, what could she expect?

"If my mother wants to accept the money for Lily, that's her business." Nathan moved closer, stopped within a few feet of Christine. "And maybe that will ease your conscience, knowing you've paid money for your father's indiscretions. I'll accept that, but then I want you to leave Magdalena and forget you ever heard the name Lily Desantro."

SHE HAD A NICE ASS. Face wasn't bad either. Harry leaned against the counter, watching Greta Servensen bend, turn, stoop, and reach as she prepared the evening meal. Lamb with sage, party of four; he wasn't invited. He'd only stopped by because he'd promised Chrissie he'd check in on her mother. Gloria was busy "exfoliating," Greta told him, and wouldn't be available for another twenty minutes.

He reached over the counter and grabbed a mushroom stuffed with crabmeat. Damn, Greta was a good cook, pretty, too, in a scrubbed clean sort of way, no frills, no makeup. Was this her preference, or was it a prerequisite to work for Gloria Blacksworth? Couldn't permit the hired help to be more beautiful than the boss, now could she?

Harry didn't have much occasion to see a pretty woman sans makeup and every other beauty product known to the cosmetic world. The women he entertained, about town and in bed, wore full armor: mascara, lipstick, eye-shadow, bronzers, fake nails, fake hair dyed and extended, fake boobs, too. But Greta looked natural, fresh, and for some insane reason this turned him on.

She was a *nice* woman. He reminded himself

that she had kids, a 1992 Toyota Corolla with a dented front fender, a mother who lived with her, for chrissake. He downed the rest of his scotch in one swallow.

"Mr. Blacksworth, would you like a piece of Black Forest Cake?" She was bent at the waist, all curves and hip, one hand clutching the refrigerator door as she looked at him.

He shook his head, tried to ignore the panty line under her white uniform. "No. And my name is Harry, not Mr. Blacksworth."

She nodded, her smile slipping.

*Jesus*, was she afraid of him? Why? Could she see inside his sick mind, tell that he was having perverted fantasies about her tight ass? *Shit.*

"Harry?" His name sounded soft and breathy on her lips, her accent giving it a sensual bounce. "Mrs. Blacksworth will be a while yet. Can I get you anything?"

*Oh, yeah, Greta, how about that tongue, to start?* "No." He lifted his glass, saluted her. "This is all I want, but I'll get it myself." Harry pushed away from the counter and hurried out of the kitchen, straight to the liquor cabinet. He poured a drink, swallowed, and squeezed his eyes shut. Another three and he'd be ready to face Gloria.

If he hadn't promised Chrissie, he'd be sitting in his hot tub at home with Bridgett doing dunk and dive on his dick. But Chrissie had fallen apart on the phone last night, going on and on about a half sister. *A thirteen-year-old kid?* What the hell was Charlie thinking?

"Hello, Harry."

Gloria entered the room in a sweep of peach silk and heavy perfume. He hated that stuff she wore. It clogged his sinuses and gave him a damned headache. He'd told her before, several times, but she said it was a Neiman Marcus exclusive, and it was Charles's favorite.

Was it? "Well, if it isn't the grieving widow."

"You said you had something to tell me about Christine." She walked to the liquor cabinet and poured herself a scotch, no ice.

Harry straightened, swirled the liquid in his glass, and said, "She's having a tough time."

Gloria sipped her scotch, two healthy sips, one right after the other. "We're all having a tough time right now."

He sat down at one end of the couch, wondered how Charlie had tolerated all the florals and stiffness of this furniture for so many years. What was wrong with honest-to-god leather? You could sink into it, let it mold itself to your body, surround you. Or even some fabric with pillows, the soft, squishy kind that reshaped itself with a person's body. But this? Chintz or whatever in the hell it was, no pillows, no extra padding, nothing but a designer label and a hard frame?

Kind of like Gloria.

"Tell me about Christine." She lounged across from him on a pink and cream flowered chair. He watched as she flipped open a small black case and pulled out a cigarette.

"Ah, what would Charlie say?"

"Go to hell, Harry."

He laughed. "Glad we can be so familiar with each other."

She sucked in a long drag, blew it out through pursed lips, her pink-tipped fingers resting on the arms of the chair, cigarette dangling.

"You know how she felt about Charlie," he said, suddenly not interested in baiting her, wanting to be done so he could get out of the house, breathe in fresh air.

"I expected it would be difficult for her."

"He was like God to her." *I shouldn't have let her go there alone.*

"He was still just a man. I mean," she took a quick puff on her cigarette, "he wasn't God. He was human, subject to human frailties, just like the rest of us."

*Human frailties.* Is that what shacking up with a mistress for fourteen years and having a child with her was called?

"I've tried to tell her for years that her father disappointed and let people down, just like the rest of us. But she never saw that, no, all she could see was her father in his three-piece suit with his briefcase and his fancy words. He never scolded her, never once told her no, not even the time she brought those four girls home from college at Easter break when she knew we had plans for Florida. I'd been waiting for months to get out of the cold, and then Charles cancelled the trip," she snapped her fingers, "just like that. He said we'd take a long weekend after they left." She lifted her glass, took a quick sip, the words slipping through her lips faster, spilling into the air, as though she were incapable of stopping them. "Of course, we never did.

"Oh, but Charles thought it was fine for the girls to stay with us, invited them to church and Easter dinner, even took them to the office, introduced them around. And not once did he apologize for canceling our trip." She tapped the ashes of her cigarette in a blue glass ashtray. "He said we should be grateful our daughter still wanted to come home, and if she brought a few friends, then it only meant she was comfortable with our home and—"

Harry raised an eyebrow. "And?" So she'd finally realized she'd revealed shades of a marriage she hadn't wanted to reveal.

"Nothing." She straightened in her chair, stubbed out the cigarette. "Do I need to call Christine?"

"No. She'll be fine." *How the hell can I say that with a straight face?*

Gloria nodded. "I just want her to know, eventually, that if I was," she paused, "firm at times, there was a reason for it."

Harry swirled the scotch in his glass, said nothing.

"I just want her to know that," she repeated.

What did she expect him to do, agree with her, take sides and say, *Yes, Gloria, you were firm because Charlie couldn't be; he was a sap when it came to discipline?* Did she think he would actually go against his brother? He'd done that once in his life and he'd paid for it, was still paying for it. She could go straight to hell if she thought he'd ever say anything against his brother again.

"Chrissie's worried about you," he said, changing the subject. "She made me promise to stop over and make sure you were okay."

"Oh." She sank back in the uncomfortable flowered chair, put a hand to her throat, the skin smooth and tanned, the diamonds on her left finger glistening. "Well, I'm managing."

He wanted to laugh in her face, tell her he knew she was *managing*; he'd witnessed that the other night at the benefit when she was parading around the floor, wearing Charlie's death like a cloak to gain sympathy and attention.

"Stop looking at me like that."

"Like what?"

"Like you think he meant nothing to me."

Harry merely lifted his glass and sipped his scotch.

"I loved him." She pushed the emphasis into the words. *"I loved him."*

"Of course you did."

"Don't patronize me. You've never loved anyone in your life, other than yourself."

She was wrong there. He loved Christine, and that's why he'd never revealed the truth about Gloria, a truth that would destroy the family. It was because of Christine that he'd been silent.

And it was because of her he would remain that way.

# 7

CHRISTINE ROLLED OVER, reached in the direction of the urgent ringing until she located her cell phone. "Hello."

"Christine? Are you okay?"

"Connor."

"Jesus, are you all right? You sound terrible."

"I'm fine."

"Well, you don't sound fine." He paused, and she pictured him riffling a hand through his thick hair, once, twice, a nervous habit he employed when he found himself in a situation he couldn't control.

"I was just sleeping," she said, pushing herself up on her elbows.

"It's five o'clock in the afternoon."

She heard the recrimination in his voice. Five o'clock was work time; business deals got made at five o'clock, even on vacation.

"I just fell asleep." Should she tell him the real reason? *I just found out I have a half sister.* No, the

Pendletons were very particular about bloodlines and heritage. They would not take kindly to learning about an illegitimacy. It didn't matter; she wasn't telling anyone about Lily Desantro.

"You must be really bored," Connor said, chuckling into the phone. "Didn't you bring your laptop? At least you could stay connected to the real world while you're out there in the boondocks."

"It's here," she said, surprised that she hadn't opened it yet, not even to check the Dow. "I've just been busy."

"Oh?" He sounded intrigued. "Doing what?"

*Driving seventy-eight miles to track down my half sister . . . confronting my father's mistress . . . and her son.* "Well, for one, trying to figure out how to operate a tub with a rubber plug." She tried for humor, anything to avoid the real question. Connor only wanted to know when she'd be on her way back to Chicago.

His next words proved this. "So, when are you coming back? I'm still hoping you'll come to New York with me."

"So I can work the deal with Glen Systems for you?"

"No, of course not."

But she knew the truth—she heard it in the split-second hesitation. He might want her there because he cared about her, but he also wanted her friendly personality seated right beside Niles Furband when he tried to land the deal. This should have upset her, and the mere fact that it didn't worried her most.

"Will you come? It's the twenty-sixth."

"I don't know." She still didn't know what she was going to do about the situation here. Should she just leave? Tell Thurman Jacobs to disburse the funds and be done with it? But what about the girl? Could she let her walk around without ever seeing her, without knowing if they shared the same color hair, the same cowlick on the right side of their forehead, the same blue eyes, Blacksworth eyes?

"I could meet you in New York on the twenty-sixth if you'd like." Connor wanted his deal; he didn't care what she was doing in the middle of nowhere that kept her so busy.

If Mr. Saro from Japan had called and spoken to him in Japanese about financial issues, Connor would have dragged in a translator, maybe two, to interpret the words in English, then he'd have analyzed them, dissected meaning and inflection, spent hours, perhaps a whole day, trying to understand.

But this, something as mundane and uneventful as a girlfriend in her dead father's cabin in the Catskills—it smacked of emotion and angst, and she knew Connor was careful about avoiding both. "I'm not sure when I'm leaving." She was suddenly tired of talking. "I might stay on another day or so, or it could be longer. I'll let you know, okay?"

"Do you want me to come up there?" He wanted to make a trip to the Catskills about as much as she wanted to throw herself naked in a pile of snow.

"No. I want to be by myself right now." There, she'd give him his out, because it would ease his conscience, and because it was true.

"Okay, then," he sighed into the phone, a long breath that she supposed was intended to make her feel a tinge of guilt for remaining undecided about the New York trip. "Let me know as soon as you can."

"Sure."

And then, this last bit, perhaps to boost her spirits. "The Dow was up two hundred points today. You should check it out."

"Thanks. Maybe I will."

*Click.* He was gone.

She placed the cell phone on the nightstand and fell back on the bed, staring at the ceiling. It was dark outside, a cocoon of blackness but for the tiniest sliver of moon sifting through the window, settling in a faint arc above her.

It was then, as she stared at the arc, followed its faint shimmering trail, that she realized the truth about her relationship with Connor Pendleton.

He'd made certain he told her about the Dow, but had never once said *I love you*.

And neither had she.

CHRISTINE SPENT THE next two days at the cabin, pondering the dilemma of Lily and following the NASDAQ. Jumping into the market was the best way to get back in control. She called her assistant, Moira, returned phone calls to clients, made recommendations, took orders.

No one needed to know she was conducting business from a card table in the Catskills, surrounded by snow and evergreens, or that she was dressed in gray sweats and a red fleece top and two pairs of Thinsulate socks.

On the third day, she decided to pay a visit to the machine shop her father had bailed out. *Stay busy, just stay busy.* She'd meet the owner and she would reassure him she planned to honor the agreement. She was also curious about the type of man, a relative stranger she guessed, her father would sign a note for, guaranteeing payment. But maybe the man wasn't a stranger; maybe he was a friend. Fourteen years was a long time to cultivate a friendship, and the fact that she didn't know upset her as much as it depressed her.

For days, she'd asked the question: Who was

Lily Desantro? But the real question was: Who was Charles Blacksworth?

She had to get away from the cabin. *Now*, before her mind drove her crazy with its incessant ranting. She pulled on her boots, stuffed her arms into a down jacket, and fought her way to the car. It took almost an hour to dig a path to the road, and another thirty minutes to clear the car and heat it up. It was freezing. She could get stuck out here, and no one would ever find her until spring when the thaw came through.

Christine drove the back road into Magdalena, fingers gripping the wheel, gravitating toward the middle when there weren't any other cars around. The snow fell, full and fat on the windshield. Her father must have driven roads like these for years, narrowed from snow piling up along the edges, slick with ice, dark, country roads, fighting change, fighting progress, just like the people who lived in the towns where the roads led, Tristan, Ennert, Magdalena.

ND Manufacturing was located about five miles from Magdalena. It was a longish-shaped brick building, weathered to a faded orange, with a flat roof supporting several metal vents and two small windows at the front entrance. A handful of buildings similar to this one ran up and down the road like brick rectangles. A parking lot stood to the left smattered with pickup trucks and older model cars,

Fords and Chevys mostly, with bumper stickers that read "Mail Pouch" and "Union Works."

She parked her car next to a blue Ford F-150 with a dented right fender and headed for the entrance. The contact person was Jack Finnegan, but he wasn't the owner, only "the man in charge of the paperwork," her father had told her. He hadn't given her the owner's name, telling her there'd be time enough for everything she needed to know later. But there hadn't been enough time; there hadn't been *any* time.

A gray-haired woman with tight curls and cat's-eye glasses perched behind a glass partition in the lobby. She looked up when Christine entered.

"May I help you?"

"I'm looking for Mr. Finnegan. Is he available?"

The older woman let out a chuckle. "Sure is. Your name?"

Christine hesitated then said, "I'm Christine Blacksworth."

"*You're* Christine?" The woman's blue eyes widened behind the cat's-eye glasses. "Charlie's daughter?"

"I am."

"Oh, my word. Oh, my goodness. Oh, my." The words rushed out in a string of breathlessness as the woman fanned herself with her hand, said again, "Oh, my."

"You knew my father?" It was a ridiculous question because, judging by the woman's reaction, she had indeed known him.

"Yes, oh, my, yes." The woman stood and thrust her hand through the open portion of the sliding window. Even standing she barely reached Christine's shoulder. "Betty Rafferty. I'm the receptionist here." She paused, let out a small laugh. "And the chief cook and bottle washer. I do a little bit of everything in this place: answering phones, filing, typing, checking time cards—" She stopped herself mid-sentence. "My lord, but we are so sorry about Charlie." She shook her head, but the curls didn't move. "So very sorry."

"Thank you." Did everyone know him, know about him? Know about Miriam and Lily, too?

"He was a wonderful man," Betty Rafferty went on, "wonderful. There wasn't a kinder person than Charlie Blacksworth. He helped us all out at one time or another, and I mean *all* of us, no matter who we were, he didn't care. Me, when my mother died and the lawyer tried to tie up her estate and charge a ton of legal fees, Charlie made a few phone calls and it was done," she snapped her bony fingers, "just like that.

"And then, when Ned Glezinski's landlord was gonna kick him out for not making his rent payments, Charlie stepped in." She lowered her voice, "We all thought he loaned Ned money, but nobody ever said, least of all Charlie. Anyways, he showed Ned how to do a budget, how to put a little aside in savings for a rainy day, and I'll be darned if Ned didn't buy a two-bedroom house down on Edgar Street last year."

Christine didn't want to hear that any good had come of her father's stay here, didn't want to even consider the possibility that he was missed by this town as much as he was missed by his friends and associates in Chicago. This place wasn't his home. These people had no right to Charles Blacksworth; they were nothing but pirates, bootlegging his name and his identity.

"And then there was Freda and Arthur Peorelli, and their son, Giovanni," she went on, stopped. "I think," she scratched her pointy chin, "I should stop before the boss comes in." She lowered her voice, leaned forward. "He and Charlie didn't quite see eye to eye."

"No?"

Betty shook her head again. "No, ma'am, they sure didn't, but then you must know that."

"Actually, I—"

"Betty!"

Christine turned and spotted the scruffy old man standing behind her, clad in jeans and a red flannel shirt rolled up to his forearms. He was wiry and small with shocks of thick white hair sticking out from under a John Deere ball cap cocked back on his forehead. Gray-white stubble peppered his cheeks, a stark contrast to the weather-beaten tan on the rest of his face. But it was his eyes that held her. They were a brilliant blue, and they were trained on her.

"Christine."

She managed to nod.

The man shot a glance toward the receptionist. "Been flappin' your gums again, Betty?" he asked, lifting a bushy white brow.

"Just making Christine feel welcome, Jack, that's all."

"I'll take over from here." He thrust out a work-worn hand. "Jack Finnegan, otherwise known as 'Old Man Jack.'"

"Mr. Finnegan." She reached for his outstretched hand, felt the calluses. "You're just the person I came to see."

"Don't think so, not if you came to see *Mister* Finnegan. Like I said, I'm Jack or Old Man Jack, plain and simple." He threw back his head and laughed, revealing random spots of silver and a row of bridgework.

"Jack, then."

"Let's go into my office," he said, winking at her. "And Betty, not a word of this to the boss, you got it?"

Betty lifted a blue-veined hand, pinched a thumb and forefinger together, and ran it along her lips. "I'm zipped, Jack."

"Good. Keep it that way. No slip-ups."

"Aye-aye." Then, "Nice to meet you, Christine. Your father was a true saint."

"Come on, before she starts praying the rosary."

Christine followed Jack Finnegan down a narrow hallway. There were offices on both sides, four altogether, small squares filled with carpet, computer, an occasional metal filing cabinet, and a desk. Jack moved past the first three and stepped into the last one, which had a copy machine where a desk would be and six filing cabinets along the back wall. There was only one chair in the tiny room, a gray swivel with black plastic arms. "Sit," he said, closing the door behind her. He kicked a box of copy paper a few feet from her and plopped down, feet spread, arms crossed over his chest.

"What can I do you for?"

"I guess first you can tell me what you make here."

"That's easy enough. Parts for farm equipment, you know, gadgets that fit on tractors, combines, bailers, and such."

"Oh, I see."

"Your dad was mighty proud of you."

It was a plain statement, meant as a compliment,

but the mere fact that these intruders felt they had a right to an opinion concerning her father angered her. "Before my father died, he made mention of a collateral loan he'd signed for ND Manufacturing. Your name was listed on the correspondence as the contact person."

Jack Finnegan scratched the back of his head. If he'd noticed the direct snub, he chose to ignore it. "That's right," he said slowly, "I'm the *contact* man."

"Who's the owner? I don't have his name."

His thin lips pulled into a smile. "No, you don't, now do you?"

"Well, I'll need his name so I can contact him."

"Are you planning to call the loan, Christine? Shut the place down?"

"No, of course not."

"'Cause I know that's not what Charlie wanted, and he'd be damned disappointed if he thought his daughter was doing this to spite him."

"I have no intention of calling the loan or changing the agreement my father made."

"Good." He stroked his stubbled chin. "That's good."

"And that's the reason I came here, to give my assurances that my father's word would be honored."

"Appreciate it. I'll pass the word along."

"Mr. Finnegan . . . Jack, what's going on?"

"Charlie bailed this place out of a rough spot. If he hadn't come through, a lot of people would have fallen on tough times, lost their jobs, their medical insurance, probably their homes. I don't know how much you know about this town, but Magdalena doesn't have an extra supply of jobs."

"I gathered that."

He nodded, pushed his cap farther back on his head. "But some people don't take kindly to accepting favors from anybody, especially if it's somebody they ain't too keen on."

She forced herself to remain quiet. If she bided her time, eventually, in a roundabout convoluted manner, with hundreds of detours, Jack Finnegan would get to the crux of the matter, the truth.

"And then you got pride," he went on. "That has to figure in somewheres, now don't it? So, you take pride, and somebody you ain't too keen on, and then you add a family member buttin' in, and, well, that just plain spells disaster."

"Yes, it does." Now they were getting somewhere.

"So, what's a body to do? The boss still needs help, still has to find a way to come up with money he ain't got and ain't got no way of gettin', leastways, on time." He leaned forward, planted his elbows on his bony knees. "I'll tell you what you do. You find a body that can get the boss to take the money, but you can't tell him where it came from," he paused, "well, not exactly where it came from."

She was starting to understand. "Are you saying the owner of this place doesn't know my father put up the collateral for his business?"

"No, ma'am, he don't know," Jack Finnegan said, shaking his head. "And he ain't gonna know, not now, not ever."

"Just how do you plan on keeping all of this a secret?"

He shrugged. "Same way we been keepin' it a secret for the past thirteen months."

"And what way is that?"

"A member of the family loaned it out, said it was insurance money."

"And does the owner believe that?"

"Ain't got no reason not to. The man's desperate. When people get like that, they don't want to go lookin' for the truth if it's gonna cause them a grief they can't handle. It's easier to just shut out that little voice that's sayin' somethin' ain't quite right."

"Well, there's no reason not to tell me who the owner is. If I want to find out, all I have to do is look up the company in Dun & Bradstreet, and all of the officers are listed."

She waited for him to say something, but he just sat there watching her, fist balled under her chin, elbows on his knees.

"Are you going to tell me?"

"Guess I'm gonna have to, now ain't I?" He let out a sigh. "You gave your word you ain't gonna cause no trouble, Christine. You said you'd honor Charlie's agreement."

"Of course I will." She just wanted a name. As long as she received a monthly check she didn't care where it came from, and if the old man wanted to keep ND Manufacturing's benefactor a secret, fine.

"The boss's old man and I went way back. I been with this company forty-three years."

*Oh, God, he was starting again with the stories.* "Just give me the name, Jack, okay? That's all I want, so I know, and I promise it'll stay between us. I give my word."

"It's Nate. Nate Desantro."

# 8

IT WAS SNOWING, GOBS of white sticking everywhere, trees, animals, cars. But Nate and Lily were tucked away inside his log cabin two miles outside of Magdalena, a world away from the storm outside. The stone fireplace crackled, filling the room with what Lily called "tree heat."

They sat next to each other on the old piano bench that had once belonged to their mother. The piano, too, had been hers, but she'd given it up years ago in favor of a paint brush and router. And Nate had gladly accepted it into his home, found solace in the sound his fingers extricated from the keys.

He reached over and grasped Lily's hands, gently placing her index fingers on the keys. "Now, when I point to you, I want you to tap the keys three times in a row, got it?"

Lily giggled. "Got it."

"Okay. I put a red mark on the ones I want you to hit. Here we go." He played the first few chords of

*Jingle Bells*, watched her face split into a smile as she waited for her part. Then he pointed to her.

Lily giggled again, raised her fingers high, aiming for the marked keys. She hit the edges of them. Once, twice, three times.

"How was that?"

"That was good, Lily. Very good."

She threw her arms around his waist, hugged him tight. "I love you, Nate."

He brushed his beard over the top of her head. "I love you, too."

"Play *Santa Claus is Coming to Town*."

"Why?" He paused, his fingers resting lightly on the keyboard. "Santa Claus already came to town, and he brought a whole sack of goodies for Lily Desantro."

She laughed. "A lot of stuff," she said, nuzzling against his flannel shirt.

"Too much. You're going to have to move to a bigger house just to find a place for all your junk."

"It's not junk, Nate."

"Okay, then, toys. Bicycle. Doll house. CD player. CDs."

She squeezed her hands tighter around his middle. "Santa didn't bring me the bike. Daddy did."

He stroked her hair. "You're right. He did."

She sniffed into his shirt and whispered, "I miss him."

"I know you do, Lily."

"I don't want him to be in Heaven."

"I know."

"Why did God have to take him?" She eased her hands from around his waist, looked up at him, her blue eyes shiny behind thick glasses. "Why, Nate?"

He was not the most God-fearing person in the world. Hell, he wondered sometimes if he even believed in God despite his twelve years at St. Gertrude's and his altar-boy duty. Maybe God was just a form to curse for the pain and suffering in the world, kind of like shooting practice with a billboard target.

Nate's life sucked. Here he was, alone at thirty-five, divorced, no children, not even a relationship with a woman that brought him gratification past a one-night stand. The only ones who brought slivers of light into his life were Lily and his mother.

The only other times he experienced anything close to joy was when he was making furniture. The feel of the wood in his hands, the smell of a fresh cut of oak or mahogany, the planning and design of a chair, a desk, a dresser, all of this brought him peace and made him forget the unfortunate circumstances of his life—the near-bankruptcy of his business, the duty to his dead father that would not permit him to leave the company, the self-imposed solitude, the plight of his mother, the hatred toward Charles Blacksworth.

Even dead, Nate hated the man. The bastard had been a coward, leading two separate lives, refusing to choose one over the other. He'd stolen the best of both worlds, wealth and prestige from one, refuge from the other. *Goddamn Charles Blacksworth and his weakness to hell.*

Nate knew about duty, knew what it meant to forge ahead when the last drops of sweat were wrung out and all a person wanted to do was scream, "Enough." His own father had died when he was twelve, left Jack Finnegan to teach Nate about the business. And he'd wanted that connection with his father, wanted it so badly that he'd gone to the shop every day, stuck his hands in oil and learned the machines, all of them, working until the smoky oil smell saturated his clothes, seeped into his pores, and there was no way out, not even when he discovered the love of crafting wood.

His mother told him that he and Charles Blacksworth were more alike than he knew. She said they were both too bound by duty to live their own lives. But she'd been wrong. He was nothing like that son of a bitch.

"Nate? Nate?"

"Huh?" He looked down at his sister, tried to clear his head.

"Do you?"

"Do I what?"

She nudged him in the shoulder. "Do you think Christine is sad, like me?"

*Christine.* "I'm sure she's sad."

"Probably crying, too." A tear trickled down her cheek.

"Probably." He wrapped his arms around her, wishing he'd never heard the Blacksworth name.

"She's so pretty, isn't she?"

"Yeah, she's pretty."

Lily was in awe of Christine Blacksworth; hero-worship was a better word. Ever since the day she'd opened Charles's briefcase and found the picture of her older half sister sitting on a white horse decked out in fancy riding gear, she'd been obsessed with her. There was an album by her nightstand filled with pictures: Christine at eight, holding a black puppy; Christine at fifteen, singing in the high school choir; Christine at sixteen in a long dress standing next to a gangly boy in braces; Christine at seventeen, holding a golf club; Christine at twenty-one, on vacation in Rome.

Christine, Christine, Christine. He knew all about her, more than he'd ever cared to, and it all came from Lily. She'd pump Charles every month, eager to glean a tidbit, mix new findings to old, constructing a hero in the likeness of Christine Blacksworth.

And until a few weeks ago, Christine Blacksworth hadn't even known Lily existed.

"Do you think Mom will ever let me get a horse?"

She meant, like the one in Christine's picture. "I don't know, Lily. Animals are a lot of work."

"I want a white one, and a fancy hat with boots."

He stroked her hair and said nothing.

"A black hat."

"Uh-huh."

"And I'll zoom, fast."

"You will, huh?"

She pulled away, her thick black hair bobbing up and down as she nodded. "Uh-huh." She clapped her hands together, yelled, "Fast!"

Nate laughed, too. "Why don't you go," he paused, smacked his own hands together, "*fast*, and put on those little dance slippers you got for Christmas, and I'll play while you twirl around the room?"

Lily giggled, clapped her hands. "And then can we have hot chocolate with marshmallows by the fire?"

"Are you sure you don't just come here for the hot chocolate?"

She let out a half-giggle, wrapped her arms around his neck, and gave him a kiss on the cheek, her lips moist, smelling faintly of peanut butter. "I love you, Nate."

"I love you too, Lily."

"Be right back." She pulled away, moved across

the room in a clumsy half-gait, legs slightly unsteady, arms swinging from side to side.

She was all that was good and pure and innocent in this world, and he'd be damned if Christine Blacksworth was going to get near her.


SHE WATCHED THE HOUSE from down the street, her car tucked between a Chevy Blazer and a Ford Astrovan. It was 7:15 in the morning, cold, bleak, cloudless. She'd been parked three houses from the Desantro home for over an hour, even though the woman at Magdalena Middle School had informed her that classes didn't start until 7:45. She wasn't taking any chances; she was going to see Lily Desantro.

The decision to stay and meet the girl had come to her in the middle of the night. She'd almost decided to pack up and head back to Chicago.

This other life made up only a fraction of his existence, four days a month, forty-eight days a year. If she did the math, and she'd done it enough these past few days to know it was only six hundred seventy-two days in comparison to four *thousand* four hundred thirty-eight days.

Why not just bleep it out of her memory, pay the Desantros their money, and forget about them? It would be so much easier.

No.

Truth settled in her gut, crawled upward, pumping through her heart, migrating to her brain. She had to meet Lily to see what she looked like, how she spoke, what she wore; she had to know everything about her.

But not as her half sister. She was Nate Desantro's half sister. She hoped the girl didn't have the same black hair, the same blue eyes as she did. *Let her be tall and slim like her mother, with hazel eyes and a thin, straight nose. Do not let her look like me; do not let her look like a Blacksworth.*

She heard the bus before she saw it: the unmistakable shifting of gears, the low rumble of brakes as it slowed, moved past her, slush splattering the windshield of the BMW. Then the lights came on, first yellow, followed by red, as the bus stopped three houses from the Desantro residence.

*Now* she was going to get her first glimpse of the girl. Two gangly boys emerged from the house to the right of the Desantros', backpacks flung over their shoulders, heads bare, they sauntered toward the bus. When they'd climbed the steps, the yellow doors closed, the lights disappeared, and the bus moved down Artisdale Street, turning left at the stop sign.

Where was Lily?

Damn, she'd wanted to be done with this.

Christine drained the last of her coffee, settled back in her seat to consider Lily's absence. A familiar grinding sound caught her attention, and she glanced in the rearview mirror. A school bus approached, this one a smaller, compact version of the earlier one. It moved past the BMW, splashing a fraction of the slush its larger counterpart had, and came to a stop in front of the Desantro home.

The screen door opened, and a young girl dressed in a red parka, hood up, bustled out of the house, book bag strapped to her back. *Lily*. Christine leaned forward, sucking in every detail, the short, bulky frame stuffed into the jacket, the oversized red mittens, the jeans, the ankle high snow boots . . . the awkward gait.

A swirl of wind gusted around the girl just as she was getting ready to step on the bus. The hood of her parka blew back, exposing a tangle of black hair. She turned then, full face, to wave goodbye to her mother.

Christine stared, tried to comprehend what she was seeing. Then she sank back in her seat and closed her eyes.

# 9

MIRIAM WAS EXPECTING Charlie's daughter. She knew she'd want answers that couldn't be found in a legal document. Nathan wouldn't be pleased if he discovered she was still here. He was only trying to protect them, especially Lily, but it was too late. The look on Christine's face said *she knew.*

"Christine." Miriam moved aside to let her in. "I was beginning to wonder if you'd gone back to Chicago."

"No. Not yet."

"Let me take your coat. Would you like some coffee? Tea, perhaps?"

"I saw her get on the bus."

Not quite an accusation, but close. "Lily's bus comes at 7:25."

"I *saw* her, Miriam. I know."

"Do you?"

"She's retarded."

She hated that word. It snuffed out the face with deliberate intention, squashing personality and character as though the person were nothing more than an unfortunate aberration. "She has Down syndrome."

"I ... nobody told me."

"No, they didn't." Miriam led the way into the living room where she sank into a rocker, Nathan's creation, and let out a long breath. "We love Lily. Your father loved her, too. We've always felt very fortunate to have been blessed with her. You find that hard to believe, don't you? You think it's merely a mother's rationalization for the imperfection of her child."

"No, no, of course not."

"It's natural to think that way when you haven't been exposed to someone like Lily, but it's a prejudice that pricks at a parent's heart, nonetheless."

"I'm sorry—"

Miriam lifted a hand to interrupt her. "I used to think that the only people who could contribute to society in a meaningful way were the geniuses. I taught gifted students for years, and I still remember the time I tried to get the Special Education teacher to let me use her room because mine was having two broken windows replaced. I wanted to boot her out of her own classroom and push her into the library. I didn't understand why she wouldn't do it, since it was obvious, to me at least, that my students were learning for a worthier cause." She pressed her fingers to her cheeks. "And it wasn't until I had Lily that I understood. *She's* the one who teaches us the things you can't find in a classroom or on an IQ test, the things that really count."

Christine sat across from her in an overstuffed floral print chair, coat still on, hands clasped in her lap. "I don't have any experience with," she faltered, "children like Lily."

"Most people don't. It's the demand for perfection in our society and the definition of that perfection that blocks out all other possibilities. If someone is different or doesn't learn in the manner educators deem essential for success, with success being defined by *Money* or *Fortune* magazine, if they value non-societal possessions and give no credence to market trend, then what?" Miriam didn't wait for an answer, didn't expect one. "They're devalued, that's what. But a person who *fits*, goes to the right school, finds the right job, marries the right person, has the right amount of kids, despite the number of Prozac she pops every day, now there's a *success*." She let out a long breath and said, "I'll get off my soapbox now. You wouldn't want to see me at school board meetings. I'm no fun, believe me." She stood up, brushed off her jeans. "I could use a cup of tea. How about you?"

"Yes, I'd like that."

"Why don't you come in the kitchen while I get it ready? I made banana bread yesterday, and Nathan hasn't been around to steal it so I've got more loaves than mouths to eat it." She filled the teapot, switched on the stove. "What made you decide to stay, Christine?"

"I imagined myself walking down the street in Chicago, New York, anywhere, seeing a girl with black hair and blue eyes, and thinking, is that Lily? I had to know."

"Of course you did." She pulled down two mugs. "What do you want to know?"

"How old is she? Exactly. And when did you discover she was . . . that there was a problem?"

Yes, she would need to know how to chronicle Lily's existence into her own life. Perhaps, she would calculate her own age, pull out a scrapbook, stare at her father's face and try to recall the feelings, see if there was ever a hint that he'd just become a father again to a daughter named Lily.

"Lily was born June eighth, 1990. I had just turned forty when I discovered I was pregnant." She lifted the kettle and poured water over the tea bags. "The doctor wanted me to have testing done because of what he termed 'advanced maternal age,' but I said no, the results wouldn't affect my decision to have the baby one way or the other."

"And my father? What did he say?"

Miriam unwrapped a banana bread, pulled a knife from the drawer, and sliced two pieces. She arranged them on a blue earthenware plate and set it in front of Christine. Then she grabbed the mugs, placed them on the table beside the bread, and sank into a chair. "He agreed."

"Just like that? No questions . . . no argument?"

She couldn't tell Christine that Charlie hadn't even known about the baby, had decided weeks before to break it off between them, so she merely said, "He was concerned for me and the baby. I'd had several miscarriages after Nathan and even delivered a baby girl." *Anna.* "But she only lived a few hours. Charlie and I talked, and, in the end, we decided that God's will be done and we said no to the testing."

"And when Lily was born, you knew right away that she had Down syndrome?"

"We knew."

"Why'd you name her Lily?"

Miriam took a sip of tea. "I'd started painting some months before. It . . . kept me busy at night." She did not want to say, "when your father was gone," but the truth of it hung in the air. "It was early summer, and I was painting one of the gardens in the backyard." She pointed to the left, toward a row of small windows that lent a view of trees and shrubs dipped in snow. "It was filled with lilies, and the colors were gorgeous—burgundy on pink, red on white, orange on yellow. When Charlie saw the painting, he said it filled him with such over-whelming happiness, the same happiness he knew he'd feel when he looked at our child. So," she took another sip of tea, "we decided if we had a girl, she'd be Lily."

"And her middle name's Eleanor."

"Yes."

"Named after my aunt."

"Yes," Miriam said softly.

They sat silent then, the meaning of Lily's middle name settling between them, wrapping itself around both women, forcing them together, pulling them apart. Charles had named his second daughter after his beloved sister, Ellie; not even Christine could make that claim.

"Sometimes, I think I will hate him for the rest of my life."

"Don't hate him, Christine. He loved you with his whole heart."

"Is that why he came to you? Why he started another family?"

"I can't explain what happened between us without sounding demeaning toward his other," she paused a second, "relationships."

"You mean my mother."

"Yes."

Christine set down her mug and met Miriam's gaze. "You know, this is almost surreal, me having tea with you as though it were perfectly normal."

Miriam chose her words carefully. "I think you have a lot of unanswered questions."

"That would be an understatement."

"But I don't think you're ready for the answers, not yet." Christine looked so much like her father sitting there, brows stitched together, eyes narrowed. Ocean-blue eyes. And her fingers, they were Charlie's fingers. *God,* but Miriam missed him.

"I'm not ready. I've been obsessing about every detail since I found out, but deep down, I don't think I want to know."

"That's understandable."

"Except for Lily. I want to meet her."

Miriam rubbed the back of her neck, trying to relieve the tightness at the base of it. "I don't think this would be a good time to meet Lily."

"She might like to know she has a half sister."

"She already knows."

"She knows about me?"

"Lily's known about you for years," Miriam said.

"Why? How?"

"Your father. Lily found your picture, the one of you on your horse, and she was mesmerized. She thought you looked like a princess, and then, when she saw one of your high school dance pictures, with you in a gown and your hair all done up, she was *sure* you were a princess."

"She knew all about me? And you, you knew, too? He even showed you pictures?"

"He loved you. He was very proud of you, and he wanted to share that with us."

Christine pushed back her chair and stood up, the sound of wood scraping the oak floor filling the tiny kitchen. "He had no right to expose me that way, to let you see inside my family. He had no right to *share* anything about us."

Right or not, he'd done it. Miriam knew all about Christine, the history of firsts: first dance, first date, first car, first day of college, first job. She knew of the less joyful times, too, the sad strips of life that left their mark, the dog that died in her arms, the boyfriend who turned out to be less than loyal, the mother who smothered and clung.

Charlie had been so careful when he spoke of Gloria, his words well-chosen, at times compassionate, most times guilt-ridden.

Miriam did not speak of her own dead husband, Nick, despite Charlie's gentle prodding and Nathan's insistent attempts to resurrect the man. Loyalty kept her silent, not to her husband, but to her son. How does a mother tell her child that the memories he holds of his father are incorrect, that the truth does not even remotely resemble the memory? How does she tell him about the gaping holes in the recall that make it all a sham?

"He told you everything about us," Christine continued, "and we didn't even know you existed."

"No, you didn't." She fingered the gold cross around her neck, pressed it against her skin. *Dear God, give me strength.*

"Do you have any idea how that makes me feel?"

"That, he regretted most of all."

She couldn't tell Christine that her father was tired of the company she worshipped, the life-style she admired, the people she called family. And she could never tell her that if it had not been for Christine herself, he might have found the strength to walk away, the courage to relieve himself of the suffocating responsibility others cast on him, and that he so dutifully accepted, and for once, just once, he might have chosen to ignore expectation, ignore duty, and follow his own course.

She could tell her none of this, and so she settled for, "He found himself in a situation where he had two families, right or wrong, and being the man your father was, he felt a duty to both."

There was a long pause, a silence that hung between both women, with nothing but the sound of a snowplow filling the gaps. Miriam waited, fingers pressed to the cross around her neck.

"I think I will never understand this, and I know

I will never accept it, but I want to be done. Lily will get her money, and we'll forget we ever met each other. Agreed?" She was in a rush now, pulling on her coat, gathering up her scarf and gloves.

"If that's how you want it."

"It is. There is one other thing. My father told me about a loan he signed for a company," she paused, "your son's company."

"I see."

"I saw Jack Finnegan the other day and he told me the whole story, how your son believes you came into a small windfall and you're the one who signed the note for him when, in reality, it was my father. Is that true?"

"Yes." She'd lied to help her son, and now, if he found out she'd merely been the front person for Charlie's money, it would be disastrous.

"I have no intention of informing your son that my father was the one who held the collateral on his business and that *I* am now the one holding the note."

"Thank you."

"As long as there's no reason to divulge anything, he'll be none the wiser."

As long as Miriam stayed away from the Blacksworths, is what she meant. "Fine," was all Miriam could muster.

"I'll be leaving in the morning. You can expect a

bank draft in the next several weeks. As for Lily, I'd at least like to see her room."

She might as well have said, *I demand to see Lily's room, or else* ... because, despite the casual tone in her voice, the threat was there; *I demand to see Lily's room, or else I might have to contact your son about the bank note.*

Miriam pushed back her chair and stood. "Follow me." She led Christine past the kitchen, down a tiny hall to a room with a sunflower painted on the door. "This is Lily's room."

She watched from the doorway as Christine stepped into the room. Lily loved the pale-yellow walls, the orange ceiling swirled with gold, the mahogany dresser Nate had made for her. Mobiles dangled overhead, glow-in-the-dark stars, brilliant sunflowers with dark-brown faces, pristine snow-flakes. A field of sunflowers covered one entire wall, Miriam's gift to Lily on her eleventh birthday. Lily said the flowers looked real, even the furry bumblebee that hovered near the corner. The bedspread was sun-yellow with a mountain of sky-blue pillows piled near the head, round and square shapes, even a few stars. A small white desk perched in one corner with a study lamp and a yellow cup stenciled in sunflowers stuffed with pens, pencils, and a ruler.

Christine moved from the mobile, to the mural, to the bedspread, even picked up the black stuffed dog on the bed, studied it, gently placed it back on top of the pillow mountain.

Then she turned and spotted the photo album on Lily's nightstand. On the cover was a picture of herself at seventeen dressed in a long, formal gown of shimmering pink, her hair piled on top of her head, tiny pink rosettes tucked in the curls. She was smiling, beautiful, and radiant . . . like the princess Lily thought she was. Miriam watched her flip through the pages, slowly, fingering one here and there, lingering, perhaps recalling the memory, the moment, the feeling. When she reached the last page, she closed the album, turned it over.

"These . . . are all of me." She stared at the closed album.

"Yes."

Christine turned toward Miriam, caught sight of the bulletin board near the door and the large glossy photograph of herself and her horse next to it. "I," she began, her voice unsteady as she moved toward the pictures. "I don't understand. Why?"

"Isn't it obvious?" Miriam said softly.

Christine reached up, touched the muzzle of the horse in the framed picture. "No." Her gaze met Miriam's, and there were tears in her eyes. "No."

"She loves you, Christine. Lily loves you."

"No," she said again, shaking her head. "No."

And then she ran past Miriam and was gone.

# 10

HARRY SHRUGGED OUT OF his suit jacket and flung it on the back of a chair. There were three chairs and a couch in his office, plenty of room to spread out and no reason to worry he'd have to move it for a client or co-worker. The only people who'd ever ventured through this door were Charlie, Chrissie, and the Mexican cleaning lady, Gladys.

The rest of them were polite, even solicitous, but how else should an employee treat the man whose brother signed their checks? They asked about his weekend, his plans, current events, the delicious veal scallopini at The Presidio. And of course, when he lingered at the coffee station in the morning, telling his most recent off-color joke, they laughed, as expected.

*Assholes.* Harry pulled out his chair and sank into it. Lunch had been exceptional today, broiled whitefish with rice pilaf, broccoli florets, and a cup of clam chowder. His belly was full, and his chest and shoulders were sore. He'd pushed himself on the machines today, spent an extra half-hour at the gym before lunch trying to work off some of the tension. He'd thought about just cutting the workout short, or skipping it altogether and heading to The Presidio and a double scotch, but his damn headache made him opt for the rowing machine instead.

Christine was the one causing him so much aggravation. *Jesus*, if this kept up, the worrying alone would kill him long before the drink ever did. She'd left a message on his voice mail late yesterday morning to tell him she'd just finished up with a meeting and was on her way back to the cabin to pack up, and then she was heading back to Chicago. She sounded hollowed out. The meeting was with the Desantro woman, and he wondered if Charlie's mistress had given her trouble.

He still couldn't believe Charlie had set himself up like this. For all of his calm brilliance, hadn't he guessed this could happen? Even Harry could figure this game out; married man screws around and fathers a child. He dies and leaves the woman a shit-load of money, but now it's not enough, and it's not just about the money. So, what does she want now? Recognition? More money? A plot next to his in the cemetery?

He should've gone with Christine and seen for himself. Who knew what kind of loony the woman might be. After all, she'd been shacked up with Charlie for fourteen years, quiet as a mouse, with a kid, too. How the hell had that all worked? And what the fuck was wrong with Charlie? If he wanted to be with her, maybe even had the unfortunate bad luck to have loved her, why hadn't he dumped Gloria, given her a truckload of tissues and a hefty settlement and told her to kiss off? Hell, he could've even offered to pay for therapy sessions and thrown in a year's worth of free prescriptions.

Maybe the timing was off. Or, maybe he'd been getting ready to do just that, or at least getting ready to think about doing it. Charlie was a methodical man, big on responsibility. *But fourteen fucking years?*

And what about the kid? Did she have the Blacksworth eyes, the black hair? It must've blown Chrissie's mind when she found out about her. This was one major screw-up, and now Charlie was gone and Harry was left to clean up the mess. That in itself was scary or hysterical, depending on how you looked at it. He'd done good, though; he'd actually paid Gloria a visit, twice, stretched out long enough to fulfill his duty and polish off two scotch neats. And the last time, he'd pulled up a chair and sat in the kitchen, talking to Greta while she stuffed a turkey. Who the hell ate all that food she fixed, anyway?

At 1:35 P.M., Christine still wasn't in her office, hadn't phoned in, either. Where the hell was she? The jolt to his gut started then, a quick nauseating pain that kicked into a slow burn. He called her house, counted four, five rings.

"Hello?"

"Jesus, Chrissie, are you okay? You sound like shit."

"I was sleeping."

"What the hell's going on? Why didn't you call last night?"

"I'm sorry. It was late; I didn't want to bother you."

"Hell, you bothered me by not calling."

"I'm sorry."

"What's wrong, Chrissie?" He gentled his tone. "What happened?"

"She's retarded, Uncle Harry."

"Who? The girl?"

"Lily. She has Down syndrome."

"Jesus." *Jesus.*

"I'm really tired. I'll talk to you later. Okay?"

"Sure, get some rest. We'll talk later." He hung up the phone, stared at the receiver. No wonder she'd been in a hurry to get out of that damn town. Retarded? He opened his bottom desk drawer, pulled out a half-empty bottle of Crown Royal and the glass he kept with it.

The phone rang, and he considered letting it go into voice mail, decided against it, thinking it might be Christine calling him back.

"Harry Blacksworth."

"Mr. Blacksworth, this is Belinda at the front desk. I'm sorry to bother you, sir, but I have a client on hold who says he needs to speak with someone about his investment right away."

"Why are you calling *me*?"

"I didn't know what else to do. Everyone else is in a meeting, and he said it was urgent."

"Belinda—you did say that was your name, right?"

"Yes, sir."

"Are you new here?"

"Yes, sir. I started last week."

"Ah." He twirled the phone cord around his finger, watched it suck the blood from the tip of it. "Well, *Belinda*, let me tell you how it is around here. I'm a very busy man, and I don't talk to other associates' clients, I don't care if the fucking bottom just fell out of their 401(k) and they're ready to jump out the window."

He unraveled the phone cord, studied his finger, which was now blue. "Do you understand?"

"Yes, sir, thank you, sir."

"Have a good day, Belinda," he said, and hung up the phone.

Then he reached for the bottle, unscrewed the cap, and poured a drink. *Busy fucking indeed.*

GLORIA PIERCED A SCALLOP, lifted it to her mouth. She'd have to compliment Greta on the meal tonight. The scallops were meaty, a golden opaque with just a hint of garlic. Charles had always loved scallops. "So, dear, tell me about your trip."

"It was fine."

"Did you find what you were looking for?"

"What do you mean?"

"Just that. Peace and state of mind. Isn't that why you went to the cabin?"

"Yes. Yes, it was."

"So?" She forked another scallop. "Tell me about it."

Christine set down her fork, took a sip of wine. "Well, the cabin was on the outskirts of town. There wasn't much there, just a grocery store, if you want to call it that, and I think a thrift shop of some sort."

"How quaint."

"But the people were very nice, actually, quite friendly."

"I can imagine the type." And she could. Old men with dentures in their pockets and women wearing their husband's overalls and snow boots.

Why anyone could even consider living in a town like that, where the butcher and the funeral director, if they had one, were the same person, was beyond her comprehension. Uncivilized, that's what it was.

"They really were nice."

"But what did you *do* all that time?"

Christine's gaze dropped to her plate. She'd barely touched her food.

"Christine? Is everything all right?"

"Yes. Fine. Just tired, I guess."

"You know, going there may have harmed more than helped. All those hours alone in that cabin, traveling the same road . . . did you see where the accident happened?"

"I saw one spot that might have been it."

"Oh, Christine." She covered her daughter's hand with her own and said, "This was too much for you. It's bad enough to know it happened; you don't need to stick your face in it."

"I had to see . . ."

"No, you didn't. If someone gets hit by a train, you don't have to touch the blood splattered on the tracks or witness the smashed body to accept the death. That only makes it worse, places a vision in your head that will never go away." She stroked her daughter's hand, lowered her voice. "I would never want to see the guardrail he hit or his car. I wouldn't even want to travel the same road he was on that night. Doing those things, gathering those details, can destroy a person."

"I know. It probably wasn't the best idea."

"Now, you have to try to forget it, busy yourself so the images fade."

"Yes, that's what I'll do."

"Good."

"Do you miss him?"

"Yes, of course I do."

"He loved you."

"Yes, he did." There was such certainty in her words, but it was her heart that held the doubt.

"I love you, too."

"And I, you. I'm hopeful," Gloria began, keeping her voice calm, "that you and I can grow even closer." She took a sip of wine, set the glass down. "It's always been you and your father, ever since my accident, and as admirable as that was, it was lonely for me. I wanted so much to be a part of what you had, and yet I was always on the outside."

"I never meant—"

"But there was a time, when you were a baby and before the accident, when you and I did everything together. Your father was always busy traveling with work or at the office, and many a day, I was the first person you saw in the morning and the last one you kissed at night. Surely you remember?"

"It's fuzzy, but I do remember bits and pieces," Christine said.

"Before the accident, it was always you and me, but then, when I fell . . . I lost so much more than a healthy body . . . I lost you."

"I'm sorry, I never meant—"

"Don't be sorry. I just want you to understand. We were so close once, as close as you and your father were. When I had the accident, I was in so much pain, he had to step in and take over. I still suffer, every day, but I push on."

"I know you do."

"He's gone, Christine. It's just you and me now. I want that closeness again."

"I want that, too, Mother." Her eyes were wet. "Very much."

"Good." Gloria smiled. "And maybe one day, you'll widen the circle, include that man of yours?"

"Connor and I are . . . an interesting match."

"You're perfect for each other. His father can't get within ten feet of either of you before he's talking about genes and what beautiful children you'll have."

"I know."

"So? You've been seeing each other almost two years. You're twenty-seven, old enough to settle down, and he's an excellent choice." She took a sip of wine. "Truly excellent."

"I don't know." Christine pierced a scallop.

"Sometimes, I think the chemistry just isn't there, like we'd make better business partners than life partners."

"Be careful what you wish for. Caring too much has its own dangers. No matter how far our society's come, one partner is always more committed than the other, and that's the one who'll be most disappointed."

"So you're saying, don't care so much?"

"I'm saying don't put such stock in chemistry and 'head over heels.'" She studied the row of diamonds on her left finger. "It's really more about considering the whole person, understanding his strengths, tolerating his weaknesses," she paused, "and compromise." The ring sparkled, brilliant under the light. "Compromise is perhaps the biggest part."

"Well, of course it is. But you can only go so far; you can't compromise *yourself*. Where would that leave you? And what about love?"

Gloria let out a small laugh. "For all of your intelligence and sophistication, you sound like a school girl. Do you know how many women who were 'head over heels' in love when they got married ended up in divorce court fighting over the silverware? In the end, they got nothing but a large legal bill and a new street address in an overcrowded development. Or they stayed married and looked the other way."

"Well, what about you and Dad? Didn't you feel that way about him?" Christine pushed her plate aside and leaned forward, gaze fixed and waiting.

"Yes, I did. I loved your father with every ounce of my being." The sad, painful truth. "But all I'm saying is, a woman's got to be practical too, have other considerations. For example, at some point, she's got to decide if she can live with a man who's slovenly, or remote, or gambles. Connor is attentive, handsome, intelligent, and very wealthy." Gloria ticked his assets off on her fingers. "What more could a woman ask for? I think the two of you would make a wonderful couple."

"I think he's more interested in a merger than a marriage."

"Well, isn't that what marriage is anyway, a merger of sorts?"

"I guess."

"Give it some thought. He adores you." *And you'll never destroy yourself with loving him too much.*

CHRISTINE TURNED OUT the light and fell into bed. She'd left work early to meet her mother at Mon Ami's for a manicure, dinner, and shopping. While Lisette snipped, clipped, filed, and painted Christine's nails, her mother had her eyebrows waxed and her lashes dyed. Dinner came next, at a fancy little French restaurant on the north side of town that served a delicious shrimp and escargot dish. And after dinner, there was shopping at a string of boutiques nearby. Christine settled on a red wool shawl that she had absolutely no use for and no idea when she would ever wear it. She didn't even think she liked it very much, but none of that had mattered at the time. She was caught up in the shopping frenzy that had sucked her in these past several weeks, buying for the sake of buying, the forty-second rush of owning something for the pure pleasure of ownership.

How could she stop when her mother thrived on the outings, planning each excursion with the thoroughness she'd given to her husband's homecoming dinners? When they were shopping, or dining out, Gloria didn't complain of pain, though she discreetly downed her little white pill at five-thirty every afternoon, usually with a glass of chardonnay.

It was the busyness that Christine embraced most, the exhaustive outings that ate up chunks of time, left no hours for remembering what she wished most to forget, Magdalena.

Connor was more available, too, and she wondered if her mother had spoken with him about finalizing the merger with her daughter. He sent flowers to the office, red roses and calla lilies (whose mere name brought back memories she was trying to forget), and scheduled evenings at the theater. An attentive Connor was hard to ignore. When he told her he'd planned a weekend in New York City to see a show, she'd been hopeful they might be heading toward a new plateau. She didn't stop to question why she'd never wanted this before, refused to consider that this sudden urgency might have something to do with her recent trip.

But desire could not hold up to reality and the truth of what life with Connor Pendleton would be like. He was the descendant of a long line of business moguls, determined to conquer, restructure, merge, whichever might prove more beneficial to his particular interests. It didn't surprise her when Niles Furband from Glen Systems showed up that first night and joined them for dinner, though Connor swore it was pure coincidence.

When she lay in his arms that night, the beat of his heart against her naked skin, his breath fanning her hair in calm, even exchange, she knew the true meaning of loneliness, knew, too, that she would never commit to this man.

Surprisingly, it was Uncle Harry who helped her acknowledge what needed to be done. He took her for sushi when she returned from New York and told her, *Connor Pendleton's an asshole who wouldn't know a good thing if it bit him in the ass.* As for her mother, he was careful, dealing around the issues of Gloria Blacksworth, instead of hammering her head on. *Do you really want to spend your life riding escalators and dodging the perfume counters at Neiman Marcus? And pissing around with your hair? Leave it alone.*

Then he shoved a drink toward her and asked her if she was more upset about her father's girlfriend or the retarded half sister.

When she didn't answer, he'd let it go, but now they were sitting in his living room, sipping sherry, and he'd put the question to her again, and this time, he wanted an answer.

"I don't know, Uncle Harry," she looked away. "It's really hard to talk about."

"Most painful things are. Look at me." He raised his glass, saluted her. "I've spent my whole goddamn life hiding a hurt that happened over thirty years ago, and I still can't get over it."

"What are you talking about?"

"We're not here to discuss me right now. You're the one we need to talk about, so let's do it. Start talking."

Was it the mistress or the daughter that bothered her most? Or was it the resentment she harbored against him for not being who he said he was?

"I think I never really knew him."

"Charlie was a tough guy to know, never wanted

to disappoint anybody, but in the end, he let himself down. He sold himself out so he could please everybody else."

"What did he want?"

"Oh, now, there's a sad fucking question."

"Tell me."

He refilled her glass, then his own. "Charlie never wanted to run the business. He wanted to be a doctor, save the whole goddamn world. But you don't tell Randolph Blacksworth you're not going to follow the plan he's laid out for you since the time you could walk, not unless you're ready to tell him to go fuck himself. It was never an issue with me, of course, because the old man never expected anything from me. It was always Charlie."

"But a doctor's a very respectable profession."

"Didn't matter. He'd even been accepted into medical school, Georgetown, I think. But once the old man put his foot down, that was it. When Charlie told me he was giving up on medical school, I told him he should tell the old man to go screw himself.

"But he was excellent with the firm; he was a natural leader.

"He was Charlie. But deep down, he'd have much rather been hunched over a microscope, studying cancer cells, than sitting in a boardroom."

"Are you saying his whole life was a lie?"

"Hell, no, I'm not saying that, but what I am saying is your father made choices, and he chose duty and responsibility, to everyone but himself. And now we find out he was only human, just like the rest of us. If he found one little slice of happiness with that Desantro woman, then let it go, at least give him that."

"You mean we were merely his *duty*, that Miriam Desantro and her daughter were the ones he really loved?"

"No. I'm saying maybe with them, he could be himself, not always the one with the answers, who makes everything right."

"You don't know that."

"I don't." His blue eyes studied her. "Neither do you. At least not yet."

"What's that supposed to mean?"

"It means there's probably only one person who knew the real Charlie Blacksworth, and unless you go back there, talk to her, and try to understand, you'll end up just like me, tormented and miserable for the rest of your fucking life."

# 11

SHE WAS COMING TODAY. Sometime, in the next several hours, Christine Blacksworth would drive into Magdalena and knock on his mother's door. And Miriam would let her in, welcome her, actually. Wasn't Christine the one who'd told them all she wanted nothing to do with them?

Why'd she have to come to Magdalena and screw everything up? What if she ran into Lily this time? Saw the truth? His mother said Christine knew all about Lily, but Nate was more concerned that Lily not find out about Christine. What would she do if she knew the person she idolized had sat at her kitchen table, walked through her bedroom?

Lily would want to meet her. She'd wanted to meet her since the day she found that damn picture of Christine on a horse, sitting there so proud . . . so fucking untouchable. And if Lily did meet her, she'd like her, and she'd want to start inviting her to school, maybe church, and just when she'd begun counting on her, Christine would go back to her real home. Just like her old man.

Lily would never understand; she believed people did what they said they'd do. She didn't know about the hidden agendas, the lies.

But his mother hadn't wanted to hear any of it. She'd told him Christine was reaching out to her, and she wasn't going to turn her away.

The money from the will had come the other day, the first of three installments. Nate called it guilt money, but Miriam said it was merely Charlie's way of taking care of his responsibilities. She'd mentioned the possibility of paying off Nate's business loan with some of it. There was more than enough, but he'd told her he'd torch the place before he accepted anything that belonged to Charles Blacksworth.

So, he'd sit here, and he'd wait. There was a six pack of Michelob in the refrigerator and a stack of wood by the fireplace.

He was ready.


CHRISTINE THOUGHT ABOUT turning the rental car around and heading back to the airport at least once every twenty miles, but the desire to *know* pushed her forward. Miriam hadn't sounded surprised to hear from her. In fact, she'd spoken as though she'd been expecting the call. When the subject of meeting Lily surfaced, she told her they'd have to "see how things went."

Her mother wasn't pleased with her decision to return to the cabin for a few days.

*Again? Why? Why do you have to go?*

*I . . . just need a little time.*

*I thought,* pause, *this was our time. We were having a grand time together, you and I.* Pause. *Weren't we?*

*Of course, Mother. But I need to do this. It's only for a few days.*

*I hope this isn't going to become a habit, like with your father.*

*No!*

*When will you be back?*

*A few days.*

*Four?*

*Yes.*

*Good. I'll fix you dinner. Seven o'clock.*

*Okay. Invite Uncle Harry, too.*

*Oh, that damn man.*

*Please?*

*All right. What about Connor?*

*No.*

*But—*

*No.*

Pause. *Don't be late. The meal will be ruined if you're late.*

And that was that. Unspoken words slid between them. *I want you here, I want you here, I want you here.*

Four days, that's all the time she had to piece together years of questions that would take a lifetime to understand.

It was early afternoon when she reached Magdalena, its streets a dirty mix of snow and slush. Plows had created mini-boulders along common areas, perfect for children playing king of the hill. Christine parked along the curb of 1167 Artisdale Street. There was an old station wagon with wood panels and a black F-150 pickup parked in the driveway. She guessed Nate Desantro was standing guard over his mother.

She made her way up the steps, the snowman and Christmas tree chimes tinkling on either side of her, and rang the bell. Nate Desantro opened the door. She hadn't remembered him quite this large, the massive shoulders stuffed into a blue and black flannel shirt, the muscular forearms exposed beneath rolled-up sleeves, the thick neck.

"My mother's been expecting you," he said.

"Thank you." She nodded and shrugged out of her coat.

He stood in front of her, blocking the hallway

that led to the living room. "For some insane reason she wants to get to know you," he said, lowering his voice. "She thinks it will help you come to terms with your old man. But don't you dare demean her, or I'll kick your ass out of here. And if she decides to let you meet Lily, I want you to keep in mind that the child worships you. She'll believe everything you tell her, understand? So, don't be like your old man and make promises you can't keep."

She didn't know what her father had told Lily, didn't know anything about the man who had lived here four days a month. And so she simply nodded and said nothing.

"My mother's in the living room." He turned his back to her and headed down the hallway.

Miriam sat in a rocker, knitting. Her fingers stilled when she saw Christine. "Christine. Hello." A smile spread across her face, accentuating the lines around her eyes and mouth.

"Thank you for agreeing to see me."

"I'm glad you called. Please," she stood up, clutched the burgundy piece she was knitting in her right hand, "can I get you something to drink? Tea? Coffee?"

"No, I'm fine, thank you."

"Well, then, something to eat. You must be hungry." She turned to her son, who was leaning against the doorway. "Nathan, would you mind, dear? I've got pumpkin roll sliced in the fridge. And put on the water for tea, too, just in case Christine changes her mind." When he'd disappeared, Miriam sat down, motioned to her. "Sit down. Make yourself comfortable."

Christine sat in the stuffed, flowered chair, the same one as last time. "What are you making?" She couldn't open the conversation with "Tell me everything about my father so I can think of him without this hate that's been ripping me up."

Miriam lifted the burgundy material in front of her. It looked like a half-finished sweater, with the neck and better part of the torso completed. "I was making this sweater for Charlie." She let it slip to her lap, her hands gripping the material in tight bunches. "He was always cold. I made him a new one every year." She shook her head, and the loose bun at the nape of her neck wobbled back and forth. "I don't know why I'm still knitting it. It's . . . just that it makes me feel close to him, almost like he's still here." She looked up. "But you haven't come to listen to me ramble on about how I miss Charlie. Tell me what you want to know, and I'll try to help."

"I'm struggling to understand this," Christine made a sweeping gesture, "all of this. Not only his death, but you, this place . . . Lily."

"It must be very painful and confusing for you."

Miriam's fingers moved over the burgundy material resting in her lap, once, twice, three times, in an absentminded caress. "Charlie worried about it all the time: how to tell you, when, even if. He used to say that of all the people who'd counted on him, you were the one he'd let down the most ... and you didn't even know it." She sighed, clutched the gold cross around her neck. "He tortured himself with that, every day, for fourteen years."

She let out a small laugh. "I met Charlie in Sal's Market, in the pickle aisle. He was looking for Kosher Dills, and I told him they were in the refrigerated section, by the herring and cream cheese. That started a discussion on Kosher refrigerated versus non-refrigerated, and twenty minutes later he'd told me about his sister dying and invited me for coffee. He needed to talk to somebody, and he seemed like a nice man, so I went."

"He and Aunt Ellie were very close." What else could she say?"

"Your father and Ellie were inseparable, from what I heard. But I always felt sorry for your Uncle Harry."

Before Christine could ask why, Nate Desantro appeared carrying a tray with a teapot painted in sunflowers, two matching cups and saucers, cream, sugar, and a sunflower plate filled with sliced pumpkin roll.

"Thank you, dear."

He set the tray down on the coffee table and said, "I'll be in the garage if you need me." He glanced a warning at Christine and left.

When the back door closed, Miriam poured the steaming tea into the cups, and said, "He's not as mean as he sounds. He's just very protective."

"I gathered that."

"His father died when he was only twelve, and he felt as though he had to become the man of the family. He didn't like it much when Charlie started coming around, to talk, share a meal. But Nathan tolerated it because I think he figured Charlie would go back to Chicago, and that would be the end of it. But when he came back here, and then Nathan found out about you and your mother," her voice drifted off, "well, he never forgave your father."

Christine gripped the cup between her hands, felt the heat seep into her fingers. *Of course he couldn't forgive him; how could he?*

"For all of his power, his responsibility to business and family, your father was not a strong man." The words slipped out as though she regretted saying them, but knew they needed to be said. "He tried so hard to make everyone happy, but he couldn't choose between us, Christine. He just couldn't."

"What did he say when he found out you were pregnant with Lily?"

She looked away. "He didn't know for a while. You see, Charlie had decided to break it off. The duplicity was killing him." Her voice dipped, filled with pain. "I didn't see him for three long, horrible months; by that time I knew I was pregnant. When he called to see how I was doing, I told him about the baby." She turned to meet Christine's gaze. "Don't hate your father, hate me. He was trying to do the right thing, but I wouldn't let him. And then, of course, when Lily was born with Down syndrome, he *couldn't* leave."

Miriam reached into her pocket, pulled out a pack of Salem Lights. "Will it bother you if I smoke?"

Christine shook her head. "My father hated smoking. My mother hid her cigarettes and only smoked when he was here."

Miriam lit her cigarette, took a long drag. "I only smoked when he wasn't here, and then only outside so he wouldn't be able to smell it in the house."

"Well, now nobody has to hide anymore."

"I guess you're right."

"I want to know everything."

"Charlie started coming to Magdalena once a month. Actually, he'd stay at his cabin, drive up here, and I'd cook for him." She smiled, blew out a thin stream of smoke. "He loved vegetable beef soup with homemade rolls. And strawberry shortcake. Those were his favorites, but then you knew that."

No, she didn't. What about veal piccata? Chicken Oscar? Chateaubriand? Had her mother ever served them vegetable beef soup *or* strawberry shortcake?

"We used to talk for hours," Miriam said. "He'd sit at the kitchen table, right where you sat the last time, and I'd be cooking, or feeding him something, and before we knew it, three or four hours had passed. It's the talking that keeps people together, Christine. Don't let anybody tell you any different. A person's got to know that somebody cares about what he has to say."

*What about talking to his wife*? Even though Gloria liked to keep her topics light, "table talk" she called it, hadn't there been a time when they'd shared issues that mattered?

"At first, Charlie was reserved; he didn't talk much, mostly listened and asked a lot of questions. I could almost see his brain working, processing my answers, filtering out his own questions." There was a second's hesitation before she added, "He was an amazing man, Christine. Truly amazing."

Christine pretended not to see the tears in the older woman's eyes.

"I'm sorry, so sorry that I hurt you." The words fell out in soft penance. "But I will never be sorry that I loved him . . . or that he loved me."

\* \* \* \* \*

HOW LONG WAS SHE going to stay? One day, two days? Four? He let out a laugh, cursed under his breath. Wouldn't it be ironic if she followed her old man's footsteps and stayed four days? Nate didn't want her staying at all; he wanted her out of here before Lily came home. But his mother had told him Christine could stay as long as she needed to.

As long as she needed to *what*? Needed to see how her old man played house in Magdalena? Needed to see how screwed up she could get trying to absorb it all? Needed to ferret out every detail of her old man's secret life so she could forgive him? Or hate him?

He couldn't hide out in the garage forever; it was fucking freezing out here. Besides, he could only check the oil and tire pressure on his mother's station wagon so many times. He slammed the hood, wiped his hands on a cloth. Fuck it. He was going to have to go back inside and face Christine Blacksworth, maybe even share a meal with her.

He zipped his jacket to just below his beard, moved to the small, scarred workbench where his father had spent many a night tinkering with one project or another, and pulled out a sketch pad. He flipped it open, grabbed a pencil, and began drawing. He didn't hear the garage door open, didn't realize someone was standing behind him until she spoke.

"Nate?"

He jumped, slammed the pad shut. "Jesus," he said, turning on Christine. "What the hell are you sneaking up on me for?"

"I wasn't sneaking up on you. Your mother sent me to tell you lunch is ready."

"How long are you planning to stay in Magdalena?" He pushed the sketch pad aside and stood. Might as well get it all out in the open now, before Lily got involved.

She shook her head, and her hair swayed across her shoulders, brushed past her cheeks. Thick, black hair, smooth, pale cheeks.

"I was planning to stay a few days."

Her words brought him back. "Four?"

"I don't know."

"Four would be an interesting choice."

She just shrugged, stuck her hands in her pockets. "I'm sorry if my being here upsets you, but I have to do this."

He looked away. He didn't want to see the sadness in those blue eyes, didn't want to admit that she might be right. Hell, he didn't want to admit that she *was* right. He'd blocked out enough issues to screw himself up for the next twenty-five years. He called it self-preservation, but wasn't it really self-destruction?

"I have to meet Lily, too."

"I know."

"Today, after school. Your mother said it would be all right."

He didn't answer. Maybe once she met Lily she'd leave and they could all get back to their lives, back to grieving and moving on in their own ways, one breath at a time. That's all you could really count on anymore—the next breath coming out of you, and sometimes you couldn't even count on that.

"Nate?"

"Yeah?"

"Thank you."

"For what?"

"For understanding. I know how hard this must be for you—"

"Stop it." He should've pushed her to leave. So what if she never came to terms with her old man's secret life? So, she could go see a shrink. It wasn't his problem.

"I just—"

"No." He shut her down again. "Don't thank me for anything. My mother thinks it's important for you to meet Lily. So fine, you'll meet Lily, maybe even play a game or two together. But then you're out, got it? You leave, and we get back to normal around here."

# 12

CHRISTINE FLIPPED ANOTHER page, stared at the picture of Lily dressed as Snow White. She must've been seven or eight at the time, wearing a blue and white gown, her heavy black hair held in place with a red band. But this Snow White wore thick glasses that distorted the shape of her blue eyes, and the smile she offered was lopsided, a hint of moist pink protruding through full lips.

She was surrounded by other children dressed in fairytale outfits: Pinnochio, Red Riding Hood, Cinderella, Peter Pan, most wearing thick glasses, which, like Lily's, hid the true color and shape of their eyes. But it wasn't the high foreheads, the flat noses, the half protrusion of thick lips that pulled Christine in, held her there, as she studied them one by one. Their physical appearances faded next to the expressions on their faces. Pure joy.

She turned another page, and then another. Here was a picture of Lily a year or so older, cheeks puffed out as she leaned over a chocolate cake glowing with candles. In the corner of the picture a man's hand rested on the table, long fingers spread wide. A gold wedding band circled his left finger. It was her father's hand.

There were pictures of Nate, too, looking younger and more relaxed, dark hair shorter, beard trimmed, skin brown from the outdoors. In one photo, he stood on a large rock in the middle of a stream, with Lily hefted high in his arms, clapping her hands and laughing. In another, Nate sat in a rocking chair, with Lily tucked against him, thumb in her mouth, sleeping. There were several others, most of them outdoor shots, traipsing through the woods with backpacks, fishing on the banks of a river, building a campfire. And in all of them, including the photo of Lily sleeping, there was a joining of brother and sister.

But when she turned another page, the dreaded truth lay before her. There were three photos of her father and Lily: one sitting side by side, arms touching as Lily opened a present; one hugging each other, eyes closed, smiles wide; and one with Lily, lifting a basketball from a box, head thrown back in laughter as her father looked on, the pleasure and love on his face undeniable.

She tried to ignore the jealousy that stabbed her. Why would she be jealous of a retarded girl? Lily

Desantro was destined to live her life on the outside of a world that demanded perfection and precision.

She flipped the page, studied the five-by-seven glossy staring back at her. Her father stood in front of a Christmas tree, wearing brown corduroy slacks and a green and black flannel shirt, Miriam at his side, nearly as tall as he was. One hand rested on her waist, the other on Lily's shoulder as she stood in front of her parents, dressed in a red velvet pantsuit trimmed in white lace, and black patent leather shoes.

It was the flannel shirt that held her attention. He was a cashmere casual dresser, or wool, even cotton. But flannel? Most of her memories of him were in suits and ties, or khakis and polo shirts.

Who was this man in flannel? Where had he come from? What was he trying to prove? Where was the Charles Blacksworth she knew, the one who ate Chateaubriand and veal piccata, not beef stew and strawberry shortcake, who celebrated catered birthdays with parties of twenty or more, not a grouping of three with a homemade two-layer cake and a double scoop of ice cream?

A horrible, nagging dread threatened to snuff out the air in her lungs, to suffocate her with new memories as she poured over picture after picture of this "family." It was all in front of her, pages of glaring memory: Charles wielding a hammer over a workbench, dressed in another flannel shirt and *jeans*; Charles with Lily standing in front of a snowman, holding a carrot in his mouth; Charles and Miriam wearing sunglasses and straw hats, waving to the camera, somewhat out of focus; Charles in the kitchen, stirring a pot of something. Beef stew? Several of the photos were a younger version of him, his hair a shade or two darker, the silver not as pronounced, the lines around his eyes less apparent.

But in all of the shots, from the earliest days when he cuddled his newborn baby in his arms to just this past Christmas, when he held up a pair of green corduroy slippers, there was a sense of calm, a quiet contentment that spoke of peace and fulfillment.

It was then, as this truth hit her, sucking the air from her lungs in one grand effort to strangle her own memories, that she thrust the album aside. Had the real Charles Blacksworth resided in Magdalena, not Chicago? And worst of all, had the daughter he loved out of duty and responsibility been herself, not Lily?

The front door opened and closed. There was the sound of boots stomping out snow, then a high, excitable, "Mom? Mom? I'm home."

Miriam rose from the rocking chair, glanced at Christine. "Are you sure you want to do this?"

*No*, she wasn't sure, but she forced herself to say, "Yes. I'm ready."

Miriam nodded, graceful in a pair of cranberry velour pants and matching cable-knit sweater. She wore a pair of faded moccasins, no socks, a fact that made Christine think of her own mother, who refused to leave the bedroom in slippers or bare feet. Miriam was beautiful, the pink staining her cheeks and lips a result of the March winds whipping over her during the brisk walk she took each morning. Her eyes were clear, translucent almost, not gobbed with liner and shadow, but framed instead by a natural fringe of dark sable. There were no rings on her work-roughened fingers, no adornments on her wrist save a simple watch, a man's watch, perhaps, with a large white face and a brown leather band. Today, the earrings she'd chosen dangled in tiny clusters of white and cranberry stones from two fine strands of silver. And, of course, she was wearing the gold cross.

Christine wondered if her father had given her the cross. Maybe it represented some greater connection, a unity of body and spirit? He'd never been a particularly religious man, had declared himself a Methodist only when pressed, though her mother liked to say they were members of the beautiful and newly renovated St. Rowan's Church rather than the smaller, darker, sister church on the other side of town that most of the members of her Junior Women's Association attended.

"I have a surprise for you, Lily, a wonderful, exciting surprise." Miriam disappeared and was talking to Lily, whose voice rose as they drew nearer.

"A present?" The words were loud, half-formed. "Can I open it?"

Miriam laughed. "Well, it's a present but not something you can open. Here, stop a minute. Let me fix your glasses; they're still all fogged up."

"I want to see! I want to see the surprise!"

"You will." Miriam reached the living room first. "There you are, Lily," she whispered. "There's your surprise."

Lily stood in the doorway, staring at Christine. She didn't move, didn't speak.

"Lily? Christine has come to visit you."

"Christine?" Lily's voice filled with part shock, part disbelief.

Christine pushed herself out of the flowered chair and managed a smile. The child was smaller than her pictures, somehow more fragile. "Hello, Lily. How are you?"

Lily took a step forward, stopped, looked at her mother.

Miriam nodded. "It's okay, Lily, go ahead."

The child hurled herself into Christine's arms. "Christine! Christine!"

In the seconds that followed, Christine forgot the circumstances that had brought her into Lily's Desantro's life, forgot the pain of betrayal and loss, forgot everything but the honest emotions of the child, blending with the scent of her hair, an apples and cinnamon concoction, the feel of her breath along Christine's neck, faint, tiny puffs of air, and the sound of Lily's small whimpers as she tried to calm herself.

"You're really here." Lily's words were muffled against Christine's sweater.

"I'm here." She raised a hand, placed it along her half sister's back. Miriam watched them from the doorway, her expression unreadable. Christine turned back to Lily, placed her other hand in the child's hair, stroked it . . . so thick . . . so soft.

Lily pulled back, smiled up into her sister's face. "You came."

"Yes. I came."

She turned to her mother. "Mom, Christine came." There was awe in her voice, and wonder. "She came."

Miriam nodded, her eyes bright. "Yes, yes, she did."

"Come see my room." Lily pulled away, grabbed Christine's hand. "It's cool. Really cool!"

Christine let herself be led to Lily's room, pretending she hadn't seen it before, didn't know about the pictures of herself plastered on the wall and stuffed in photo albums. But when she stepped over the threshold, she saw the room all over again, this time through Lily's eyes.

Lily pulled her from one object to another, clutching her hand tightly, spilling out stories, relaying memories and interpretations. There was the heart-shaped prism hanging from the window on a yellow ribbon, *a gift from Daddy*, she'd said, that cast pale pink designs on the wall when the wind blew over it. And the yellow basket of stuffed animals, mostly dogs, all with names, tucked near the bed in case her favorite, Jesse, got lonely. There was a collection of smooth, flat rocks piled in a brandy snifter, white, pink, gray, a few black, most of which she and Nate had picked from the stream running along his property.

Lily's room transformed into a treasure chest told from a child's perspective, minute details unearthed, bits and scraps of memory whose retelling left poignant longings, soft-spoken, reverent whispers, exposing more about the private life of Charles Blacksworth and his family than any detective ever could.

*Daddy used to lay with me when we had thunder and lightning.*

*Daddy sang "You are My Sunshine" to me every time he came.*

*Daddy tried to make Mom a birthday cake one time and burned it.* Giggle, giggle. *He set off all of the smoke alarms.*

*Daddy said he kept a special calendar where he marked off all the days until he could see me again.*

And then, the one that stripped away years of well-planned orchestrations and dutiful responses to expose the truth: *Daddy cried sometimes when he left.*

HE SHOULDN'T HAVE agreed to let her come; he should have told Lily she'd have to wait one more day, and then he'd bring her over and they'd have their time together, music, dancing, pizza if she wanted it. But somehow, Lily had gotten it into her head that what she wanted was for Christine to come, too.

He'd tried to coax his sister into seeing the right side of it. *This is our time, Lily, family time, just you and me.* But she'd told him Christine *was* family. He'd tried another tactic. *I don't really like to play for anybody but you, Lily. And Christine might be embarrassed if you ask her to dance. I think she's shy.* This was a lie. It hadn't worked anyway.

So now Christine Blacksworth sat ten feet behind him in his living room on the green and blue plaid couch worn thin around the edges, with Lily squished next to her, shoulder to shoulder, waiting for Nate to start playing. Lily had been yakking nonstop since she'd laid eyes on Christine. *What did you get for Christmas? Do you have lots of snow in Chicago? What color is your bedroom? Do you miss Dad?*

The woman should have just made up some excuse, like she had to stay and help Miriam bake cookies. Hell, she probably didn't know what a kitchen was, let alone a cookie recipe. He guessed he should respect her for not lying to Lily, for making the trip when she had to feel as uncomfortable as he did. Okay, he'd give her that, but still, a Blacksworth in his house, sitting on his couch?

He leafed through the music and settled on "Greensleeves." Nate might have been able to tolerate the whole Charles Blacksworth situation until the bastard began to permeate every corner of Nate's world.

It started slowly, first his mother: *Charlie was admiring the desk you made me,* or *I'm sending you a container of vegetable beef soup. Charlie loved it.* Zing. It was always there, his goddamn presence, lurking just below the surface, waiting to jump out, a reminder of who he was, what he'd stolen.

And then the town started: *That old Charlie, he sure knows his numbers, said he'd help me apply for a loan,* and *Charlie says mutual funds are the way to go right now. You ought to talk to him, Nate, see if he can help you with the business.* Charles Blacksworth had invaded Magdalena, taken the town where Nate had been raised, where his father had sweated years of hard work at a business that eventually killed him, and replaced the memories and the allegiance to the Desantro family with his perfect diction and dollar-cost averaging.

When Lily was born there'd been that split-second after the doctor had said "Down syndrome" that Nate thought Charles might leave. *Now she'll see what a bastard he really is,* he'd thought. *Now she'll see. He'll go back to his other family.*

But he hadn't left. He'd stayed. And that had surprised Nate most of all.

"Nate. Did you find the song yet?" Lily was standing behind him.

"Got it, right here," he said, smoothing the pages open. "Ready?"

"Uh-huh. Christine and I are going to dance. Dance, dance, dance. Right, Christine?"

He waited, curious to see how she was going to try and get out of this one. Vice president of Blacksworth and Company Investments of Chicago, dancing in her stocking feet with her thirteen-year-old half sister in a log cabin located in the obscure town of Magdalena, New York. *Never happen.*

"Of course we are." Her voice fell out thin and shaky. "We're going to dance."

*Well, well, well . . .*

Lily and Christine did dance, first to "Greensleeves," then "Dance of the Sugar Plum Fairies," subdued versions that dwindled and stalled, rolled into Elton John's "Crocodile Rock," and ended with Billy Joel's "Only the Good Die Young." He pictured Lily moving in half-jerky steps, round and round, clutching Christine's hand, one arm planted on her waist. He wanted to turn around, but forced himself to keep his back to them as he played, even when Christine joined in with Lily to sing the chorus in "Crocodile Rock."

He finished the last chords of "Only the Good Die Young" and stroked the length of the keyboard, once, twice, three times, signaling to Lily that music time was over. She ran up to him, flung her arms around his shoulders.

"Thank you, thank you, thank you, Nate!"

He reached up, patted her hand. "Good. I'm glad you enjoyed it."

"Next time, I'll play. And you can dance with Christine."

*Right.* "You play too fast, Lily." He turned around and pulled her onto his lap. "I'd look like the Energizer Bunny."

She giggled, patted his beard. "I'll play verrrry slooowww."

"You're silly, you know that?"

Another giggle. "So are you, Energizer Bunny."

He smiled. "Let's go fix some hot chocolate and cinnamon toast. Then we need to get you home before Mom starts calling, wondering what happened to you."

"Nate? Can we stay here tonight?"

"Of course you can't stay here tonight. We have to get you and Christine back home."

"I think Christine wants to stay." She turned to her half sister. "Don't you want to stay, Christine?"

"Lily—"

Nate cut her off. "And just where would she sleep, missy? In the tub?"

"No." Lily shook her head, giggled again. She pointed a finger at him. "She could sleep in your room."

"I don't think so."

"And you could sleep on the couch."

"And you can sleep at home, in your own bed, which is where I'm taking you as soon as you have your snack." He pushed back the bench, stood up, careful to avoid looking in Christine's direction.

"I'll help, Nate." Lily scrambled off the couch and started after him.

"Why don't you just keep Christine company? I'll be back in a few minutes."

"Okay. Don't forget the—"

"—extra marshmallows."

"Right. Do you want extra marshmallows in your hot chocolate, Christine?"

Slight hesitation. "Sure, that'd be fine."

Nate disappeared into the kitchen, thankful for a few minutes' respite. He'd drink the hot chocolate, but what he really wanted was a shot of Jack Daniel's.

Lily never meant anything by her questions, but they stirred up a whole lot of emotion that people spent thousands of dollars in therapy trying to justify and certainly didn't want aired out in general conversation. In a society that valued politeness over truth, where malice and subterfuge were common-place, even accepted, Lily's frankness was labeled an eccentricity of her "condition." (Fuck the bastards; they couldn't even say "Down syndrome.")

"Can I help?"

Christine stood in the doorway, watching him. She lifted a hand, pale and soft-looking against her pink sweater, and gestured toward the other room. "Lily fell asleep. I think the dancing wore her out," she said.

"She's not used to being up this late." He moved the pan of milk to a different burner, flipped off the heat. "You can have hot chocolate if you want," he said, reaching into the cabinet above him, "but I've got something else in mind." He pulled the half-empty bottle of Jack Daniel's down, turned to her. "What'll it be?"

She blushed, a faint shade of pink that matched her sweater. "I'll take the hot chocolate."

"Suit yourself." He poured the steaming milk into a mug, stirred it until it mixed with the cocoa and the tiny marshmallows popped to the top. He handed the mug to Christine, then fixed his own drink.

"Thank you for letting me come tonight." She sipped at her hot chocolate. "I appreciate it."

He shrugged. "Lily wanted you to hear the music."

"I know, but you didn't have to agree."

"I did it for Lily." He took a drink, enjoyed the burn.

"And I also want to thank you for not making a scene when your mother invited me to stay."

"Jesus, you really think I'm an asshole, don't you?" He downed the rest of his drink, poured another. "You might not be one of my favorite people," he said, his back to her, "but even I wouldn't send you on the road in weather like we had last night."

"But you could have made your opinion very public, and you chose not to."

He turned and saluted her with his glass. "Like I said, I'm not that much of an asshole. Besides, after this trip, I don't expect we'll see you again, anyway, so what's a night or two in Magdalena?"

# 13

CHRISTINE SAT ON the edge of the bed and watched Lily rummage through a box in her closet. "Here they are." She pulled out a stack of what looked like books. "I've got them all." She clutched them to her small chest as she moved toward Christine, her glasses slightly cockeyed on the bridge of her nose. Lily pushed them up with her forearm and plopped the stack of books on the bed.

But they weren't books. They were calendars.

Thirteen of them.

Lily pulled one from the pile, flipped it open. "Mom wrote in these until I was old enough to do it myself." She pointed to a date. "See. October nineteenth, 'Dad comes home.' October twentieth, 'hayride and pick out pumpkin.' October twenty-first, 'carve pumpkin—make pumpkin cookies.' October twenty-second, 'Dad leaves.'"

Christine ran a hand over the page, fingering the half-scribble covering those dates. She gently flipped to the next page. *November,* "'Dad comes home. Eat turkey and pumpkin pie. Make birdfeeders. Take pictures/Dad leaves.'" *December,* "'Dad comes home. Decorate tree/hot choc. w/ m mallows. Presents! Purple bike! Dad leaves.'"

"I have thirteen of these," Lily said, shuffling the calendars in her hands. "Most are of horses, 'cause those are my favorite. One, two, three," she counted through thirteen. "Ask me when Dad came, any year," she spread them out on the bed, "and I can show you." She smiled up at Christine. "I can show you all of them."

No. *No.*

"And now . . ." Lily scrambled off the bed and ran to the calendar on the wall. She eased it off its hook and scurried back, "Now I can start to write your visits, too. See," she pointed to Thursday's date. "March seventeenth—'Meet Christine! Very pretty!' March eighteenth—'Sing and dance at Nate's.' March nineteenth—I didn't write anything for that yet," she giggled, "'cause that's today."

Lily expected her to come back, like her father had done. She thought it was just that simple; pick a date on the calendar and show up, no questions asked, no history to confront, no guilt.

"Oh! Wait!" Lily jumped off the bed, ran to her dresser. "I want to show you something." She pulled open the top drawer, rifled through it. It was a beautiful dresser, dark, with a high gloss, cherry, or mahogany. Had Nate made it for Lily?

"Here it is." Lily held up a small box in her right hand, the innocent pleasure in her voice seeping through her words. "I have to keep it safe." She moved closer, protecting the box with both hands. "Dad said this is very special. There's no more like it." She sat on the edge of the bed next to Christine. Her glasses had slid part-way down her nose again, and she smiled as she opened the box and carefully removed the gold pocket watch.

Christine didn't have to turn it over to know the initials R.E.B. would be inscribed on the back, or that there'd be a small dent on the side from the time Uncle Harry threw it across the room, saying "the damn thing should be buried with the old man so it could rot in hell with him."

They'd all heard the stories of how Randolph Ellis Blacksworth had carried the pocket watch every day for fifty-four years, had consulted it in the middle of business deals, from the early days of renting a one-room office on Michigan Avenue to the later years, when he negotiated global contracts and put his name on his own building. The watch represented power and determination, gleaned through hard work and perseverance. Charles had earned the right to own it, and Christine had hoped to do the same.

She'd assumed it had been lost in the accident, or, perhaps, stolen in the transportation of her father's body from one location to another. What bitter irony that it should end up in Lily's hands.

"Want to hold it?" Lily's soft words reached her, strangling her with their innocence.

"No."

"It's okay." She held the pocket watch out to her. "You'll be careful."

Christine accepted it, cradled it in the palm of her hand. *This* was what she'd been waiting for, strived for years to achieve.

And it had been given to Lily, *the other daughter*.


CHRISSIE HADN'T EATEN more than three bites since Greta brought out the pork tenderloin. She hadn't touched her salad either, and she usually loved that radicchio shit. Harry had eaten all of his salad tonight, iceberg with red onion, served separately. He thought old Gloria's tweezed eyebrows were going to jump to her scalp when Greta set the plate in front of him. He hadn't asked Greta to do it, hadn't even thought he'd made that big a deal of hating "the other lettuce." Gloria had made some comment about iceberg lettuce containing absolutely no nutritional value whatsoever, and that it was filled with nothing but water. So, Harry told her that's why he ate it; so he didn't have to dilute his scotch, and she should try it.

Now she wasn't talking to him. Well, it wasn't the first time he'd gotten the cold shoulder. But she wouldn't shut him off completely, not with company present, and he guessed Connor Pendleton was company, asshole that he was. Couldn't the jerk see that something was wrong with Chrissie? Didn't he notice the listlessness in her voice? *Shit*, how could he when he wouldn't shut up about that stupid-ass deal he had going in New York?

Harry slid a glance at Chrissie. *Fuck it*, he'd told her to forget about the damn watch. Charlie had probably given it to the kid because it was shiny and it caught her eye. Or *maybe* he'd wanted to put an end to the expectations behind that goddamn watch, relegate it back where it belonged, a piece of shiny hardware, period. No sense mentioning that possibility, so he'd stick with the shiny-object-to-the-retarded-kid theory. Chrissie might not like it, but she'd probably buy it.

"Christine." He didn't miss the edge in Gloria's voice, a slight jarring that upset the languid fluidity that usually accompanied dinner conversations at the Blacksworths'. "You've barely spoken two words since we sat down. Are you feeling ill?"

Chrissie's gaze darted to Harry. "I'm fine, just a little tired."

"Well, of course you're tired, traipsing back to that godforsaken cabin in the middle of nowhere." She forked a piece of cucumber. "You're probably on the verge of a cold. I'm sure the heating was inadequate, and you've always been prone to colds in the winter."

"I think I'm just tired."

"You're acting more than tired. That's how colds start." She lifted her wine glass and took a healthy sip. "Usually indefinable, spreading through the body, making a person feel miserable long before he's identified the culprit as a cold."

"Mother, I'm fine. I'm just really tired."

"Well, I don't care if you're sick or tired. I'm just glad you're home." Connor Pendleton laid his hand over Chrissie's. "Back where you belong."

*Oh Jesus, give me a break. . . .*

"And these next few weeks, you just need to relax and take it easy." He stroked the back of her hand, "Leave the office at five, go to bed at nine."

"That will never happen." Gloria looked on, her lips pulled into a tight smile.

"Of course it will." Connor grinned at Chrissie, a flash of white against tanned skin. "My girl just needs somebody to make sure she does what she's supposed to." The stroking started again. "Pick her up from work, take her to dinner, tuck her in." Chrissie's hand lay lifeless under Connor's earnest ministrations.

"And after she's rested up," he winked at Gloria, "say around the twenty-second of next month, we'll head to New York for a show."

Chrissie pulled her hand away. "I can't go on the twenty-second."

"Let's see how you feel. If you're not up to it, I'll change the flight. I booked the reservations yesterday." He dropped his voice to a low, persuasive rumble. "I'm going to take care of you, Christine. I want to."

*Oh, God, the bullshit was getting deep.* What he really meant was he wanted to take care of Chrissie's *interests*, her money and her position. Being the shrewd businessman he was, he'd undoubtedly detected his sliding loss of market share in regard to Christine's affections.

"I can't go."

Connor Pendleton rubbed his jaw, first one side, then the other. He was too damn good-looking; Harry never trusted "pretty" men. If you could imagine them slimmed down, wigged up, shaved, and painted, and if the visual were almost credible, then they weren't to be trusted. No guy should be able to pass as a switch-hitter.

*What the hell did Chrissie see in him?*

"Of course, you can go." Gloria was chipping in like a mother hen again. "Nobody turns down trips to New York. There's an exquisite Neiman Marcus there."

"I may just have to bring both of you."

"Yes, Connor, you may indeed."

Harry sucked in the rest of his scotch. Swallowing the burn was the only thing that kept him from telling them both to *shut the fuck up.* They were driving him nuts, Gloria with her goo-goo-eyed banter and Connor Pendleton with his smooth-ass sucking up. Nothing was worse than watching a middle-aged woman coo under the attention of a younger man, a prospective son-in-law, no less. Who the hell did she think she was, another Mrs. Robinson? It was enough to make Harry puke.

Nobody was paying attention to Chrissie, except Harry. He'd heard her the first time, understood the meaning beneath the quiet words and expected the others would, too.

But they were too busy playing games with one another. Gloria wanted that asshole for a son-in-law, to secure the name, the position, the power, to ensure that her daughter's life became as meaningless, as dull and desperate as her own. And Connor Pendleton, he wanted Blacksworth and Company.

"Why can't you go, Chrissie?" Harry asked. *Tell them.*

Gloria and Connor Pendleton looked at Harry as though he were fifteen minutes behind in the conversation. But at least they did have the good grace to turn to Chrissie.

"I can't go to New York because I'll be back at the cabin on the twenty-second."

Silence.

"You . . ." Gloria sputtered, stalled.

"The cabin?" Connor Pendleton picked up. "What the hell for? You just got back."

Chrissie looked at Harry.

*Fuck*, it was about the watch. "Maybe she's got to sort things out," he said, "and the only place to sort them out is hundreds of miles away from everything." *Half lie, half truth.*

"She doesn't need to go anywhere," Gloria said. "Christine, I'll call Roger, have him prescribe something for you."

"I don't need any pills."

"Just for a little while. Until you adjust to your father's"—she caught herself before the word "death" slipped out—"not being here."

That was the problem with the whole goddamn world; nobody had balls enough to call a spade a spade. Dead was dead. It was a hell of a lot more permanent than a milquetoast "not being here."

"You'll be surprised how they make everything more manageable."

"Mother, I need to go back there for a few days."

Gloria took a long sip, or was it a gulp, of wine? "Please don't go back there."

"It's just a few days."

"Just a few? Is it just *four*? What about next month? And the next?" Gloria's voice grew more agitated. "Until the months turn into years and still, still it won't be enough."

"No. That's not my intention."

"It wasn't your father's *intention*, either." She was going ballistic now, nostrils flaring, eyes narrowed. "It was never his intention, Christine, but it happened nonetheless, and there wasn't a damn thing I could do about it."

*Jesus.* Did she know?

"It was only four days a month, wasn't it?" This from Connor Pendleton. "Christ, he could have been doing a hell of a lot worse than holing up in a cabin a couple days a month."

Gloria stumbled to recover. "You're right, of course, you're right. I didn't mean anything by it. It's just that," she sniffed, "I don't want to lose you, Christine."

"Oh, Mother," Chrissie reached across the table and grabbed Gloria's hand, "you aren't going to lose me. I'll always be here for you. Besides, it's only four days."

Thank God Greta entered the dining room just then, carrying a platter of pork tenderloin and brown-sugared carrots. The rest of the meal took place in relative calm with occasional spurts of conversation, mostly geared toward Gloria's role as committee chair in the upcoming West Mount Memorial Spring Fashion Show. On and on it went, with Connor Pendleton piping in like a Boy Scout, offering his services, smiling at Chrissie, stroking her hand, her shoulder, her back. There he was patting her goddamn back again.

She was shutting down right in front of them, withdrawing inside herself, farther down, farther yet, until nothing remained but the shell that carried her. The real Chrissie Blacksworth, the one who laughed, and cried, loved and even hated, that one was buried beneath layers of polite sedateness.

Because Gloria Blacksworth could never, not in a million fucking years, handle the truth. *She's going back to see the kid, Gloria, Charlie's kid, the thirteen-year-old he fathered with his mistress. What do you think of that, Gloria? Huh? What do you think of that?*

Connor Pendleton excused himself shortly after dinner. *I'm expecting a call from Tokyo, possible merger.* For all of his back-patting and promises to Chrissie, the guy was still a businessman first, boyfriend and significant other second.

Harry hung around after Chrissie and Connor left. What he needed to say to Gloria would take no more than a minute or two. He poured himself a scotch and waited.

She sat in one of her straight-backed flowered

chairs. The night had withered her like a rose too long without water.

"I don't want you laying a guilt trip on Chrissie. She's got enough on her mind right now without you trying to make her feel sorry for you and guilty that she wants to stay close to her father."

"Leave me alone." She lit a cigarette, sucked in hard. "I want you to leave now. My back is killing me."

"That old back injury sure serves a lot of different purposes, doesn't it? Gets you out of doing things you don't want to do, lets you do things you do want to do," he paused, "even acts as a form of bribery on occasion, for those who would behave differently toward you, if not for your back."

"Shut up."

He let out a laugh, sat down on the edge of a chair. "You and I, we're from the same mold, Gloria. It's just that I don't try to hide my inadequacies, while you, well, you smother them in expensive perfume, fancy clothes, and a bad back."

"I'm not going to sit here and listen to this." She stubbed out her cigarette in the shiny blue ashtray and stood up. "You know the way out."

"Do you think Charlie ever knew about us?"

When she met his gaze there was hatred in her eyes, and fear. "We agreed we'd never mention this," she snarled.

"Charlie's dead, now. Unless you think he's floating around in this room somewhere."

Her jaw twitched just a little. "We agreed."

"Yeah, we did."

"For God's sake, if you can't honor your word for Charles's sake, then do it for Christine." She laid a hand over her smooth throat. "This would devastate her."

"Not to mention what it would do to your role as mother."

"Fuck you."

"We did that already, remember? I know it's been a long time, but surely you recall at least some of the sordid details?" He moved toward her. "I do. Hell, I recall more than I want to."

She took a step back, then another.

"Oh, don't flatter yourself, Gloria. It wasn't so good that I'd remember it that many years; that's not it at all. It's the guilt that keeps it fresh in my mind. I betrayed my own brother, and I've had to live with that all these years, sitting at his table, accepting his friendship, even his love, and all the while knowing what I'd done. Don't you ever just want to fuckin' shoot yourself and be done?"

"I try not to think about it. It was a mistake for which I've paid dearly."

"Really? How so?"

She shook her head. "I have my own pain."

"Are you on the back thing again? Take a few more Vicodin and you won't feel a thing."

"What do you want? Is it money? Have the creditors finally caught up with you?"

Harry laughed. "Now, I'm really insulted. You think I'm after *your* money? You don't have any money, Gloria. That was Charlie's money, not yours."

"I'm a very wealthy woman now."

"Good for you. I'm sure that young stud who was sniffing up your dress at the West Mount Memorial function knows that too."

"I'm going to bed."

"Now there's an offer I can refuse."

"It wasn't an offer."

"Good." He straightened and lowered his voice. "But this is: leave Christine alone, and I'll keep quiet about our past indiscretions. Got it?"

"I've got it." She drew in a deep breath, held it, let it out slowly. "May you rot in hell, Harry Blacksworth."

He threw back his head and let out a loud laugh. "You can count on it. You can goddamn fucking count on it."

# 14

SHE COULDN'T GET THEM out of her head.
Uncle Harry accused her of thinking too
much, working and reworking words and situations,
chipping away at them until there was nothing left,
sometimes not even the truth. Maybe he was right.
Maybe she did that when the answers staring back
at her weren't what she expected. Like now.

She wanted to force the Desantros into her
subconscious, but it was useless. Images and conversations kept resurfacing, gnawing away, until there
was a gaping hole that flooded her brain with Lily
and Miriam, even Nate.

How could she feel more uncertain at twenty-
seven than she had at seventeen? Ten years ago she'd
had a plan, an objective that started with advanced
education, and ended in running Blacksworth and
Company alongside her father, with friends, family,
maybe even marriage and a child gathered up
along the way. It was a simple plan, mapped out of

arrogance and naiveté. Why wouldn't she believe the world was waiting for her, Christine Elizabeth Blacksworth, to file through life, ticking off the list she'd compiled at seventeen, achieving her goals, lauding accomplishments and successes, living life—*right on schedule*? But no one had prepared her for the possibility of a plan gone bad.

That would equate failure, which was not an option. *Try hard enough, long enough, and you will succeed.* She'd believed her father's words, just like she'd believed everything he told her.

But now?

She couldn't picture herself with Connor, night after night, stretched out beside him on his black leather couch, discussing stocks and trends and harboring nothing in her heart, no spark, no desire, no love. She'd tried to mold her feelings into love, but it was useless.

Her mother would be so disappointed. She'd wanted this union so much.

It wasn't right that she'd agreed to go back to Magdalena. And it wasn't right that Lily was occupying large blocks of her mind these days or that Miriam's sage words kept seeping into her consciousness when she least expected it. It wasn't even right that she should remember the conversation she'd had with Nate the night Lily fell asleep on his couch while he was fixing hot chocolate. He'd been almost half-friendly, the bottle of Jack Daniel's resting on the countertop as he answered questions about his company, told her how his father had started the business out of nothing, how Nate himself had spent hours there, from the time he was just a kid. The words flowed from his lips, loosened through whiskey and reminiscing, as though he were recapping someone else's life, not his own. It wasn't until she'd asked him if he'd made the beautiful cabinets in his kitchen that he'd given her a curt nod, then clammed up.

None of it was right, not Nate, or Miriam, or Lily, but they were all there, nonetheless, with pulses of their own, living, breathing threats, pulling her, challenging her to turn away, begging her to come back.

She had no choice; she'd go to Magdalena, finish what she'd started. And then she'd be done.


IT WAS ALL A GODDAMN setup. Harry recognized her work, the bitch. And how fucking convenient was it that she just so happened to fall the night before Chrissie's trip?

It was all staged, had to be—the invitation to The Presidio, with Harry included, which was a first; the demand that it be that night, not a few days before as Chrissie had suggested; and the request that the gathering be in public, not in Gloria's home.

Harry figured it was so she could have witnesses when she took the big dive, and of course, sympathy and attention. Afterward, he understood why he'd been invited; she wanted him to witness the accident, see her on the ground writhing in pain so there would be no way he'd be able to call her a liar.

Well, he still called her a goddamn liar, just a bit more orchestrated, deluged with exquisite calculation, but still a liar. He didn't recall the exact moment her foot missed the step—accidentally or intentionally?—hurling her down a flight of thirteen stairs, but he did remember the cries of pain spilling from her mouth, the look of pure terror on Chrissie's face. And the onlookers, poor damn Armand, the guests, the valet, rushing to her, solicitous, all on cue. Only Harry had stood back, taking it all in, watching, waiting.

The ambulance arrived, the attendants placing Gloria on a backboard, careful of spinal injuries. *She has a history of back problems.* The swell of the crowd had increased, as many as three deep, murmuring, catching snatches of information, throwing them back.

*She slipped on the step . . . her heel caught.*

*I think the step was wet.*

*Will she sue?*

*. . . history of back problems . . .*

*Gloria Blacksworth . . . husband died a few months ago . . .*

*I think the step was wet.*

*Will she sue?*

*. . . widow . . . Blacksworth and Company . . .*

*God, look at her, the ankle's huge . . .*

*. . . poor thing . . . horrible . . .*

*Will she sue?*

Speculation continued as everyone stood by, waiting for scraps of information, a look, a gesture, a nod even, that might indicate Gloria Blacksworth's condition.

Harry went to the hospital only because Chrissie had ridden with her mother in the ambulance and would need a way home once Gloria was settled. No doubt they'd keep her in the hospital for observation. How was she going to slip a cigarette? Or a nip of Crown Royal? He'd bet she hadn't considered that, or maybe that little black case she carried was tucked away inside her purse; maybe there was a flask in there, too, and the bottle of Vicodin.

It was all a plan, implemented the night before Chrissie took off for the cabin. What daughter could leave her mother in a hospital bed and take off to "be by herself" or, as truth would have it, to spend time with her father's mistress and her daughter? Good old-fashioned guilt, and Gloria sure knew how to use it.

It was almost 11 P.M. when Chrissie showed up in the waiting room. Harry had visited the café twice, once for a ham on rye and then later for a piece of cherry pie and coffee. The cashier wasn't half bad-looking either, kind of reminded him of Greta, same blonde hair scooped up in a bun, same shape, but younger. Turned out she was a freshman at Loyola, too young, even for him.

Chrissie sank down in the brown vinyl chair beside him. "She's sleeping. They scheduled surgery for nine tomorrow morning."

He nodded. *Round one to Gloria.*

"It was a clean break, thank God. The doctor said ankles can be tricky, but with therapy she should have full recovery."

"I guess she's lucky." *Lucky shit, she knew exactly what she was doing.*

"I'm glad she's okay. It could've been a lot worse."

"So, I guess this means you're not going out of town tomorrow."

"I can't. There's no way I can leave Mother right now."

*Exactly according to plan . . .*

"Why are you looking at me like that? I can't leave her, Uncle Harry."

"What are you going to tell the kid?"

"The truth, I guess. My mother fell down a flight of stairs and had to have surgery."

*Correction . . . your mother threw herself down a flight of stairs . . .*

"Are you going to plan another trip? Next month?"

"I don't know. I think so." She dragged her hands over her face. "I just don't know."

"Kind of odd the way it worked out, isn't it?"

"What?"

"Well, here it is, the night before you leave on a trip your mother doesn't want you to take, and she goes and crashes down a flight of steps and busts an ankle. What in the hell are the odds of something like that happening?"

"It was an accident, Uncle Harry."

"Did I say it wasn't?"

"No, but don't go getting any ideas."

"Okay, so it was an accident." He rubbed his jaw. He'd have to take it easy or he'd lose her; she'd be so busy defending her mother she'd never consider any other possibilities. "Anyway, what kind of person would throw herself down a fight of stairs to keep her daughter from doing something she didn't want her to do?"

"A nut case . . . someone who's deranged . . ."

"Right."

"And she's neither one of those."

"True." He let her relax a little, then hit her with, "Of course, if a person were really desperate, then maybe she'd be driven to do something like that."

"Uncle Harry, stop it, okay? I'm tired and I'm hungry."

"Sure. I'm sorry, kid." He stood up, grabbed his trench coat, and held out a hand. "Come on. Let's see if we can find you a burger. Maybe a Big Mac and fries, like in the old days when you were a scrawny little runt in pigtails, huh?"

She grabbed his hand, worked out a small smile. "Thanks, Uncle Harry."

He laughed. "Don't thank me until after you've eaten. Indigestion comes with age, you know."

"No, I mean thank you for coming here, for being with me. I know you and my mother don't always see eye to eye, but I appreciate you making the effort."

"Sure, kid." He pulled her into his arms. She was the best part of his fucked-up life.

"Uncle Harry?"

"Hmmm?" He'd do anything for her.

"It was an accident."

And if Gloria ever pulled a stunt like this again, he'd do what he had to do. By God he would.

"SHE'S NOT COMING, is she?" It was just a guess, but he'd watched his mother's smile falter, then fade, seconds after she'd answered the phone.

"No."

"*I knew it.*"

She sank into a chair. "She said her mother fell last night and broke her ankle."

"Right."

They'd been sitting at the kitchen table waiting for Lily to finish dressing. She'd wanted to do everything herself today, even her hair, so she could show Christine. When the phone rang, he'd almost reached for it, thinking it might be Christine. But then he'd changed his mind. Maybe a small part of him had been hoping she'd show. "Do you want me to tell Lily?"

"No. I need to do this."

He hated seeing her like this, as though she'd been stabbed in the gut and left to bleed dry. Why didn't she ever learn with these people? The Blacksworths wanted to play both sides of the fence, no matter who paid the price, even a child.

"Did you really think she'd come back?" he asked.

"I did."

"Why, because the Blacksworths are such noble people who always honor their word?"

"Don't, Nate, please, not today."

"She won't be back again. Lily will be waiting for her the whole goddamn month and she'll never show. We were just a novelty for her; don't you see that? This way, she cuts you off now, with this mother's-broken-ankle excuse, and just kind of eases out of it, maybe even tells Lily she'll come next month and then invents another reason why she can't make it. Hell, after a while, it will all start to blur, and one day she'll wonder if it happened at all."

"I think you're wrong, Nate. I think Christine did want to understand her father's reasons for coming here."

"Maybe she got it already; she just didn't like what she learned."

"No, that wasn't the impression I got."

"You believe in everybody. They all sell you a bill of goods, and you just believe them."

"There's a lot of good in people—you just have to give them a chance."

"That's called letting them take advantage of you. That woman's not interested in you or Lily or anybody who's going to inconvenience her lifestyle or tarnish the Blacksworth name."

"Christine—"

"Is she here?" Lily bounced into the kitchen, mouth open, eyes bright beneath her thick glasses. She wore black corduroy pants and a red shirt with eight shiny white buttons, all done exactly right. Nate knew the button count on the shirt because he'd helped her redo them on several occasions. It was her "special" shirt, the one she wore to church, the movies, school recitals, and now to meet Christine, only Christine wasn't coming. *Damn her.*

Once again, human nature proved to be just as untrustworthy as it always was, and still, still, his mother acted surprised.

"Where is she? Where's Christine?" Lily moved past them to peek out the back window. "I think I heard her."

"Christine isn't here, Lily."

"Oh." Her smile slipped. "When's she coming?" She took another step toward her mother, picked at a shiny button. "Did she call?"

"Yes, she called. Come here, dear." Lily clasped Miriam's hands, held tightly. "Christine's mother was in an accident last night. She fell down a flight of stairs and broke her ankle."

"Christine's not coming?"

"No, she's not."

"But she said she'd come. She promised." Her voice squeaked; her lower lip started to wobble.

"I'm sorry, Lily, she can't come."

*"But she promised."*

"Her mother needs her right now."

"I need her too!" She yanked her hands away and tucked them under her armpits. "I need her too!"

"Lily, stop."

"I've been waiting twenty-seven days."

"I know, dear."

"She promised!" Her small chest heaved up and down, as the tears started. "She promised—"

Miriam pulled her into her arms. "I know." She smoothed her daughter's thick hair, stroked her back. "Christine's mother is hurt, Lily. She's in the hospital, and Christine can't leave her alone right now." More stroking. "You wouldn't leave me if I were in the hospital, would you?"

"No." It was a small word, muffled by tears and the cloth of her mother's shirt.

"I know you wouldn't. If Christine could be here, she would be." She ignored Nate's hard stare, went on, "I know she'd be here."

He watched the tears pool in his sister's eyes. *Damn it*, why had their mother ever agreed to let that woman come to Magdalena?

"I got all dressed," Lily murmured, "all by myself. I just wanted her to come back."

"I know."

This is what happened when you trusted a Blacksworth. The crying went on and on, Lily's small body trembling with sobs.

"I'll bet Christine's really scared." Lily stilled, inched away. Her eyes grew bright beneath her thick lenses. "I'll make her a card."

"That's a good idea. But, you know we can't send it, Lily."

"I know. I'm just going to keep it for when she comes back."

# 15

HARRY LET HIMSELF in the front door. He could hear Greta moving around in the kitchen, cupboards and drawers opening and closing, water running. She'd made bread today, or maybe it was rolls he smelled, the sourdough kind with butter smothered on top. What would it be like to come home, just once, to real apple pie filling his senses, not the manufactured aroma of an apple air freshener? He'd never know, of course. His women didn't cook, and hiring someone like Greta, or even hiring Greta herself, was out of the question. How could he fuck Bridgett on the kitchen table with Greta mashing potatoes next to him?

He could never hire Greta as a cook or house-keeper or whatever in the hell she was. How long would it take before he forgot she was a decent woman with two kids and tried to bang her? One day? Two? He just had to picture her bending over the oven, that nice ass full and tight against the white of her uniform, and bam, he'd be after her.

He heard her humming, some soft little tune that made him picture her lips, teeth, tongue. *Jesus*, he was sick. He shrugged out of his coat and headed for the staircase. It was mid-afternoon and Chrissie was still at work, which was why he'd decided to make the trip now. The poor kid looked worn out from popping in to visit her mother every morning and every night, squeezing a few hours of work in between, then running around the city picking up magazines, books, lotions, anything that might speed Gloria's recovery. The damn bitch was wringing the life from Chrissie, one damned aromatherapy candle at a time.

But that was all about to end.

The bedroom stood at the top of the stairs, to the right. Harry eased the double doors open and stepped inside. It was different than he remembered it, no crimson and gold walls with matching curtains and bedspread, poured out in lavish excess, smothered in heat and sensuality. Even the carpeting was gone, a dark red that later he thought of as blood red, seeping betrayal, harboring secret remnants of sweat and lust within its thick piles. The new carpet was the palest blue, the color of an ice pond.

This new décor suited Gloria. He bet she'd picked it from a showroom window, down to the stuffed white cat sitting on the rocker. Or she could have gotten the idea from a *House Beautiful* cover. There were blue stripes, some pale, some almost white, and peach, at least he thought it was peach, covering the walls, the curtains, a few pillows. And then she'd gone and mixed a flower pattern, peach and blue with white, on the rest of the pillows and the bedspread, or was the technical term comforter? He guessed *House Beautiful* would consider the room elegant, but Harry had one word for it: dead.

He took a step toward the bed. She lay on her side with her back facing him, two pillows wedged between her legs to elevate the cast on her right ankle. He struggled for air; the goddamn stripes were closing in on him. He took another step, tried to suck in a clean breath, inhaled the heavy scent of her perfume.

The years rolled away, and she was on the bed, straddling him, head thrown back, long blonde hair brushing his thighs. She was moaning, over and over and over, and he was pumping into her, harder and harder and harder. . . .

*Jesus Christ*, he was going to puke. Harry breathed in through his mouth, once, twice, three times.

"Christine?" Gloria's voice sounded groggy with sleep, or Vicodin, or booze, probably all three. "Is that you, Christine?"

Harry took one more open-mouthed breath. "No. It's not Christine."

She swung around, winced from the sudden movement. "What are *you* doing here?"

"Don't get up for me. I'll just come around to the other side of the bed so you don't hurt your, ah," he paused, "injury." *Okay, okay, I can do this.*

"I want you to leave." She rolled onto her back, eased into a half-sitting position.

"In a minute."

"What do you want?"

She was still beautiful, her skin smooth, unwrinkled, no lines around her neck or eyes. Her features were small and delicate, the nose, chin, cheeks, lips all flawless, the blonde hair fluffed and shiny. She wore a peach lounging outfit made of silk, or perhaps it was satin? She could pass for a full ten years younger than fifty-four, but then why shouldn't she when she spent her existence perfecting herself, escaping the reality of life, denying the inevitability of death?

In some ways, he and Gloria were very much alike.

*God*, the thought sickened him. He would do this for Chrissie and now, for himself, to prove that he and Gloria *weren't* the same.

"I said, what do you want?"

Harry sank into a blue-striped chair by the

bed, kicked his feet out in front of him. "Do you get Botox injections?"

She stared at him.

"I mean, really, do you? You're a beautiful woman, I'll give you that, but you're fifty-four, Gloria, you realize that, don't you, and not a line, no wrinkles, nothing? How can that be?" He crossed his arms over his chest, watched her tiny nostrils flair, her jaw clench. "You do, don't you?"

*"What do you want?"*

She wasn't taking the bait. Why the hell was he doing this anyway? What did he care if she injected her whole goddamn body with Botox? He'd grabbed the first thought that crossed his mind, anything to blot out the memories of her young body working him, slick, hot. She'd had a birthmark on the inside of her thigh, strawberry, shaped like a heart . . . *Jesus Christ!*

"I know your game, Gloria." He forced himself to meet her gaze. "I've always known your game."

"I had an accident, for God's sake. I broke my ankle." She pointed to her right leg. "Even you, limited intelligence that you possess, can see that."

"I know you broke your ankle. I saw you break it; me and fifty or so other people saw you break it. Witnesses, right? That's what we were."

"I have no idea what you're talking about."

"Witnesses to the accident," he said, keeping

his voice calm. "It was a brilliant idea, and for just a second you almost had me. But then I thought why would Gloria request, or rather, *demand,* as I recall, that we dine at The Presidio the night before Chrissie plans to leave? And why in God's name would she make a point to invite me when we both know we hate each other's guts? The answer came to me as I watched you lying on the floor, and all the people around you, the *witnesses,* and Chrissie, right by your side. Then I knew; you'd staged the whole fall to keep her from leaving." He leaned forward, lowered his voice, "You threw yourself down those stairs so your daughter would cancel her trip."

"The Crown Royal's pickling your brain, Harry."

"And you knew she'd cancel it because that's the kind of person she is."

"You're crazy. You need professional help."

"You think so? Maybe we should check into rehab together. I'll go for the booze; you go for the pills."

"I broke my ankle."

"I know. You also did something else. It's called manipulation."

"I told you—"

"Listen. This is the way it is; you leave Chrissie alone. No more of this guilt-trip, stay-with-mama shit. If she wants to go away, to the cabin or goddamn Alaska, you let her go. If you think about pulling this shit again, you better throw yourself in front of a semi because when I'm through, you'll wish you had."

"Is that meant to instill fear?"

"Goddamn right it is. You try this again, I'm telling her. You got it?"

"Even you're not that big a fool."

"I mean it, Gloria. I'll spill it all, how you and I used to screw right here in this room while Charlie was in London earning a goddamn living to keep you decked out in diamonds and a Mercedes."

She pulled her lips together, tight, keeping whatever words she meant to say inside.

If he thought he could get away with it, he'd reach over and squeeze that goddamn *unlined* neck she was so proud of until he'd choked the last pulse out of her. He clenched his fists and fixed his gaze on her neck. He could do it; he could kill her right now for her part in all this. But what about Chrissie? It would kill her, too. Harry unclenched his fists, forced his gaze from the smooth, unlined silkiness of her neck.

She was talking again. Was that nervousness or fear in her voice? "We both live in our private hells, Harry. God made certain of that. I haven't looked at you once in the past twenty-eight years without remembering how we betrayed Charles. And yet I had to welcome you into our home, invite you to our table, engage in conversation with you, and *pretend* nothing had happened."

"So, you've got a conscience after all."

"I hate you, Harry Blacksworth." She reached for the cigarette case on her nightstand, flipped it open. "We were only together six times; many of the women I know have been far more indiscreet."

"And were they screwing their husband's brother?"

Her head jerked up. "You were no innocent, Harry. You were dying to take something that belonged to your brother."

"And I've never stopped paying for it."

She blew out a long thin line of smoke and studied her cigarette. "Neither have I."

The striped walls began closing in on him, red seeping through pale blue, pulling him back, threatening to soak him in deceit. He shot out of his chair. "I just hope to God Charlie never knew."

"Of course he never knew. Why would you say such a thing?"

"Because if I thought he knew, I'd blow my fucking brains out."

"He didn't know."

The red was gone; the stripes were crisp and cold. "Leave Chrissie alone, lay off the guilt trips, and I'll keep quiet. Start coming up with ailments, or reasons to keep her by your side, and I'll tell her about us."

Gloria puffed on her cigarette, muttered, "Bastard."

"And then I'll tell her the rest."

"You wouldn't do that to her."

"If it were the only way I could save her from you, I would. I'd tell her the whole fucking truth, every last detail." He snatched the cigarette from her fingers, stubbed it out in the blue ashtray next to a small mountain of butts. "Charlie hated it when you smoked."

"Charles is dead."

He grabbed the pack of Salem Lights from the nightstand and threw it across the room. "Then goddamnit, show his memory a little respect."

"Fuck you, Harry Blacksworth, fuck you!"

*Good.* Harry turned and headed for the door, sucking in sips of air. *Feel it, Gloria, feel the rage and let it strangle you.* He closed the door behind him and drew in a clean breath of air, one free of perfume and memories.

Then he threw back his head and laughed.


*IT WAS AN ACCIDENT.*

Gloria eased herself onto her side, moaned as the pillow slipped from between her knees, jarring her right ankle. It had been two hours since Harry bombarded her bedroom, stealing first her slumber and then her peace of mind.

She let out a second moan that had nothing to do with her ankle. Why would he accuse her of manipulating her own accident?

People lost their footing every day, slipped, tripped, stumbled. That's why these mishaps were called accidents, why engineers were continually designing new products such as non-skid surfaces and shoes with improved traction.

Did Christine believe she'd orchestrated her own fall, too? Is that why she'd been so erratic lately? Surely, she must know her own mother would never do such a thing.

True, she hadn't wanted her daughter to return to the cabin, had all but begged her not to go. But to fake her own accident to keep her here?

She never should've taken the Valium that day. It was one thing to self-medicate in familiar surroundings, but to pop Vicodin and Valium and then negotiate thirteen steps at The Presidio, down, not up, unassisted; well, that had proved disastrous.

If she could've avoided the steps, none of this would've happened. She knew how to balance her pills, move through her days in a shimmer of fuzziness that no one detected. And when sleep eluded her, an occasional Ambien got her through the night and much of the next morning.

It was talk of another trip that pushed her to the Valium. Christine had no business going back there.

*It was an accident.* Christine knew that, didn't she? Goddamn Harry Blacksworth and his worthless existence. And he'd thought she had no remorse. . . .

Charles had been standing by their bed the day she'd realized he really loved her, despite the missed anniversary, the remoteness, the constant travel. But by then, it was too late.

*How could you, Gloria?* She could still picture him in their bedroom, so handsome, so wounded, the small foil packet in his outstretched hand. *How could you?*

She'd tried hard to be valiant, make him believe. *What is it?* And then leaning closer, gasping, *Where did that come from? Someone's been in our bed! Oh my God, Charles!*

And he, all the while watching her, the silver packet screaming infidelity in his outstretched palm. . . . *My cuff link fell under the bed . . . I bent to pick it up . . .*

*I'll speak to Anna. I hired her nephew and his girlfriend two weeks ago to clean the windows and chandeliers. They must've snuck in here . . . oh, my God, how disgusting.*

*I already spoke with Anna. It wasn't her nephew—*

*It had to have been him and his—*

*Anna told me she followed them from room to room to supervise their work. They never came near this bedroom, Gloria.*

*She's lying to keep her job.*

*Stop it.* He'd thrown the packet on the bed and said, *It was you.*

She'd crumpled at his feet. *I'm sorry . . . I'm sorry . . .*

*I want a divorce.*

*No!* She'd clutched his pant leg. *No, please!*

*I'll move out. You can stay in the house until we sell it.*

*No. No, Charles. You can't leave me.* And then, because she was desperate, and because it was true, *I'm pregnant.*

He'd stayed in the guest room until after the baby was born, vowing that if the child didn't look like a Blacksworth, he *would* divorce her.

Gloria reached for the bottle of Vicodin, popped off the cap. But he hadn't divorced her; Christine had been born with a full head of midnight hair and the bluest eyes any doctor had ever seen. Blacksworth eyes.

And Charles died never knowing the Blacksworth blood running through Christine's veins might not be his.

# 16

SHE WAS STANDING IN front of Nate Desantro's home. Yes, she was four days late, but she'd come. That should count for something. She'd planned on waiting a month and going on the next scheduled date, but her mother had insisted she make the trip this month.

She'd scheduled the next available flight, and now here she was. Christine pressed the doorbell, waited. Bocelli's "Canto Della Terra" swirled around her, climbing, clinging. Maybe Nate couldn't hear her. She pressed the doorbell a second time.

He was the only person who could make this visit work; that's why she'd come here first. If he would just try to understand why she'd not been here four days ago, then maybe they could form a truce of sorts. After all, there was Lily to think about. She rang the bell one last time and slowly turned the knob.

He was in the kitchen, his back to her, stirring

something at the stove. Tomatoes and garlic? Sautéed onions? Whatever it was, it sure beat the hamburger and chips she'd eaten on the plane.

She'd almost reached the kitchen when he turned around. "Jesus! You scared the hell out of me."

"I'm sorry. I rang the doorbell," she gestured toward the stereo, "but I guess you couldn't hear it."

He turned back to the stove, flipped off the burner, and set the pan aside. His hair was damp, slicked back, probably from a recent shower, and he'd trimmed his beard and mustache, which made him look half civilized.

"What are you doing here?"

"I had to see Lily. I promised her."

"You're four days late."

"I know. My mother broke her ankle, and she had to have surgery. I couldn't come until she was settled."

He turned back to the stove. "You didn't need to come."

She moved beside him so she could see his face. "Yes, I did. I promised Lily."

"Have you seen her yet?"

"No. I wanted to come here first, make sure you weren't going to give me a hard time when I visit her."

"Depends on what the arrangement is. Is this a

one-time stop, or are you planning to mark her on your calendar every month like your old man did?"

"I . . . I hadn't thought much past this visit."

"Well, you'd better, before you see Lily." He stirred the sauce, a tomato and zucchini mixture. "She'll expect you to come every month, just like your old man did. So, if that's not part of your plan, then end it now. Don't give her hope where there isn't any."

"I wouldn't do that."

He stared at her. "People do it all the time, Christine. You know that."

"Well, not intentionally . . ."

"Sure they do. Haven't you ever gotten a phone call, maybe from a friend who wanted you to do something, and you knew there wasn't a snowball's chance in hell you were going to do it, but you didn't have the guts to just say no?"

"I guess—"

"You know you have. It's human nature, the best and the worst of it. We're trying to save another person's feelings, dangling a shred of hope in front of him a little longer, because we don't want to make him feel bad, or worse, make *ourselves* look bad."

"Are you saying you've never done that?"

He shrugged.

"I won't do that to Lily. I give you my word," she said.

He didn't respond to that. "Are you hungry?"

And with that, the subject of Lily and man's adept ability to deceive others and preserve his own image was closed, shifting instead to topics of food and wine, safe subjects. She actually enjoyed his dry sense of humor as he relayed tips on different ways to cook pasta, most of them learned through first-hand experience, ranging from a campfire setting with a ten-pound iron skillet to a motor boat and a two-burner hot plate.

"I can't believe you could think of food in the middle of a storm." She laughed. "Just the thought of putting anything in my stomach with the boat tossing and turning would send me straight to the railing."

"I said we cooked it." A smile slid across his mouth. "I didn't say we *ate* it."

"Ah, the truth emerges."

He sipped his wine. "It usually does, in one form or another."

She set down her fork. "Nate?" When he met her gaze, she said, "Just give me a chance with Lily, okay? That's all I'm asking."

"You ask a lot."

"I won't let her down."

"I'll think about it." He twirled a forkful of linguine. "So, Christine Elizabeth Blacksworth, do you have any cooking stories?"

"No, sad to say, I'm a mess in the kitchen. How'd you know my middle name?"

"Are you kidding? With Lily in the house, I know more about you than I know about my ex-wife."

"Ex-wife?"

"Yeah, I had one of those. You?"

"No."

"Why not?"

She shrugged, fixed her gaze on a piece of zucchini. "I just never . . . took the big step."

"It can be a step or a dive, depending on the person and the situation."

"I take it yours was more than a step?"

"It was a damn parachute jump without the parachute."

"Oh. Sorry."

"Don't be. She's remarried to some bank executive who keeps her happy with houses and cars. Log cabins and pickups weren't her style. She's much happier now."

"Good."

"What was the name of that guy you were seeing? Lily used to draw hearts with your initials inside. Colin? Curt?"

"Connor."

"That's it, Connor. What happened to him?"

"He's still around."

"Don't sound so excited."

"I'm not. We're just friends."

"Does he know?"

"He should."

"Trying to dump him, huh?"

"No." She looked away. "It's not that. Connor's a nice guy; everybody likes him."

"Except you."

"I like him."

"'Like' doesn't make for a marriage."

"Connor Pendleton's a great guy."

"Okay, Connor Pendleton's a great guy. You don't have to convince me. I'm not the one marrying him."

"Neither am I."

"Then tell the poor schlep before he buys the ring and orders the monogrammed towels."

She rubbed her temples. "I've tried."

"Remember what I was saying about giving hope where there isn't any? If you're done with the guy, you should give it to him straight up, no sugar."

"It's not that easy." He didn't have to live with her mother's disappointment.

"It never is."

MIRIAM WIPED HER HANDS on an old towel crusted with color. She'd been working on this piece for months. It was an oil of Lily on a four-foot canvas. Charlie had been so excited about it, had sat beside her as she blended tans and pinks with off-white to find just the right hue for their daughter's skin tone. He'd be pleased with the results, a pale ivory dusted on the cheeks with pink. And she'd gotten the eyes right, too, a vibrant sea-blue that changed with the seasons. Charlie's eyes.

God, but she missed him. She shook a cigarette out of its pack, lit it, and sucked in a deep pull of smoke. It had been seventy-seven days since she'd lost him. The pain remained sharp, the tears just below the surface though she tried to keep them hidden from Lily and Nate. What good would it do to let them see that sometimes she just wanted to curl up and disappear inside herself?

They all depended on her: Lily, Nate, the town. Charlie had depended on her, too. The world didn't know the real Charlie Blacksworth was riddled with self-doubt, tormented by guilt of decision and inde-cision, whether to choose love over duty, desire over expectation.

She'd cried when he was gone from her, back to his other home, and she was alone in the queen-sized bed, wrapped in the easy folds of the chenille spread. When they were together she hid her desperate longing to keep him there, instead waiting until he'd backed out of the drive to snatch a ciga-rette and two quick shots of Johnny Walker Red—

to steady herself, which ultimately failed and only made her feel worse.

But then morning would come, and with it Lily and reminders of how bleak her life had been before. It was true that one could be more alone with someone than by oneself. She'd always thought the idea foolish, a poet's version of love gone awry, but that was before her baby girl's death, before marriage to Nick Desantro became nothing but a piece of paper blessed by St. Gertrude's Church. That's when she knew loneliness, sleeping beside a husband turned stranger, passing through the motions of polite existence, day after day, speaking but saying nothing, meaning nothing, feeling nothing. Nate had been her only light, her salvation.

The loneliness she'd felt with her husband and the one she'd known when Charlie was gone were different—with Nick it was his *presence* that evoked the feeling; with Charlie, it was his *absence*. And then came the deaths. Nick's brought relief, Charlie's sorrow. Both times, Nate was by her side.

She loved her son, prayed for his happiness each Sunday at Mass and all the moments in between. If God would grant her one wish, it would be that Nate would bury the hatred he carried for Charlie once and for all with the anger that scarred his life and blotted out his ability to see goodness. Had that same hatred caused his breakup with Patrice?

Had she felt the pain of his wounded soul and been unable or uninterested enough to pull him out?

A mother knows her children's weaknesses, even if she sometimes refuses to acknowledge them. When Nick died, perhaps it was guilt that prevented her from speaking up each time Nate immortalized his father, creating images and situations that were so much grander than the actual man had ever been. She'd believed that, given time, Nate's misplaced loyalty would fade and replace itself with a future where Nick Desantro was a vague memory, loved, respected, but put in the past.

But it had continued, molded and changed until Nate decided the only way he could truly honor his father would be to carry on in the family business. It didn't matter that Nate loved furniture making; ND Manufacturing was his duty.

So, when Charlie Blacksworth came into her life, there was no chance Nate would approve. How could he when Charlie represented everything his own father had not—educated, articulate, city-born, wealthy . . . caring? To welcome such a man into his life would be to disrespect his own father.

She'd wanted to tell him hundreds of times just what kind of man his father had been. She'd practiced the words so many times that they sat in her subconscious, ready to spring to instant recall. Even the pauses and enunciations were well-tuned. *He couldn't even face his baby daughter when she was dying. Did you know that?* Pause. *Anna died in my arms, and he couldn't face her. Do you know where he was?* Another pause. *In O'Reilly's Bar, that's where, all night. What kind of honor is that, Nathan?*

But she couldn't strip the image her son had so carefully created, year after year, layer upon layer, of beliefs wrapped in supposition, most of them groundless, all of them untrue.

And so she said nothing.


LILY WAS ALMOST ASLEEP when she smelled it, sweet, flowery, familiar. She lay very still, sniffing into the half-darkness. Was she dreaming? Was her mind playing tricks again like it sometimes did, making her wonder if what she saw or smelled or heard was in a dream?

She turned just a little, lifted her nose in the air, sniffed again. The scent grew stronger, heavier, filling both nostrils. It wasn't a dream! She was wide awake, and still she smelled it.

"Christine?" Lily whispered into the darkness. "Christine?" *Please, please, please, let it be you.*

"Lily?"

"Christine!" She jumped up, scrunched her eyes to see. Someone stood next to her, same size, same shape as Christine, but fuzzy. Lily swiped a hand over the nightstand, found her glasses, and shoved them on her face.

"Christine!" *It was her!* Even in the half-dark, she could tell it was her.

"Your mom said you went to bed a little while ago, but sometimes it takes a bit for you to fall asleep." Christine sat on the edge of the bed. Her hair was long and fluffy tonight. "I'm sorry if I woke you."

Lily giggled. "I smelled you." She giggled again, moved closer to Christine, and grabbed her sister's hand. "Like flowers."

"Oh, my perfume."

"Yeah."

"You like it?"

"Hmmhmmm." She touched her sister's hair, *so smooth, so soft.*

"I'll put some on you tomorrow if you want."

"Okay." *The best sister in the whole world.*

"Okay."

"Is your mom better?"

"Yes, she's doing better."

Lily stroked her hair again. "You are so beautiful."

"You are so beautiful too."

Lily threw her arms around Christine's neck. "I love you." She squeezed tight, burying her nose in Christine's hair, inhaling the flower perfume. "I love you, I love you, I love you."

# 17

MARCH IN MAGDALENA was brutal. Rain and hail pelted the town on and off for the better part of three hours, bombarding rooftops, ripping immature branches from their fragile frames, filling the streets, forcing man and animal alike to seek shelter.

Christine peered through the slats of the white wooden blinds. She was in Miriam's living room, having her second cup of green tea and her third slice of poppy seed bread. The rain had settled to a steady drizzle, much less threatening than the earlier downpour. The winds had diminished too, fizzling to sporadic mini-gusts that swirled and then died.

It was her second night in Magdalena. Lily had gone to bed an hour ago, but her presence still circled the room. They'd spent the day inside playing checkers, Go Fish, KerPlunk, making Playdough spaghetti, smearing Crayola paint on a white sheet of paper and coloring in a *My Little Pony* coloring book.

Lily had chattered nonstop about everything—her new red shoes, the blue jay in the bird feeder outside, the loud horn in Nate's truck, the wind and rain, but she always circled back to the same subject.

*Christine? I want to ride a horse like yours.*

*Lady Annabelle?*

*Uh-huh.*

*Maybe someday you will.*

*Dad promised for my fourteenth birthday. I want to wear a hat like yours, too.*

*The one in the picture? The black riding hat?*

*Yup. Just like you.*

*Maybe for your birthday.*

*Yup.* Giggle. *Maybe for my birthday.*

*Lady Annabelle was a very gentle horse. You would've liked her.*

*Yup.* Lily's lips curved into a big smile. *On my birthday, Christine, I'm gonna ride a horse just like yours and wear a hat, too, just like yours.* She poked Christine in the arm, giggled. *Yup, just like yours.*

On her birthday. . . .

Lily was wriggling her way into Christine's thoughts more than she liked to admit, making her wonder, just for the briefest of seconds, if her father hadn't spent hour after hour wishing he were here, in this town, in this house. Away from Chicago and Christine and her mother, away from everything that reminded him of his other life.

Her own life was a mess; she wanted to delve into the existence her father had shared with these people, dissect it, piece it back together, and yet there was that other part of her that considered running back to Chicago, sinking into her work, and pretending she'd never heard of Magdalena or the Desantros.

Uncle Harry thought she'd come back only because of the watch. That was part of it, but not the whole reason. She pictured it lying in Lily's pink jewelry case beside the fold-up ballerina with the net tutu. She'd had a case like that when she was about six or seven. It wound up from the back and played "Some Day My Prince Will Come," just like Lily's. But it hadn't had Randolph Blacksworth's pocket watch resting on the pink velvet lining.

"Christine?" Miriam called from across the room.

*Why? Why didn't you love me enough, Dad? Why'd you give what was mine to someone else? You had no right . . .*

"Christine?"

"Yes?" *You had no right . . . damn you . . .*

"That was Nathan on the phone." Miriam sat down on the flowered chair, reached for her tea. "He sounds horrible; his cold is going into his chest."

When had the phone rung?

"And he's got a horrible cough."

Christine moved away from the window and turned to Miriam. "Is he taking anything?"

"He either takes nothing, which is what he's doing right now, or he takes a double dose of everything."

"Does he have anything there? Robitussin? Tylenol Cough and Cold?"

"He says he does." She sipped her tea, breathed out a long sigh. Tonight she wore a salmon sweater and jeans with gray hunting socks and moccasins. And she looked absurdly elegant. "But having it and taking it are two different things where my son's concerned."

Maybe that's why he hadn't been around today; maybe it had nothing to do with her being here.

"I've got a pot of chicken soup simmering on the stove." She pointed a work-roughened hand toward the kitchen. "That's what he needs to open him up. A bowl of chicken soup and good old-fashioned Vick's VapoRub, just like when he was a boy." She paused, rubbed her cheek. "Some things never change. Have you ever noticed that, Christine? Think about it: You grow up, move out, and still, some things just never change?"

Yes, she'd noticed.

"Don't you think we all tend to revert back to our childhood roles when our parents are around?"

"I guess so."

"I know so." She slid a piece of poppyseed bread onto a napkin. "I've done it myself. I can be a successful, independent woman three hundred sixty-three days out of the year and then, the two days my parents come to visit me, *bam*, I revert back to the shy little girl who used to trip over a one-inch rug and fall flat on her face." She let out a small laugh. "I'm no longer a well-respected artist; I'm the little girl sitting at the kitchen table smearing finger-paint on a piece of freezer paper and waiting for my mother to tell me it's beautiful."

Christine said nothing. How many times had she looked to her father for approval, tolerated her mother's critical evaluation of her looks, her life-style. How many times had she been the little girl in the corner, waiting?

"Nate's a fighter, though. He hates it when I hover; that's what he calls it, 'hovering'. He's never let me take care of him, not since his father died, said it was his duty to care for *me*. Can you imagine a twelve-year-old saying that? I remember . . ." Her voice drifted, stilled. When she spoke again, a sadness clung to her words, filling in the gaps. "He just needs somebody to care about him, not *for* him. Anybody can iron a shirt, wash a few clothes, and cook a meal. For heaven's sake, a cleaning lady can do that. Nate needs some-body who'll stand beside him, maybe even stand up to him if need be." She sighed, rubbed her eyes. "Not those silly women, either, the ones who flit in and out of his life like butterflies. He shoos them away before they can light."

"I'm sure he'll find someone."

"I just hope he's not too headstrong to admit it when he does. Love doesn't always come according to plan."

"So I've heard."

"Sometimes there is no plan; it just appears. And if we're very lucky, we see it, and we seize it quickly," her voice drifted off, ". . . because once it's gone, it's gone."

*Is that what you and my father did, seized it quickly?*

"Don't close yourself off to possibilities or people, no matter how absurd they might seem." She tilted her head to study Christine, and a dangle-bead earring brushed her neck. Her lips curved into a small, knowing smile. "Since Nate will probably lie there and be miserable all night, the least he can do is try some soup. I was thinking about taking a container over to him."

"You can't go outside in this weather. I'll take it to him."

"If you don't mind . . ." Her smile deepened, spread to her eyes.

"No, not at all." She followed Miriam into the kitchen, wondering if she'd ever had any intention of going to her son's house.

# 18

SHE SHOULD HAVE BEEN here by now. Nate coughed and pulled on a flannel shirt. His mother had called forty-five minutes ago to say Christine was on her way with chicken soup. So where was she? The back roads to his house were black and wet. What if she'd taken a wrong turn? Or run into a ditch?

It pissed him off that they hadn't just left him alone. He knew it wasn't Christine's idea to pay him a visit; his mother's handiwork was written all over the chicken soup. He could just picture her making the damn soup, worrying about him, insisting he take medicine, drink fluids, like he was a goddamn baby. So what if he felt like shit? He'd be fine, once his head stopped pounding and he could lose the damn cough. All he wanted was to be left alone.

Now he had to go looking for Christine. *Great*, just what he wanted to do on this god-awful night. He pulled on his jacket, checked his watch again. No sense calling his mother—she'd worry herself sick if he told her Christine hadn't showed. He'd drive around first, check her route. He hoped she wasn't in a ditch somewhere. That would involve a tow truck and at least an hour to get her out.

*Shit.*

He was sweating to death one minute, freezing his ass off the next. He grabbed his cell phone, stuffed it in his jacket, and headed out the door.

The rain started again, making it difficult to see more than a few feet past the windshield. He squinted into the darkness, trying to scour the sides of the road, searching for her car. What had she rented this time? It was a Saab, wasn't it? Black? He'd only had a quick glimpse of it the first night when she came to see him. *Damn*, he should've paid closer attention, but hell, how could he have known he'd have to play investigator later on?

The first mile and a half turned up nothing. The roads were slick, some parts pooled in water, forcing him to go slow. His mother never should have let Christine out on these roads tonight. What did a city girl know about driving back roads in weather like this? All for some goddamn chicken soup. He coughed, coughed again. The hacking started then, hurting his lungs, making it hard to keep his eyes on the road. His mother's damn soup was going to get him killed.

*Christ.*

A chill ran through his body. He reached over, flicked the heater on high. There was a bend in the road ahead, a slight curve that ended in a straight stretch, and it was there, part way into the bend, that he saw the faint stream of light in the ditch, noticed the crushed guardrails, and finally, the tail end of a dark car jutting out.

He pulled the truck alongside the road and jumped out. Wind and rain battered his body, whipped around him, making it difficult to work his way down the ditch.

"Christine!" he yelled into the storm. "Christine!" Was she lying inside, bleeding or unconscious? He slipped and slid his way to the front of the Saab.

"Christine!"

She was huddled inside, unmoving. Nate tried to open the driver's door, but it was smashed in at the handle. He maneuvered to the other side and yanked the passenger door open.

"Christine!" He reached in, touched her hair. "Are you all right?"

She whimpered. Her face was streaked with blood, her right eye swollen shut. "Nate. Help me."

"It's okay. I'll get you out of here." He reached for her shoulder, stopped. What if she'd hurt her neck? Or back? Then she wasn't supposed to move, was she? He'd have to call 911 and they'd send out medics, lift her out on a board. Wasn't that how it worked? He ran a hand over his forehead. *Christ*, he was burning up.

"Nate. Help me."

He forced himself not to look at her right eye or the patches of blood drying on her face, smeared on her nose, chin, forehead. Instead, he concentrated on her left eye, staring into it in the faint light enveloping the front seat, trying to remember the blueness of it, ocean blue, like Lily's.

"I'm going to call 911, get you some help."

"No. Please." She touched her face, felt the swelling around her right eye. "I'm okay."

"What about your neck? Your back?"

She straightened against the seat, winced. "I'm okay, Nate. Please. Just get me out of here."

He stayed focused on her good eye. "You might need stitches." His gaze slid sideways. There was too damn much blood. *She should go to the hospital, shouldn't she?*

"I need to get out of here." She tried to open the driver's door. "I need to get out of here," she said again, throwing her shoulder against the door, once, twice, three times. "I need to get out of here!"

"Okay, just calm down. We'll get you out. Just relax. Grab on to my arms; hold tight."

She clutched his forearms, her grip biting through his jacket as he eased her from the seat. "I thought . . . I thought . . ." Her whole body started shaking.

"It's okay." Nate lifted her into his arms, tucked her against his chest as he made his way out of the car and up the ditch. He'd deal with the car later. She was shivering, from cold, rain, fear, he didn't know, but hell, who could blame her when she'd ended up in a ditch, just like her old man?

He opened the truck door, helped her in, then ran to the other side. "Here." He pulled a handful of McDonald's napkins from the glove compartment. He turned on the ignition and cranked up the heat. *Damn*, he was roasting again, but she was shivering beside him. Nate unbuttoned his jacket and flicked the heat up another notch. "I'll take you to my house first and get you cleaned up before we head to my Mom's, all right?"

She nodded. "Thank you."

They drove in silence, and, when they reached his cabin, Nate parked the truck at the top of the driveway and helped her out. The rain had eased to a slow drizzle. Christine leaned against him, almost into him, her shoulders sagging, her steps slow.

This was not the Christine Blacksworth who'd presented herself at his mother's front door three months ago demanding to see Lily. This woman was tired, and afraid. . . .

In the brightness of his kitchen, she looked like

a prizefighter who'd taken one too many punches to the face. Brilliant purples and blues seeped over her swollen eye; dried blood streaked her face in crusty patches.

He pushed back a lock of hair. "Let's get you cleaned up," he said, his voice almost gentle. He fixed her a cup of hot tea with a splash of Jack Daniel's and then set about working on her. She held an icepack to her swollen eye while he filled a pan of warm water and proceeded to swab each section of her face with a damp washcloth. "It doesn't look like you've got any huge gashes," he said, studying a small cut above her right eyebrow. "Just this nick above your eyebrow is all. I think the blood came from your nose when you hit the steering wheel."

"I don't want to see my eye."

He would've thought she'd ask for a mirror by now.

"Well," he busied himself wringing out the washcloth, "it's not a pretty sight right now, but give it a day or two."

She shrugged. "It's not the black eye that bothers me . . ."

He looked up. "So, what is it?"

"The questions. Everyone will want to know what happened—you know, where, how—and I'll have to relive it over and over."

"So wear dark glasses."

"In my office?"

"Take some time off."

"That won't get me away from my mother. She'll find me."

"So tell her to mind her own business."

"Obviously, you've never met my mother."

"Obviously."

She was quiet then, pulling into herself, shutting down the outside world. He let her be, concentrating on a patch of dried blood on her left cheekbone. He knew all about being poked and prodded like a goddamn lab rat, pushed through a maze of questions for answers you didn't know or didn't want to admit you knew. It was a real pain in the ass. When Patrice had moved out, the town couldn't help but wonder, *Where'd she go? How long will she be gone?* And then, later, as time passed and the Nissan Maxima she drove still hadn't been seen around town, there was real concern in their voices: *When did you say she was coming back? Where'd you say she was?* And finally, when the mailman stopped delivering Patrice Desantro's mail to Nate's address, only the very bold ones ventured forward. *Is she coming back, Nate?*

It happened again when Charles died, all the questions, interrogations actually, wanting to know everything, trying to dig deep enough to understand what had happened, why, how? *Why* him, why

Charlie Blacksworth? *How* could such a tragedy have happened? His mother had been oblivious to their motives, had answered them all, given them responses that were grief-filled, and *still* it wasn't enough.

The real question was not, "How could such a tragedy happen to a man like Charlie Blacksworth?" The *real* question on the town's mind pulsed just below the surface, frightening in its persistency, paralyzing in its randomness. "How can we prevent a tragedy like that from happening to us?" That's what they really wanted to know.

Because no matter what the experts said, or the church preached, or logic dictated, deep down, everybody thinks they're going to live a hell of a long life, maybe not forever, but damn close to it.

"Nate?"

"Yeah?" He dipped the cloth in the pink water.

"Thank you," she hesitated, "for everything."

She studied him out of one eye, making him feel that she was seeing more than she usually did with two eyes. He shrugged, "No big deal."

"It is, considering . . . everything."

The blood on her face was almost gone. Her hair was gnarled and matted to her scalp. and there was a bruise on her forehead, a small cut above her eyebrow, and of course, the monster right eye.

Christine Blacksworth sat in front of him, bloodied and bruised, looking extremely vulnerable and, in some twisted, bizarre way, more beautiful than he'd ever seen her before. Was it the sheer helplessness that made her appear so attractive? Or maybe it was the two shots of Jack Daniel's and the fever making him hallucinate.

*Fuck.*

He turned away, dropped the washcloth in the bowl. "I should get you back."

"Can I just stay here tonight, please? I don't think I can handle having Miriam see me like this."

"It's not going to be much better tomorrow. In fact, it'll probably be worse."

"I just need a little time."

"Christine—"

"Just give me a blanket, Nate, and I'll sleep right on the couch. I won't bother you, I promise."

He should take her back to his mother's, right now. She didn't belong here. Hell, he'd already gotten more involved than he'd intended.

"Nate? Please?"

"All right," he heard himself saying.

"Thank you."

"I'll take the couch; you can have my bed."

"No—"

"You're taking the bed, or I'm taking you back." He coughed, coughed again. "Your whole body's going to be sore tomorrow, and if you sleep on a couch it'll be ten times worse."

"Oh. Thank you."

"The bathroom's down the hall," he said as he made his way to the bedroom. What the hell was he doing? He yanked open his dresser drawer, pulled out a maroon Black Dog T-shirt and a pair of old gray sweats that were too small for him, and tossed them on the bed.

"Thank you."

She stood in the doorway watching him, her face and body cast in shadow. For just a second she wasn't Christine Blacksworth, she was merely a woman in his bedroom. There'd been a string of them since Patrice left, meaningless, brief encounters ending before they began. It was the way he wanted it—memories and faces blurred by Jack Daniel's and darkness, a guarantee that no face would stand out, no touch, no voice . . . no woman.

The hacking started then and he turned away, tried to stop it. His chest ached, his head pounded, and he was burning up. He coughed again.

"You sound horrible."

She was coming toward him, her face illuminated by the small bedside lamp. He shook his head, cleared his throat. He should've taken her home. *Jesus, what a fucking mistake.*

"Nate?"

"I'm fine."

"But—"

"I said I'm fine." He yanked a pillow off the bed, grabbed an extra blanket. "Get some sleep."

He left her standing there in the middle of his bedroom and made his way to the couch. He didn't want her concern; he didn't want anything from her. He stifled another cough, plunked down his pillow and blanket, and called his mother to tell her Christine's car had slid into a ditch, a minor mishap, no big deal, she'd see her in the morning. He was careful to focus on the car, not the way he'd found her bloodied, with her right eye swollen shut. His mother would see for herself soon enough. When he'd assured her that Christine was fine, *honest, Ma*, he hung up the phone, coughed again, and fell into a restless sleep.

The screaming woke him, piercing, horrible cries. Nate bolted off the couch and ran to the bedroom. "Christine?"

She was sitting up in bed, head and arms thrashing like a wild woman. "No! No!"

"Christine!"

She stilled, opened her left eye. The right was little more than a slit. "Nate!" She scrambled across the bed, grabbed his waist. "Nate." Her shoulders started heaving, and she clung tighter.

"It's okay." He put his arms around her. "You must've had a bad dream."

"I . . . I . . ." she gasped, sucked in air, "I dreamed I was going to . . . to . . ."

"No." He stroked her hair.

"Like . . . my Dad. I was going to die just . . . like him."

Nate eased her hands from around his waist, sat down on the edge of the bed. "Look at me, Christine." He kept his voice soft and low, like he did when Lily was afraid of something. "It was a bad dream. That's all."

The tears started then, a great outpouring of grief and pain and fear. Her shoulders shook with the force of it, and she fell into him, thrusting her arms around his middle. "I saw him in the car, Nate," she sobbed. "Dead, in the car."

"Don't," he whispered, "don't do that to yourself."

More agony poured out. "I was covered in blood."

He put his arms around her and pulled her close. "You're safe now, do you hear me? Nothing's going to happen. You're safe."

In the semi-darkness of his bedroom with the wind and rain battering against the cabin walls, he held her in his arms until the whimpering faded into exhaustion and she drifted off to sleep. As he lay down beside her, he studied her swollen face, memorized it. Then he pulled the afghan around them and turned out the light.

# 19

"YOU KNOW, IT'S probably a good idea Connor's not coming tonight," her mother said, gazing at Christine over her glass of chardonnay. A pair of crutches with lamb's wool covering the tops rested on the chair next to her, the only visible sign she'd endured surgery less than two weeks ago; the other indicator, aside from the bottle of Valium, was the compact air cast on her right ankle, well-hidden under the green and gold tablecloth. "At least until the unsightliness of the swelling goes down a bit."

"I didn't want him here."

"Of course you didn't." She leaned forward, lowered her voice, "A black eye is not something you want to parade around showing everyone, especially a prospective husband."

"That's not what—"

"Hello!" The front door slammed, and Uncle Harry strode in carrying a vase filled with tulips. "How's my black-eyed girl—Jesus!"

"Hello, Uncle Harry."

"Good God, girl, you said you had a black eye; you didn't say a train rolled over you." He set the vase on the table and looked down at her. "Honey, are you all right?"

It was the tenderness in his voice that almost made her cry out, *No, Uncle Harry, no, I'm not all right. I'm falling apart. Help me, help me.* Instead, she forced herself to say, "I'm fine."

"Shit." He reached out and touched her cheek.

"I told Christine this is a warning—she should be done with the cabin. Back roads are treacherous," her mother said. "They can be lethal; we all know that."

Uncle Harry shot her a warning look, but she merely shrugged and picked up her wine glass.

Was this how her father had felt every time he returned from Magdalena, disjointed, flushed with remembering, moving his mouth in conversation while his heart remained in the white house on Artisdale Street? Had her mother exhausted him the way she was exhausting Christine tonight, question after question, well-planned, perhaps even rehearsed, to elicit what? An answer? Conversation? Guilt?

The prime rib would be superb, the potatoes au gratin exquisite, the green beans almondine perfect. And yet, she found herself longing for a simple white ceramic bowl filled with vegetable soup.

What kind of daughter would be thinking about her father's mistress and her family when her own mother had gone to such measures to create a welcome home dinner for her?

And yet she couldn't help herself; the visions bombarded her brain, memories pouring into it, taking hold: Nate lifting her from the car, Nate wiping the blood from her face, Miriam turning away so Christine wouldn't see her tears, Lily throwing her small arms around Christine's waist, Nate lying beside her asleep.

Nate Desantro had shocked her almost as much as the accident had. She'd glimpsed a side of him she'd doubted he had, one that was tender, concerned. He could have ignored her wishes, taken her back to his mother's, and yet he hadn't. And when he'd found her screaming in his bed, he could have pulled the afghan around her and told her to go back to sleep, or worse, ignored the screaming altogether. And yet he'd held her until she fell asleep and then stayed with her.

She'd tried to thank him the next day, feeling awkward and self-conscious to have revealed such weakness to him, but he'd brushed it off and then disappeared as soon as he dropped her at his mother's. She hadn't seen him the rest of that day or today. She'd headed for the airport, and still there'd been no word from him. Something had happened between them the other night. She knew it, and she knew that he knew it, too.

"If you don't feel up to going in to the office for a few days, take a break," Uncle Harry said. "I'll cover for you."

Uncle Harry believed in taking as many "breaks" as he could in one week of work. And his idea of covering would be to tell everyone who asked that it was "None of your goddamn business."

"Thanks, Uncle Harry. But I'm okay, really. I need to get back to work."

"I'll be there bright and early then, in case you need me to run interference for you."

"Thanks."

"Why can't you just tell them the truth?" This from her mother.

*The truth?* Uncle Harry spoke first. "Of course we'll tell them the truth," he said. "What the hell else would we tell them?"

She lifted her shoulders in a delicate shrug. She wore a pale blue silk pantsuit tonight, and three strands of pearls. "You made it sound as though you were considering some kind of," she paused and her gaze traveled over both of them, "subterfuge."

"You watch too much television, Gloria," Uncle Harry said, laughing. "We're not spies, for chrissakes."

"A lie then."

"Hell, we're not going to lie. We'll tell them exactly what happened." He met Christine's gaze, held it. "Won't we, Chrissie? You slid off the road and bumped your head on the steering wheel. End of story."

"This road," her mother's voice grew weak, "it's the one leading to the cabin?"

"Right."

"The same one that Charles . . ." her voice faded.

"The same one," Uncle Harry said.

"Dear God." She closed her eyes, pinched the bridge of her nose. Her long, coral nails sparkled under the chandelier light.

"Please, Mother, I'm fine, everything's fine."

"This time." She dabbed at her eyes. "Everything's fine *this* time, but what about the next or the one after that? Your father, now you . . . Don't go back, Christine. Please don't go back."

HARRY SLIPPED INTO THE kitchen looking for a slice of Greta's lemon meringue pie, actually, looking for Greta, too. The granite countertops were wiped clean. Hell, he might have caught her if he hadn't gotten stuck with Gloria and her theatrics. She'd made herself teary-eyed and nearly hysterical, going on and on about omens and begging Chrissie not to go back to the cabin. He'd wanted to tell her not to goddamn worry about it because Chrissie wasn't going to the *cabin*, hadn't been there in months.

Gloria knew how to play people, he'd give her that—a sniff here, a teardrop there, never enough to screw up her makeup, of course, and she had them all swarming over her, forgetting what they'd wanted to do that disagreed with her. Even her fucking ankle, for chrissakes. Was that a set up or what? He was still pissed that he couldn't go to The Presidio anymore without somebody running up to him and asking about her.

He opened the refrigerator, pulled out two slices of prime rib, and stuffed them in his mouth. Maybe he should think about making Mi Hermana's Restaurante his regular spot from now on; at least he wouldn't be bombarded with questions about Gloria every time he walked in. He grabbed another slice of prime rib and headed out the back door.

He missed the mussels and linguine at The Presidio. Maybe Mi Hermana's Restaurante would make them for him. But he preferred Italian to Mexican. So couldn't they change the spices? He was so involved with his restaurant dilemma that he almost ran into Greta rounding the corner of the sidewalk leading to the driveway.

"Jesus, Greta! You scared the hell out of me."

"I'm sorry, Mr. Blacks—"

"Harry, remember?"

She hesitated. "Harry. I'm sorry, but it's my car. It won't start."

"Oh." He knew something about cars, had considered racing them several years back, but the 5:00 A.M. practice runs had killed the notion.

She fiddled with her purse. "I was going back inside to call a taxi."

"I'll take you home."

"No—"

"I'll take you home." *Jesus*, was she like the rest of them, thinking he wasn't capable of performing even the most menial of tasks?

"It's all the way across town, twenty minutes away."

"So, we'd better get moving." He started walking toward his car.

"I have to pick up my children at the sitter's. It's another ten minutes past me; that's a thirty-minute drive from here."

Harry shoved his hands in his pockets, sighed. "I can do the math." Why did women have to be so difficult, so damned hell bent on figuring out every nuance?

"Besides, one of the children is in a car seat," she pointed in the direction of her Toyota Corolla. "I'd have to bring that, too. Thank you, Mr.—" she caught herself, "Harry, but this is too much to ask of you."

*Jesus*, women drove him crazy. He started back

up the driveway and held out his hand. "Give me the keys, and I'll get the car seat. Not another word, Greta, I mean it. You're driving me fucking nuts."

She barely said a word for the first fifteen minutes of the drive. He watched her out of the corner of his eye, hands pressed tightly on her knees, back hardly touching the leather, eyes fixed straight ahead. She needed to relax. She was acting like he was a complete stranger or a kidnapper, for chrissake. Didn't she know she should feel honored? Harry Blacksworth never did people favors. Didn't she at least know that much about him?

Maybe she did, and maybe that was the problem. He was starting to think he'd have been better off pulling out a fifty and letting her call the damn cab.

"Turn up here," she said, pointing to the right. "Take this road to Brookside, then turn left."

Harry turned, noticed the change in scenery. It didn't take an Einstein to figure out they were now in the low-rent district. The houses were tiny boxes, some vinyl, some wood, folded and stuffed onto a piece of property with a scrap of front yard and a strip of side driveway. A few homes had awnings over the front stoop and wrought-iron railings supporting cement steps. If there was a garage, it was detached, in the back, and he guessed was used to store anything that wasn't an automobile.

It was sure a hell of a lot different than Essex

Estates. Was that why she hadn't wanted him to drive her home? As if he cared. But what did he know, really? He'd never been without, not even a meal unless he was trying to shave off a few pounds after the holidays. But he'd bet Greta knew about not having; he bet she knew a hell of a lot about it.

"I thought your mother lived with you." He pulled that from nowhere, and couldn't even say why.

"She does."

"Then why isn't she watching your kids?"

"She had a meeting tonight."

"With a man?" he said, trying to loosen her up.

"With Father Mahoney at church."

"Oh, well, you know what they say about those priests."

"Is everything a joke with you, Harry? Is nothing sacred?"

"Hey, I didn't mean anything by it. I was just trying to get you to relax. Hell, you're sitting there like a scared rabbit. Did I do something to offend you? Other than the priest joke, I mean."

Her shoulders eased a bit, and she slipped back against the leather seat. "No. It isn't you."

He waited for her to continue. Okay, it wasn't him, so what was it? "Greta?" A full minute between sentences was fifty-five seconds too long, and yet he'd given her the opportunity, just in case, and still she remained silent. "What's on your mind? If it isn't me, what is it?"

"I'm not comfortable with you doing this."

"What? Driving you home?"

She nodded.

"You don't trust my driving? I'm going too fast? I'll slow down." He lifted his foot off the gas. "There, though I was only eight miles over the limit." He flashed her a smile. "That's practically a crawl for me."

"Your driving is fine, but you shouldn't be doing this." She turned to face him. "You're driving your sister-in-law's cook to pick up her children in a car that cost more than her home."

"So?"

"So it isn't right."

"You think you don't deserve to be in this car? You think your kids don't?" She didn't answer. "You think my goddamn excuse for a sister-in-law is better than you because she was *born* into money, because she *married* into it? And me, Christ, don't tell me you've got me on some goddamn pedestal, too."

"No, Harry, I don't think you're better than me, or that Mrs. Blacksworth is, but I do think I need to remember where *I* belong. That way, I don't start to want things I can never have, things that could destroy me with the wanting, even though I know they'll never make me happy. I can go home at night to my second-hand stove and cook pot roast instead of filet mignon and be completely happy because I know it's how God meant things to be, and I will not feel the least bit of jealousy or want."

"That's bullshit."

"It's the truth."

"You mean to tell me you wouldn't like to have a little bit of this life?" He swept his hand over the seat. "Feel the leather, sink your fingers into it. And what about the houses, the trips, the bank accounts? You'd rather live hand-to-mouth in some shit hole for the rest of your days, cleaning up after some rich bitch?"

"I'm proud of my work. It's decent and honest."

"Okay, okay, but is that all you want? Don't you have a dream, you know, something you'd really like to do, if you could erase the limits?"

She didn't answer at first, and he thought maybe she wasn't going to. "I have dreams." The words came out softly, slowly, as though she weren't used to speaking them aloud. "In Germany, my grandparents owned a restaurant. When they came to the United States, they wanted to start one here, but my grandfather died, and my grandmother couldn't bear the thought of carrying out their dream alone. So she taught her children and then her grandchildren how to cook and bake according to tradition.

That's my dream, Harry, to start a restaurant, for my grandparents, my children, and myself."

"That's a very noble dream, Greta."

Her full lips slipped into a faint smile. "Yes, it is. And you, Harry, do you have a dream?"

"Me? Hell, Greta, I'm living my dream every day; I can go anywhere I want, do anything I want, buy anything I want. If that isn't a dream, what is?" He said the words with gusto, pushed out of his lungs full force, and only he knew the emptiness behind them, the lies that draped the pathetic truth; his dreams had been stripped years ago, his hope crushed, leaving him with nothing, nothing at all.

# 20

LILY STARED OUT THE window, head tilted skyward, faint whispers slipping through her lips.

"Lily?" Christine entered the bedroom and stood beside her half sister. "What are you doing?"

"Shhh." She lifted a finger to her lips.

"Sorry," Christine lowered her voice. "What are you doing?"

A smile streaked Lily's face like a burst of sunshine. "Talking to Daddy." Her eyes remained glued to a patch of bluish-white sky. "Up there, in Heaven," she said, pointing a finger skyward.

"Oh."

"Do you ever talk to Daddy in Heaven?"

"I guess I do, sometimes."

"I miss him." Her lower lip started to wobble. "A lot."

"I know. Me, too."

"I wish he wasn't dead."

"Me, too."

"I want to go to Heaven, so I can see him again."

"Lily . . . you have to die first and then you go to Heaven."

She nodded her head, "I know. Some day . . . some day, I want to go to Heaven." Her voice shook, fell apart. "Miss him, miss him." The tears started then, great sobs of grief spilling down her cheeks, pouring over her small body.

"Oh, Lily," Christine reached for her, "I know . . ." She folded her into her arms, stroked her back. "I know."

Lily's shoulders started to shake. "Daddy, Daddy . . ."

Her grief seeped into Christine, filling her, deep, deeper, until every inch of her body was saturated with loss. Christine had made only a few trips to Magdalena, and already she sensed its growing power over her, the pull of one small town and its people. Against her will, without consent or even acknowledgment, she found herself counting days, gazing out windows, thinking thoughts that had nothing to do with life in Chicago, her *real* life.

*Was* Chicago her real life? Did she still belong there with the Blacksworth name and all that it implied, or did she belong here, in Magdalena, with her father's mistress and illegitimate daughter? And Nate?

She hadn't seen him since the night of the accident. Miriam had her own thoughts on why. *Something happened between you two that night, something happened and you know it. He knows it, too. Why do you think he's avoiding you?*

Christine supposed they did need to talk, but the thought of it made her uneasy. He wasn't the most pleasant person to be around when he got into one of his moods, which was most of the time. Odd, that she could recognize his moods. And yet there was another side of him that was kind, decent; she'd witnessed it with Lily and again the night of the accident, though she was sure he hadn't wanted her to see it.

Lily's crying quieted to a soft whimper, muffled in the folds of Christine's sweater. "It's okay, Lily." She stroked her thick hair. "It's okay."

Lily sniffed and looked up. "Can we look at pictures of Dad? It makes me less sad."

"Sure. Of course, we can."

"I'll go get them." She scrambled out of Christine's arms and hurried to the bookshelf. Row after row of books, lined up by size and shape, crowded the top three shelves. But it was the bottom one that drew Lily's attention; there were four albums, pink vinyl, stacked on top of one another. She pulled them out, carried them to the bed, and plopped them down on the sunflower comforter. She looked up at Christine and smiled. "Now we can *see* Daddy when we talk to him."

HE HEARD THE CAR in the driveway and knew it was her. Who else would be coming uninvited? Nate went back to the plans in front of him. He was going to build his mother a curio cabinet with recessed lights. The wiring was always the trickiest part with these kinds of projects. *A car door opened, closed.* If you messed up the wiring you were pretty well screwed. *Why was she here? Was Lily with her?* Then you had to start all over, and wood wasn't cheap. *It would be better if Lily were with her.* Black cherry garnered top dollar, but mahogany and maple cost a pretty penny, too. *What was there to talk about, anyway?* Maple was his mother's favorite; the curio was going to be maple. *Nothing, there was nothing to talk about.*

Footsteps, he heard them coming up the drive. *She was alone.*

He didn't answer the doorbell the first time, waited instead for her to press it again before he pushed back his chair and moved toward the front door. So what if he looked like hell in his flannel shirt and faded jeans? He'd gone into work at ten last night to fix a machine that was down and didn't get home until two. So what?

He opened the door. *God*, she was beautiful, even with the fading purple and blue seeped into the skin around her right eye. Somehow, it made her more exotic-looking, more fragile. She wore jeans and a flannel shirt with an oversized jean jacket that looked like the one he'd given his mother years ago.

"Hello, Nate."

He nodded, stepped aside to let her pass. "What brings you here?" She smelled of lavender and roses.

"I needed to talk to you," she said, shrugging out of her jacket, "and I figured if I wanted to see you, I'd have to come out here."

"I've been busy."

"I'm sure you have been. What's this?" She pointed to the drawing on the kitchen table.

"I'm making my mother a curio for her birthday."

"Impressive."

"What did you want to talk about?"

She pulled out a chair and sat down. "I came to thank you again for helping me the night of the accident and," she hesitated, "to apologize for misjudging you."

"No thanks necessary. Or apologies."

"You give this mean, gruff show, like you don't care about anything or anybody except your mother and Lily, and, well, that's not true."

"Yes, it is."

"No, Nate, it's not. I saw it that night, the way you took care of me when you could have just as soon dumped me at your mother's. But you didn't, and I can't say many people in your position wouldn't have."

"In my position?" What, now she thought he was a pansy-ass do-gooder?

"You know, your position, my position, our history."

"We have no history." His gaze flitted across her lips, full, pink, soft. He turned away, opened the cupboard over the stove, and pulled out his bottle of Jack Daniel's. *What the hell was wrong with him?* He poured a shot, downed it in one swallow. *Christ.* He'd been looking at her lips, thinking about them, the feel, the taste, as though he wanted to.... He poured another shot, drank that too, and then turned around.

"We have no history," he repeated.

"We do, Nate, whether we like it or not," she said. "I think I'm finally realizing that."

"Don't think about it."

"I can't help it, can you?"

He didn't answer.

"I came to this town hating Lily, hating the Desantro name. I didn't want to try and understand anything other than *my* pain, *my* betrayal. I wanted to meet my father's mistress, get her face ingrained in my brain so the hurt would stay fresh, the pain always just below the surface, and then I wanted to pay her off and leave. But then I met Miriam, and I *couldn't* hate her. And Lily . . . no one can hate Lily."

"I hated your father."

She didn't answer at first. "I think they really loved each other."

"Probably, but that wasn't the point."

She met his gaze, her eyes a vibrant blue. "I think he didn't love my mother the way he loved yours," her voice cracked, split, fell apart. "He did love my mother, though, in his own way."

"He should've made a choice; it wasn't fair to either side." It was the weakness of Charles Blacksworth that left him raw, even after all these years.

"It would've killed my mother. Even now, I worry I'll slip up, maybe she'll get suspicious about where I go every month, who I'm seeing."

"You think she had no idea that your father had somebody on the side?"

"No, she never knew about your mother . . . or Lily."

Nate grabbed a glass, poured her a shot. "Drink this," he shoved it toward her, refilled his own. "No woman sleeps with a man that many years and doesn't know when he's double-dipping."

"I'm telling you, she doesn't know. You should've seen how she used to spend days planning these huge welcome home dinners for him. Do you think she'd do that if she knew he was returning from seeing your mother?"

He shrugged. "Depends on the arrangement. Maybe she got money and a house, and he got his freedom."

"Their marriage wasn't 'arranged.'" She took a sip of whiskey, coughed. "They did things together, like a couple."

"Maybe they didn't sleep together anymore."

"They did. They slept in the same room, I know that."

"Maybe they slept in the same room but they didn't *sleep* together, as in exercising conjugal rights."

She polished off the rest of her drink, coughed twice. "She doesn't know, and she isn't going to find out."

"Fine. Just don't be surprised if down the road you don't find out I was right."

"Are you trying to rip apart every piece of my parents' marriage?" She didn't give him time to answer. "Why? So you can punish me for being a Blacksworth? Do you really hate me that much?"

"I don't hate you," he said, and realized it was true.

"Then why are you trying to punish me?"

"I'm not." She looked so fragile, sitting there

gripping the empty shot glass, so alone. "It's just that," he searched for the right words, words that he didn't even know how to say, "you're an intelligent woman, and I don't want to see you get blindsided."

"By whom? My own mother?"

Now he sounded like an asshole. "You're right. I guess I'm way off base." So what if the mother knew?

"You are." She pushed back her chair and stood. "Thanks for the drink."

He watched her shrug into her jacket, the one he thought was his old one. It looked good on her, made her seem more relaxed, the faded jean material bringing out the highlights in her hair. He felt like a shit. Why hadn't he just shut up, let her believe her story? Why'd he have to push just to prove a point?

"Christine, I'm sorry." He was behind her, reaching out to touch her shoulder. "I was out of line."

When she turned to face him there was pain in her eyes. "I need to hold onto this, Nate. *I need to*; it's the only way I can keep from hating him."

"I'm sorry." And he was.

Her eyes filled with tears, pooled, spilled down her cheeks. He reached out to catch one, his fingers stroking across her soft skin. "Don't cry." The simple request only made the tears fall faster. "Christine." He traced a tear to her chin, wiped it away with his thumb. "Please don't cry." And then he was leaning toward her, close, closer, until his lips touched hers, soft at first, feather-light, his breath fanning her face. She moved toward him, and pressed her hands against his chest.

He tasted the salt of her tears, traced her lips with his tongue. It only made him want more. She was strength and softness, light and dark. He reached for her, eased her against his body.

*More.*

It was the moan that brought him back, reminded him what he was doing, and with whom. He broke the kiss and pulled back.

"This is insanity."

She looked away.

"What the hell's wrong with me?"

"It was just a kiss." Still, she wasn't looking at him.

"Was it? Do you mean you didn't want more?" He waited for her answer, and when she didn't respond he went on, "Because I sure as hell did."

"Wanting and doing aren't the same," she said. "I want a lot of things, but I don't go after all of them."

"What do you do?"

"Exercise self-control."

That made him laugh. Leave it to her to compartmentalize what had just happened. "So, you're exercising self-control with me?"

"I didn't say that."

"You didn't have to."

Finally, she looked at him. "It was just a kiss."

Her attempt to treat it like nothing more than a handshake angered him. He'd done a hell of a lot more than kissing with more women than he could remember, but none of them had been entrenched in family history like this one.

"So, let it go, okay? You were trying to make me feel better, and since you aren't much for words, you tried something else." She lifted her shoulders. "And it worked. I'm not crying anymore. Okay? I'm all better."

"Shut up," he said, pulling her toward him, "just shut the fuck up." When his mouth covered hers this time it was demanding, possessive, his tongue fierce between her lips, searching, taking, leaving no doubt that he wanted this kiss, that he would make her want it, too. He continued until she whimpered against him, locked her fingers behind his neck, and pressed her body into his. He gentled the kiss, his tongue mating with hers, sucking, pulling her into his mouth.

"Nate," she breathed his name.

He cupped her buttocks, pressed her against him. "Don't think, just feel."

"I can't think . . ."

"Good."

"This *is* insanity."

"I know." His mouth was on her neck now, working its way inside the opening of her shirt to more skin, beautiful, glorious skin.

"Nate?"

"Hmmm?" He flicked open the top button of her shirt. Who would have thought flannel could be such a turn-on?

"Look at me."

"I am looking at you, baby." And that bra, low-cut peach with lace ... front clasp ... his favorite ... he was in Heaven. ...

"Nate, *look* at me."

The desperation in her voice yanked him back, forced him to meet her gaze. "Are you okay?"

"I just want you to know that right now I'm not thinking about who you are or who I am, or why we should never be together." She reached out and stroked his cheek.

He kissed her then, a swelling of need that gripped his soul, swirled into his consciousness, consuming him and yet at the same time warning, *Beware ... beware. ...*

But he didn't hear the words; his heart was pounding too loudly, his need beating too fiercely against his body, as he slowly unbuttoned Christine's shirt and began the delicious freefall into oblivion.

# 21

THE SWEETNESS OF brown sugar and cinnamon drifted through the house, crawling up the stairs, seeping through the small cracks in the windows to dissipate in the spring air. Miriam was baking cinnamon rolls, Christine's favorite. Actually, she'd acquired several favorites since she'd begun visiting Magdalena: marinara sauce with linguine, meatloaf smothered in gravy, vegetable soup (with a rutabaga for sweetness), pumpkin rolls, and oatmeal chocolate chip cookies. Four months ago, she didn't know the difference between a rutabaga and a parsnip. But Miriam had taught her this, had taught her, too, about cooking from scratch, what constituted "a pinch" and how to use a rolling pin.

At home, the kitchen was reserved for people with foreign accents who wore white uniforms and white shoes. But Miriam's time in the kitchen was a form of art, created with media such as flour and eggs, used to convey her caring for others, friends as well as family. She whipped up chicken noodle soup for the neighbor with a cold, spaghetti sauce and homemade noodles for the widower who still couldn't force himself to cook a meal without thinking of his deceased wife, banana and pumpkin breads for the church. The giving went on and on. Names and faces didn't matter—it was the need that took precedence, weighing heavy on Miriam's soul, luring her back into the kitchen, until she'd created food for their family, their cause.

But food wasn't the only pull of this room. The warm, unassuming presence of the woman herself let Christine ease into conversations she'd never had with her own mother. *Why do some women feel their only value is in their body? Why do they continue to stuff their shapes into too-tight dresses, their feet into stilettos, their brains into closed vaults that can't breathe and subsequently suffocate? Why do they tuck and nip and smooth when the ultimate beauty isn't on the surface at all? And why do they not see this?*

"Would you like another cup of coffee?"

"I'll get it." Christine slid out of her chair, picked up her cup. "How about you? Are you ready for another?"

"This is my second pot," Miriam said. "Decaf or not, I think I've had enough."

"You could sleep until six some morning, you know. You won't shrivel up and disappear. Trust me, lots of people don't see daylight until much, much later."

"But there's nothing like the silence of early morning. Your father used to love to sit on the back porch with his first cup of coffee, just gazing out at the hills. He looked so peaceful then; I would watch him from the other room, wondering what he was thinking about, where his mind was. I always wanted to know," her voice drifted off.

"Didn't you ever ask?"

She set down the hot pad she'd been holding. "Once, in the beginning. It was too painful, so I never asked again."

"Still, most women wouldn't stop at one time."

"There were too many parts of our lives that we couldn't change. I didn't want to start questioning him again because I knew once I started I wouldn't be able to stop. I'd want to know every detail—what kind of coffee cup did he use, where did he have his shirts laundered, who cut his hair? The questions would never stop, and I wasn't going to do that to him, to us." Her gaze was honest as she added, "Or to myself. I loved him, and I was not going to destroy that with questions I had no right asking."

Christine opened her mouth and the words fell out, "Blacksworth and Company mug, Custom Dry Cleaning, Mario." It was the least she could do, one small gift.

"Thank you."

"If there's ... anything else you would like to know, maybe I can help."

Miriam nodded, her eyes wet.

Life was filled with so many twists and turns, like the sides of a prism, giving off light; what seemed wrong before seemed almost right when viewed from a different angle.

"Christine." The sadness lifted from her face, shifted to concern.

"Yes?"

"I know it's none of my business, and I just gave you a big talk about not asking questions, but I care about you, and Nate's my son. I don't want to see either one of you get hurt."

She should've known Nate's call last night wouldn't be the end of the conversation. What mother wouldn't inquire when her son told her the daughter of the man he's hated for years is staying overnight? And when she'd come in the back door this morning, hair still wet from a shower, Miriam had glanced up from the pot of soup she was stirring and offered a quiet smile, nothing more.

What to say? *I don't know what's happening between us? Last night he touched me in a way no man's ever touched me before? I woke up in the middle of the night just to look at him, this stranger lying next to me who'd stripped my defenses?*

"Nate's my son. He's a wonderful person, kind, considerate, caring, but there's a hard streak running through him that keeps him from forming relationships, lasting ones, anyway."

She did not want to hear this, not right now. "Miriam—"

"Hear me out, Christine. Please. You're Charlie's daughter; I would do anything to protect you, and Nate, well, that goes without saying. But a mother sees her child's shortcomings, even if she doesn't admit to them very often."

"Miriam, this is all very premature. We . . . I . . ."

"You know Nate's never forgiven your father for not choosing between his life here and the one in Chicago. He still doesn't understand that, for me, those four days were enough. Maybe I should have told him the truth about his own father, how living beside him after Anna died was lonelier than being alone, but I couldn't bring myself to shatter the illusion he'd created. But I'm afraid he might try to punish your father through you." She took a deep breath and pushed out the words. "Do you understand what I'm saying? He harbors such hate, I worry he'll use you just because you're a Blacksworth."

Miriam's words hit Christine, throwing her whole world off-center. Had he merely been using her last night?

"And then I worry, too, that perhaps it isn't that

at all, perhaps Nate's falling for you. I remember how he used to stare at your pictures when Lily showed him her album, the ones of you a few years ago and more recently. Maybe it wasn't all hate he felt when he looked at you; maybe deep down it was an unwilling attraction."

"Would that be so bad if he were attracted to me?"

"It could be if you didn't share that same attraction, or," her smile was sad, pained, "if he fell in love with you, and a cruel twist of fate forced him to live a life he condemned your father and me for, all these years."

"But if we loved each other—"

"What, Christine? If you loved each other it would be enough, like it was for your father and me? No, it wouldn't be enough; it would be the worst form of torture for him. That's why, deep down, I don't think he'll *let* himself love you, Christine, and that's what scares me most."


GLORIA SIPPED HER chardonnay and took in the surroundings, pleased that even now, several weeks after the accident, her presence still evoked a kind of quiet command among the employees of The Presidio. It was evident in the number of trips Armand had made to her table, inquiring about the food, the service, for God's sake, the butter rosettes. Was the prime rib pink enough for her liking? Had the waiter seen to her needs? Did she prefer butter rosettes or perhaps a cream pat substitute? The poor man spoke with an earnest concern but underneath she saw it for what it was: fear.

He was afraid of her. They were all afraid of her. Sad, that such lavish attention could be garnered on the person posing the greatest threat. And she knew that Armand and his entourage were petrified that she'd take them to court, cry to the judge over the surgery, the pain, the agony of rehab she'd endured, all because of a slippery step at The Presidio. There was power in this, great power.

Harry Blacksworth was fit to be tied that she was now almost as much a regular as he. She secretly delighted in his obvious aggravation, though she remained civil, even cordial, during their encounters. Being at odds with her dead husband's brother in such a public venue would lead only to questions.

"Mrs. Blacksworth, may I get you another chardonnay while you wait for your guest?" Armand stood before her looking very European in his black suit, a maroon silk scarf tucked into the breast pocket.

She handed him her glass. "Thank you, Armand, I think I will."

He flashed her a smile and took the glass. The bow was almost imperceptible, but she noticed it.

The man's deference to her must infuriate Harry. It certainly cramped his style. She'd heard he'd taken to having his lunch at Mi Hermana's Restaurante most days. *Good.* Let him think about her every time he passed The Presidio. Harry Blacksworth thought he was the only one who could make a person's life miserable, but he was wrong. It might take her longer, but she'd see to it that she disrupted his life, even if it was as simple a consideration as where to have lunch.

He had no right to tell her how to handle her own daughter. Christine was her daughter, *hers*, and no amount of threats from him would change that fact. If he thought she was going to sit by and watch Christine make a mess of her life, then Harry underestimated her.

The meeting with Connor this evening, masked as a casual dinner engagement, was all part of the plan. Connor was Christine's future—handsome, attentive, heir to a fortune, a man Christine cared about and would come to love eventually, though never obsessively. The perfect combination for a comfortable life.

"There you are, Gloria." Connor Pendleton shrugged out of his trench coat, gave her a peck on the cheek, and sank into the chair beside her. "Sorry I'm late." He flashed her a smile. "I was talking to Tokyo."

"That's quite all right. I understand."

"We're close to doing a deal with them that could open up the market in Asia."

"I'm very happy for you."

"I'm heading to London next week." He nodded to Armand as he placed a bourbon on the rocks in front of him.

"I love London."

"I'm working on a possible merger. Huge deal. I want Christine to go with me, Gloria."

"Have you asked her?" She slipped a cigarette from its case. Let Armand tell her The Presidio was no smoking.

"Not yet. Christ, I can't get a minute alone with her anymore." He sipped his bourbon. "You know how she's been these last few months. Ever since Charles died, it's like she doesn't recognize her own life, for God's sake. She flits off to that damnable cabin every month without even thinking about it, but if I ask her to go anywhere, she turns me down flat. What the hell's going on, Gloria?"

She lit her cigarette, inhaled. "Perhaps you need to make your intentions known."

"What do you mean?"

"You've done quite a bit of talking. You say you love her, you want to be with her, but what have you actually done to prove it? Sometimes, women want action more than words."

"I've tried that. Remember the trip to New York? She flat-out refused to go, said it interfered with her *other* trip, though how the hell that became a regular thing, I'll never know."

"Connor." She could picture Connor and Christine's wedding photo in the *Chicago Tribune*. "Buy the ring. Give it to her."

"You think so?"

*Christine Blacksworth Pendleton, what a powerful name.* "Of course I do."

He finished his drink and reached for her hand. "Thanks, Gloria. I don't know what I'd do without you."

Her smile widened. It was wonderful to be appreciated. "We're going to be family, Connor. We'll stick together, you and I. You'll see, everything will be just fine."

# 22

SHE WAS ALREADY counting the hours until she could leave again. What was it that pulled her to Magdalena even when she was hundreds of miles away?

There were the obvious reasons: Miriam and Lily, but what else? What part did Nate play in her increasing desire to return? He stole great gaps of time throughout her day, filling her mind with memories, hopes that he might call her, confess he was thinking of her too, perhaps tell her he missed her, and then the enormous stretch of revelation . . . .confide he couldn't wait to see her again.

Of course, he didn't call.

Was Miriam right? Had he been using her to punish her father?

There was one other possible reason for her growing attraction to Magdalena.

Her mother.

She just wouldn't stop pushing and pulling,

making demands, even if they were subtle. *Greta cooked five pounds of prime rib and I need you to come for dinner tonight ... bring Connor, too. ... I bought us tickets to the theater ... Come, keep me company. ... Bloomingdale's is having a sale ... let me buy you that new coat you've been looking at. ...*

The quiet demands bombarded her until she ignored the phone, let her mother's voice fill the answering machine with dates and times. Was this how her father had felt? Had her mother overtaken him like a sweet elixir seeping into his veins, suffocating him with excessive consideration? Or had that merely been control?

The fact that Christine was sitting at The Presidio right now, waiting for Connor to meet her for dinner, was in some way her mother's doing. He might have called Christine, even made the reservations, but her mother was behind it.

"Christine."

Connor. His teeth were so white, his skin a deep golden bronze, even in spring, all the results of bleaching kits and tanning beds. She tried to envision Nate sticking a bleaching tray in his mouth or cramming himself onto a tanning bed. It would never happen.

"It's great to see you." His husky voice spilled over her, lending just the right inflection to speech, pitch, expression. He leaned down to kiss her.

She turned her face just in time so the kiss he'd intended for her lips grazed her cheek. He smiled and straightened, as though her action was acceptable, even normal.

"I've missed you."

She couldn't say she missed him, too. It would be too great a lie. She looked down at her wine glass, fingered the stem. "You said you needed to see me, that something had come up and you needed to talk to me right away."

"That's right. Something has come up." His smile faded. "Something of a most urgent nature."

"What? Is someone in your family ill?"

"No, nothing like that; you know my family, fit as race horses."

"Ever since Dad died, I get nervous when people say they have something 'urgent' to tell me."

He reached over and covered his hand with hers. "I do have something urgent to tell you, but I'd like to think it's going to make you happy, not nervous." He laughed, stroked the back of her hand. "Well, it might make you a little nervous, but it's a good nervous."

"You got the Tokyo deal."

"I did. Pendleton Securities is acquiring Rendo Investments."

"That's wonderful."

"The old man's pretty pleased, but you know he'll never come right out and admit it."

"I'm very happy for you."

"Thanks. But that isn't the urgent news I wanted to discuss." He reached into his pocket, pulled out a small black box, and laid it between them.

She forced herself to breathe. "What is it?"

He flipped open the box, angled it toward her. "It's our future. Marry me, Christine."

An enormous marquis diamond ring rested in the center of a creamy satin lining. It winked and glistened in the light, haunting her with promises she didn't want, tormenting her with a love she couldn't accept.

"Say something."

"I . . . I don't know what to say."

"How about, 'I'll marry you, Connor. I'll be your wife'?"

She knew he meant well and that, in his own way, he loved her. But it wasn't enough. He'd give her diamond rings, necklaces, trips, houses, cars, probably even a child or two, but he'd never be able to give her the one gift she needed: himself. That would be reserved for Tokyo and London and all the other cities and business engagements that would mark him as a world-class businessman, capable of negotiating and facilitating the ultimate deal.

"I can't." And besides, she didn't love him.

"I don't understand." His hand slipped away; he ran it through his perfect wavy hair.

"I can't, Connor," she said again, this time meeting his gaze. "I'm sorry."

"Christine, you can't just walk away like this. What have we been building these past two years? What was that all about?"

He'd never understand, so she merely said, "Consider it a due diligence of sorts."

"Oh, I see; you being the acquiring party who's decided not to do the deal?"

"It's a little more complicated than that."

"I don't understand you. Ever since your father died and you started taking off to that damn cabin, things haven't been the same. What the hell's going on up there?"

"Nothing."

"Then what's the attraction and why does it have to be the same days every month? Have you got somebody waiting for you up there? A mountain man, maybe?" He let out a harsh laugh.

"Why can't you just accept the fact that I don't want to marry you? Why does there have to be another person involved?"

"Is there?"

"No."

"You're making a big mistake, Christine."

"I'm sorry, Connor. I never meant to hurt you."

He snapped the velvet box shut and stood. "I'm not used to disappointment, but I'll deal with it."

He shrugged into his trench coat, stuffed the ring in his pants pocket. "But I'm not so sure about your mother."

"My mother? Does she know about this?"

"Of course. Doesn't Gloria know everything?"


"YOU'RE LATE."

"Just settle down, Gloria. Twenty minutes is fashionable where I come from."

She glanced at the tall, thin man with the slight stoop. She'd thought he was the epitome of a cowboy the first time she saw him, brown and leathery in cowboy boots and a black Stetson. But fourteen years had weathered him even more, toughened his skin like the hides on his granddaddy's Hereford farm he liked to tell her about. Lester Conroy was a Texas man, born and bred, and no matter that he'd lived in Chicago these past eighteen years, he would go to his grave a Texan.

"Well, Gloria, what you got for me this time?" He hitched up his jeans, rested bony fingers on his belt.

"It's my daughter, Christine." The man might look like a backwoods hillbilly with manure on his boots, but he was the best private investigator in the state of Illinois. He'd been setting traps for unsuspecting victims since his early days tracking fox and coyote on his granddaddy's ranch. The only difference between then and now, according to Lester, was that this prey walked on two feet, and the reward was a hell of a lot sweeter.

"Beautiful girl."

"She's been taking off every month, says she's going to her father's cabin in the Catskills."

Lester let out a low whistle. "You think she's going somewhere else?"

"It's a possibility." *God*, but she hated to admit it.

"I'll check it out."

She nodded, not meeting his gaze.

"You want me to let you know all the details, same as before?"

"Yes. I want to know everything."

"Consider it done."

"Good." She sucked in a deep breath, forced a smile. "Pour us a drink, Lester."

"You still drinking Crown Royal, straight up?"

"For times like these, it's the only thing that works."

"I hear you, Gloria." He started toward the bar, paused. "Damn shame about your husband. After all this time, I felt like I knew him."

"Nobody knew Charles, Lester, nobody."


CHRISTINE TURNED THE rented Saab off the interstate and headed toward Magdalena. Sixteen more miles and she'd be back in the town that was becoming more like home with each passing month. Beside her in a flat wooden box were the ribbons she and Lady Annabelle had won over the years: twelve first places, six seconds, and four thirds. She planned to give them to Lily, detail the events, and how she'd won or lost each. Next month was Lily's fourteenth birthday, and with it came her most anticipated present of all—a ride on a white horse, just like Christine's.

Lily had been waiting a whole year for this gift, a promise made by their father on her thirteenth birthday. Miriam had told Christine how she'd hesitated at first, pulled under by fear for her daughter's safety, but, after Charlie's death, she'd realized she had to let Lily ride her horse; it was Charlie's last gift to her, the one she'd remember the rest of her life.

Christine was excited to see Lily on a horse. She'd already ordered a riding habit, the same cream jodhpurs, black jacket, and black hat she'd worn in the picture Lily had hanging in her room. That was Lily's favorite picture; it had been their father's favorite, too.

*Their father.*

She no longer thought of him as *my* father, *Lily's* father; he was their father. *Lily was her sister.*

When she pulled up in front of 1167 Artisdale, the front door flew open and Lily came running out, her thick black pigtails bouncing, arms flying in front of her, face shining. "Christine! Christine!"

"Lily!"

"I missed you! I missed you!" She flung her arms around Christine's waist, hugged tight.

Christine buried her face in her sister's hair and whispered, "I missed you, too."

"Come inside." Lily grabbed her hand. "We have a surprise."

"Wait a second." She opened the car door, reached for the wooden box. "I have a surprise for you, too."

Lily's gaze slid over the box, and her blue eyes grew wide. "You first," she said, squeezing Christine's hand and pulling her toward the house.

Miriam was waiting for them in the kitchen, wearing a bright yellow T-shirt and jeans, hair hanging down her back in a loose braid. She was humming under her breath, sprinkling coconut on top of a two-layer cake. "Hello, Christine."

"Hello, Miriam." She walked over and hugged her.

"It's good to see you, dear."

"You, too." The fact that she meant it had stopped surprising her two months ago.

"Can I tell her now, Mom?" Lily pressed her hands together, squeezing them with impatience and excitement.

"Now's as good a time as any." Miriam set the knife down and moved the cake to the center of the table.

Lily let out a squeal, reached behind her, and pulled out two gifts. "Happy Birthday, Christine!"

"How did you know?" Her twenty-eighth birthday had been last Thursday. She'd gotten a silk shawl and a Louis Vuitton handbag from her mother and a diamond pendant necklace from Uncle Harry. From Connor, fortunately, she'd received nothing, not even a phone call.

"I know your birthday," Lily said. "May fifteenth. You're twenty-eight."

"That's an old lady, isn't it?"

"Yeah, very old," Lily giggled. "Here. Open mine first." She shoved the package into Christine's hands.

"Thank you, Lily." The gift was taped several times, the paper crumpled at the corners. She tore the wrapping, slid the plain white box out, and lifted the top. Nestled on a fluff of pressed cotton was a clear shiny stone in the shape of a heart attached to a silver chain. "It's beautiful." She fingered the heart, carefully lifted it out of the box.

"Lily picked it out herself," Miriam said.

Christine unclasped the necklace, placed it around her neck. "Miriam, will you help me with it?"

"Certainly." She hooked the glass necklace and moved toward Lily. "What do you think?"

Lily beamed, her blue eyes shiny through her thick glasses. "Now she has two necklaces. Mine and the other sparkly one," she said, pointing to Uncle Harry's birthday gift.

"I love them both because they're from two very special people."

"Me," Lily said.

"Yes, you."

"Who gave you the other one?"

"My—" she started, corrected herself, "our Uncle Harry. Did Dad tell you anything about him?"

"I know Uncle Harry." Her smile spread. "He was the baby in the family. Like me."

"That's right."

Lily beamed. "Uncle Harry," she murmured.

"He's not a baby, though."

"Nope. I'm not a baby, either."

"No, you aren't. Twenty-two more days and you'll be fourteen. I brought you an early gift."

"You finish opening yours first."

"I won't argue with that." She tore the wrapping from the square package, pushed aside swirls of tissue paper to get to the gift, a dark bowl nestled in bubble wrap. It was one of Miriam's bowls, black cherry with a smooth finish. "Miriam." She ran her fingers along the fine grain. "It's beautiful."

"Put your cheek against it," Lily said. "Feel how soft it is."

She did. It felt like satin. . . .

Lily eyed the box on the table. "My turn, okay, Christine?"

"Your turn." She handed her sister the box, watched her slide her bottom lip over her teeth as she opened it. "Ribbons! Ribbons!" Lily reached in and pulled out a fistful, waving them in the air.

"These are the ribbons Lady Annabelle and I won."

"They're mine?" Awe spread through her voice, as though she'd been gifted a great treasure, and perhaps in some way she had; Christine had given her a glimpse into her own childhood, a journey with a horse and rider Lily had long loved and admired. But she'd offered forth another gift as well: acceptance.

Miriam turned away, cleared her throat. "Let's sing 'Happy Birthday' so we can eat this cake!" Her voice cracked on the last word, and when her gaze swept over Lily, who was clutching the ribbons against her chest, there were tears in her eyes.

# 23

*D*AMNIT, HE WAS NOT going to feel guilty. So what if they were all celebrating her birthday? So what if she'd casually asked his mother if he were coming? So fucking what?

Nate pulled a beer out of the refrigerator, twisted the cap open. Damn if he'd feel guilty; he wouldn't. He knew it was going to be like this, knew there'd be the phone calls, even if they were from his mother, wondering where, when, why? *Shit*, hadn't they both said they were making a big mistake? Insanity was the word he'd used, wasn't it? Or had she said it? It didn't matter; either way, they'd been right.

They never should have slept together, never in five fucking million years. But deep down he knew he'd do it all over again, given half a chance. And that's what was driving him insane. He shouldn't *want* to be with her again, taste her, bury himself deep inside that heat. They were enemies, or as close to enemies as civilized people could get. He had no right thinking about her, and she had no right expecting him to come to her goddamn birthday party.

He took a long pull on his beer. Three more days, then she'd be gone. He could get through it, probably wouldn't even have to see her if she'd just take the hint and stay away from his place. Or he could shack up with Natalie Servetti for the next few days. Big tits but she talked too much. *Fuck*, he didn't want to screw Natalie. All he wanted was to stay in his own house, in his own bed, and he'd give his right nut to have Christine Blacksworth in it with him. That's why he knew he was screwed up, why he knew he couldn't trust himself to be alone with her.

Halfway through his second beer he decided to load the truck and head up to Boone's Peak to fish and finish off his six-pack in peace. By the time he stopped at Mertha's Kettle for a chili dog and fries, it would be dark. So he was a chicken shit? So he'd thought of this whole scheme in less than two minutes as a way to avoid seeing her? So fucking what?

He was on his way to get the cooler from the garage when he heard the car door. *Damn.* Ten more minutes and he would've been gone. Now he'd have to deal with it, with her. Nate opened the door before Christine had a chance to knock.

"People usually wait for invitations before they come barging into other people's homes."

"I need to talk to you."

"This isn't a good time." He was blocking the doorway, forcing her to remain below him on the wooden steps.

"Oh." Her gaze moved over his half-opened shirt, took in the unfastened belt buckle.

Let her think he was screwing somebody; it was better that way. "Like I said, I'm busy."

Her face turned a dull red, the color of the tulips in his mother's front bed. He watched her stumble to pull herself together. *Jesus*, she was beautiful—the eyes, a brilliant blue; the skin, perfect; the lips, full, pink. He cleared his throat, crossed his arms over his chest. "Good to see you again, Christine. Hope you had a nice trip down here." Civil, ordinary words, relegating their night together as incidental, unimportant, a body filling a need, nothing more, certainly nothing that might be misunderstood as the beginnings of a relationship.

She backed away from him, one step, two, then three, her gaze never leaving his. "I thought . . ." Bewilderment seeped into those beautiful eyes, and pain, yes, fuck it, pain. "Never mind." She turned and walked to her car, head high, movements slow, purposeful. Not once did she look back.

He didn't take his eyes off her until the Saab had rounded a bend and was out of sight. He stood in the doorway listening to the fading hum of the car's motor, picturing the exact stretch of road the tires would be hitting. When the sound disappeared he was left, once again, alone.


HE DIDN'T WORK ON Saturdays unless they were shorthanded or a machine went down. Then he'd spend the day, sleeves rolled up, alongside his men, doing what needed to be done to keep production going. The company supported eighty-nine families, and Nate felt responsible for all of them. If they were willing to work, he'd do his damndest to give them jobs, the same way his father had. Nick Desantro had sweated blood for the company. There were still a handful of lifers around, men and women who'd been with ND Manufacturing thirty-five years or more.

Jack Finnegan was a lifer; he was the one who taught Nate the business when his father died. Jack was the most trustworthy person Nate knew, a husband of forty-two years, father to five, grandfather to seventeen, and the best damn fly fisherman for fifty miles around. He lived two and a half miles from the shop, worked every Saturday, no matter the weather or the occasion; when his youngest daughter Sara Elizabeth got married two years ago, Jack worked the morning shift and made it to St. Gertrude's by noon.

It was Saturday; all machines were running, all jobs were on time, but Nate was at work, poring over inventory sheets. It was a pain-in-the-ass job, but it was a hell of a lot better than sitting at home feeling like a shit for what he'd done to Christine yesterday. *Stay busy, stay busy. Don't think about it.*

The plan might have worked if Jack hadn't meandered into his office, plunked his skinny ass in a chair, and said, "What the hell are you doing here?"

Nate kept his eyes on the sheets in front of him. "Inventory."

"Inventory? Hell, you ain't done inventory in ten years."

"That's why I'm doing it, to get back on track."

"What's her name, Nate?"

"Don't know what you're talking about."

"When a man does something he ain't done in ten years, something everybody hates doin', there's a woman involved."

Nate shrugged. "No, just trying to find a way to tighten up inventory."

"If you say so."

The old man was no fool. He saw a hell of a lot more than he owned up to. Most of the time he just kept it to himself, unless Nate was involved, then he took it as his duty to point out the trouble spots.

"There's no woman," he said again.

"Not even that Blacksworth gal, Charlie's daughter? What's her name?"

"Christine."

"That's right. Christine. What about her?"

"What about her?"

"Seems like I remember hearing your mother say something about the two of you—"

He looked up, met the old man's curious gaze. "There's nothing there."

"Too bad. She sounds like a great gal. Not bad to look at either."

"How would you know?"

Jack's gaze flickered. "I seen pictures of her. Charlie showed me lots of times. He was real proud of her."

Nate went back to his papers. The sooner he ended this conversation, the better. He'd come here so he wouldn't have to think about her, and now Jack was trying to open up a full-blown discussion. *Christ*, couldn't anybody just mind their own business? And what was his mother doing, telling Jack about him and Christine? Was she going to tell all of her church friends, too? And the neighbors up and down Artisdale Street? Why not just place an ad in the *Magdalena Press*: *Nate Desantro and Christine Blacksworth new couple, mother rejoices?*

"Jack!" The door flew open and Betty Rafferty stood there, balancing eight reams of copy paper in front of her. "Oh, Nate. I'm sorry. What are you doing here?"

"Inventory," Jack said.

"Inventory? You never—"

"I know, I know," Nate cut her off. "Today, I'm starting something new, okay?"

She shrugged, set the paper on the table in the corner. "I thought you were in here by yourself," she said to Jack, "reading the paper with your feet propped up."

"Yeah, yeah, that's me, the loafer."

Nate welcomed the disruption. Normally, he avoided Betty; her mindless chatter gave him a headache, but today he was glad for anything to divert Jack and his fishing expedition.

"Well, I'll leave you two alone. Nate, if you're hungry, there's blueberry muffins and banana bread in the lunch room, though I can't say how much of the bread will be left if you don't get to it soon. You know Ray loves my banana bread, says it's just like his mother used to make." She crossed her arms over her chest and nodded. "The trick's in the sour cream. I use a cup, not the fat-free kind, either, and I'll tell you, it does make a difference."

Nate rubbed his jaw. *Jesus*, but the woman could talk.

"Stop flappin' and start workin', Betty."

"I was just saying hello to Nate." Her voice

slipped into a warm, conspiratorial whisper. "Talked to your mother the other day. She sounds real good."

"She's getting along."

Betty's lips curved into a wide smile. "Hear you're seeing Charlie's daughter."

"Betty—"

She held up a hand. "That's fine, nothing wrong with that, nothing at all. Must just be the Lord's will." She looked at the ceiling. "You just never know how things are going to work out, now do you?" She winked at him. "She's a real looker, too, and nice, real nice. I think you two are perfect for each other. Perfect. Much better than the last one you had." She waved at both men, turned, and headed for the door. "Well, toodles," she called behind her, "I've got loads to do before noon."

Nate waited for the door to click before he spoke. "Jack?"

The old man was studying a frayed shoelace on his work boot. "Hmmm?"

"What's going on? Did my mother come in here and broadcast my personal life to everybody?"

"Don't listen to Betty. She don't know what she's sayin'. You know she's got a bigger mouth than that fifteen-pound widemouth I caught at the lake last year."

"Was my mother here?"

Jack pushed back his ball cap, scratched his

head. "Come to think of it, she did stop by one day last week. You was visiting a customer, I think."

"And nobody bothered to tell me she was here?"

He shrugged. "It wasn't no big deal. She stopped in, brought some corn muffins, said hello, and goodbye."

"After she told you all about Christine Blacksworth."

"That's right; that's about it."

Nate leaned back in his chair, crossed his arms over his chest. "We go back a long way, Jack. I trust you more than just about anybody I can think of."

"Thanks, Nate. Feeling's mutual."

"So I'm going to trust you to tell me how the hell Betty knew what Christine looked like and, worse, how she acted. Tell me, Jack, and by God, if you value our friendship, it better be the truth."

# 24

MIRIAM CARRIED THE laundry basket outside and set it down. It was a perfect day for drying clothes, sheets especially. She lifted Lily's sunflower sheet from the basket, folded it in half, and pinned it to the line. Tonight, when she crawled into bed, Lily would smell the fresh air on her sheets, rub her face in the soft fabric, and say that it felt like summer and sunshine.

Winter was gone, though it had stretched far into April, and spring had taken root, pushed the bulbs to the surface, sprouted their delicate heads in bursts of red, pink, white, and yellow that were now fading and shriveling to a dull greenish brown. Christine and Lily had visited Abbott's Greenhouse early this morning and returned with enough vegetable plants and seed packets for the entire street. They'd spent a good part of the day planting Big Boy tomatoes, broccoli, bell peppers, zucchini, lettuce, cucumbers, beans, even two blackberry bushes on the far corner of the property.

Miriam turned toward the eight-by-ten patch of dirt, staked out with markers reading *cucumbers, beans, zucchini,* and cages housing drooping tomato plants. Almost two seasons had passed since Charlie's death, close to five months since she'd heard his voice, watched the even movement of his chest as he slept, smelled him on her sheets. It was already a lifetime, and yet she could still remember the touch, the smell, the sound of him in painful detail. A few mornings ago, as she lay on his side of the bed, she had thought she heard him, was certain she smelled him. The sensations were so real, so ordinary, and yet anticipated, that later she wondered if her wanting had merely created the illusion.

Was this what happened when half of a whole was gone? Was the other person destined to wander through life, aching, empty, searching?

Thank God for Lily and Nate. She clutched a pillowcase to her chest. *Thank God for Christine, too.*

She was thinking of Charlie and how proud he'd be to see his daughters together that she didn't hear Nate's pickup pull in the driveway. It wasn't until he was ten feet from her that she turned.

"Where is she?"

The anger in his voice spilled over his body, seeped into his eyes, through his face, to the set of his jaw, just like his father's used to when he was on the verge of a rampage.

"Good heavens, Nathan, what's wrong?"

"Where's Christine?"

"In the house with Lily. Why?"

He ignored her question, turned and headed for the back door.

"Nathan." She dropped the pillowcase in the laundry basket. "What's going on?" She hurried after him, grabbed his arm.

"Let me take care of this. It's got nothing to do with you."

"I don't understand—"

"You will, soon enough."

He flung open the screen door and stepped inside. Lily was pouring two glasses of juice in the kitchen. "Hi, Nate. Want some grape juice?"

"No, thanks, Lily." His tone gentled. "Where's Christine?"

"In the living room." Her lips pulled into a wide smile. "Playing war. I'm winning."

"I have to talk to her right away. I want you to go to your room until I tell you to come out."

"Why? Are you mad at me?"

"No, Lily," Miriam said. "This is adult talk, that's all."

Lily set down her juice glass. "There's Christine's juice," she said, pulling her lower lip through her teeth.

"Good. Now, go."

"Don't yell, Nate."

"I'm not yelling, Lily, but I'm losing my patience."

She turned and ran out of the room. Nate headed for the living room with Miriam close behind.

"Nate? What's wrong?" Christine sat on the floor, legs tucked under her Indian-style.

"When were you going to tell me? After I was indebted to you even more, then you were going to spring it on me, so you could play me like a puppet? Was that your goddamn plan?"

"What are you talking about?"

"ND Manufacturing. The note. I know your name is on it."

Miriam leaned against the wall, took several deep breaths. *Dear God, not this way, not now.*

"How . . . how did you find out?"

"Do you think I'm stupid? Do you think my people aren't loyal to me?" He didn't wait for an answer. "Jack Finnegan told me all about it, how you came to visit him, told him you held the note but didn't want me to find out."

"I only wanted to help."

"Help? By coercing my own mother into letting you take over the note? That was helping? So you could control the company, control me?"

She met Miriam's gaze, then looked away.

"No more bullshit, Christine. How'd you do it? Threaten my mother with exposing Lily if she didn't sign? Huh? Tell me, is that how you people do business in Chicago? Rule through intimidation?"

"No—"

"Forget it. I don't want to know. Everything you say is a lie anyway." He stood in the middle of the living room, fists clenched, rage pouring out of every word he spoke. "I want you to leave, now, and don't come back. Lily shouldn't be around someone like you."

"Nathan, wait." Miriam forced the words out of her mouth.

"No, Ma, let me take care of this."

"No, Nathan." She had to speak up, had to tell him the truth. "Christine didn't bribe me or coerce me." *Oh, God, forgive me.* "The loan wasn't mine in the first place."

"What?"

"It was never my note, Nathan." She moved toward him, placed a hand on his arm. "You were having such a hard time keeping everything together, and I knew if you just had a little help—"

"Whose name was on the note?"

She sensed the second he figured it all out; his body tensed, and his breath stilled.

There was no way around the truth, not any longer. "Charlie signed the note."

He deflated then in one giant rush of air. "Blacksworth."

"It was the only way, Nate."

He shrugged off her hand. "And then, of course, Christine showed up and just stepped right in and took over. All this time, I thought it was the Desantro will prevailing, and it wasn't—it was the Blacksworth money that pulled us out."

"Please don't do this, Nathan."

"You know, I would rather have let it all fold than take money from them."

"What about your people? Don't the employees deserve a fair chance?"

"Not if I had to sell my own soul to help them out."

"You didn't, Nathan. Charlie simply gave you time to recover; you're doing the rest."

He dragged both hands over his face. "What would the old man say now? His own son has to take money from his mother's lover to keep the company afloat. That's pathetic, don't you think?"

"I think it says Charlie believed in you."

"The old man would tell him to take that belief and go fuck himself."

"Stop it, Nathan."

"You think Charlie Blacksworth's so wonderful, maybe the town should build a statue to honor his greatness. Huh? What do you think about that?" He spread his arms wide. "I think I'll start a petition, see how many names I can collect."

"You're out of line."

"I never remember you saying such wonderful things about my father, your *husband*."

She said nothing. How could she tell him that she'd felt nothing but relief when his father died?

"Wasn't he good enough, Ma? Were his hands too dirty for you?"

"Nathan! Stop!"

"I want to know. I've always wanted to know. Why didn't you cry over Dad at night the way you used to when your lover was gone? He was your husband, for chrissake, *my father*. Charles Blacksworth was nothing but a weak bastard who wanted the best of both worlds."

"He was an honorable man who loved me and Lily."

"Don't bring Lily into this; this has nothing to do with her. She was his daughter; of course he loved her."

"All parents don't love their children, Nathan, especially if they're born with," she paused, gathered strength, "a deficiency."

"You're saying we should all clap our hands because he loved his own daughter?"

"I'm saying some men would have run away."

"Only a coward."

"Dear God, I thought I was protecting you by not telling you the truth, but I think I've done more harm. Maybe if I would've just gotten it all out at the beginning things would have been different; you and Charlie might have actually gotten along."

"I have no idea what you're talking about."

"You will." Her mouth pulled into a sad, faint smile. "When your father and I married, we were very much in love and so happy when you were born. We couldn't wait to have another child, but instead I lost three babies before my fifth month. Something happens to a couple when they lose a baby; it makes them desperate, even irrational, the wanting is so deep, the loss so bleak. After a few years, we began to worry we'd never have another child. But finally, I was pregnant again, and this time, I didn't miscarry. We couldn't wait for the new baby, boy or girl, we didn't care." She blinked hard, swallowed. "Your sister, Anna Nicolina, was born three weeks early." The tears started then, spilling down her cheeks, onto her chin, her neck. "The top of her head was missing. She only lived two hours. I stroked her tiny body, praying to God for some kind of miracle and all the while knowing there was no hope. They let me hold her while she took her last breaths."

"Jesus, why didn't you ever tell me?"

She sniffed, swiped both hands across her

cheeks. "Because then I would have had to tell you that your father was at O'Reilly's Bar when your little sister died. I would've had to tell you that he deserted us, told me it was better she died. And then I would have had to admit to the hatred that filled my soul from the moment he spoke those words until he took his last breath on the shop floor. I would've had to tell you that your hero, the man you thought was next to God, had rejected his own daughter."

Nate looked away, closed his eyes.

"So I kept silent all these years. I did nothing to stop the animosity you felt for Charlie because I thought I'd destroy your love for your father, but now I see my silence is destroying your chance for happiness, for peace. Charlie may have been a weak man, Nathan, but he loved Lily." She touched her son's arm. "Stop this anger before it destroys you."

He stared at her, the pain and bewilderment of her revelation stretching across his face. He opened his mouth to speak, but no words came out. Then he turned and was gone.

## 25

HARRY TOOK A BITE of his ham sandwich and watched Greta reach for a glass bowl on the top shelf of her cupboard. *Nice.* His gaze followed the strong lines of her back, the firmness of her ass stretched over white shorts. *Very nice.*

He was sitting at a small oak table in Greta Servensen's tiny kitchen on Wendell Street eating the best damned ham and Swiss he could remember. He'd become a regular here, since the night Greta's car died at Gloria's and he'd given her a ride home. No matter where he was going, a banquet, dinner, the theater, and no matter where he'd come from, golfing, a bar, a benefit, he invariably ended up at Greta's, for a cup of coffee, to talk; hell, who knew why he ended up here, he just did. She didn't seem to mind; actually, after the initial shyness of having a man in her kitchen, he might even say she looked forward to seeing him.

And he looked forward to seeing her, too; not in

the confines of Gloria's buttoned-up house, where she had to wear a white-box uniform and old-lady tie shoes, but here, in her own home, with that golden hair falling down her back and those bare legs, strong and tanned.

She was killing him, bit by bit, with that laugh, those legs, that smile. *Oh, God*, she had no idea how bad he wanted to take her, right here, spread-eagled on the kitchen table. Every fucking time he walked through that door, he fought with himself, Doctor Jekyll and Mister Hyde: one part reveling in the pureness of their growing friendship, the cleanness of it, and the other saturated with lust and visions of her naked body covering his.

He could fuck any woman he wanted; hell, he'd been doing that for years. But friendship, especially with a woman—now that was rare.

"Harry, can I get you another seltzer?"

He shook his head, "No, thanks, I'm fine." Look at him, Harry Blacksworth, drinking seltzer water. What he really wanted was a scotch neat, but that would have to wait.

"Would you like another sandwich? Maybe half?"

"I haven't finished this one yet." He rubbed his stomach. "God, I'm going to have to start living at the gym just to work off what you've been feeding me."

She smiled. "I don't think so, Harry." Her voice softened. "You look perfect."

He looked away, tore into his sandwich. *Jesus*, now why'd she have to say that? He kept his eyes on the blue and white plate in front of him. *Shit*, she was supposed to be his friend; couldn't she tell how hard he was trying to keep it that way?

"Harry?"

"What?" He needed to go home, right now.

"What's the matter?"

He heard the concern in her voice, all soft and sincere, slithering over him, wrapping itself around his cock, tormenting the hell out of him. He needed to go home right now and call Bridgett.

"Harry?"

"Nothing. Okay? Nothing's the matter."

She was leaning against the sink, her long, golden hair falling around her, pale blue shirt unbuttoned at the neck, revealing a swell of breast. He pushed the plate away, stood up.

"I've gotta go." *Now*, he had to get out of here *now*.

"But I made you lemon meringue pie."

There was the hurt in her voice, making him feel like a class-one asshole. He couldn't help it; he was a class-one asshole.

"Take some with you."

That was it. "I don't want your goddamn pie. Do

you understand?" He took a step toward her, then another until he had her backed against the sink.

"Harry?"

Her eyes turned a liquid blue, her lips parted, and her head fell back. He knew the actions for what they were, though he doubted she understood herself. Desire. Women had been looking at him like this since he was a teenager, offering themselves up to him. And he'd been taking since then, too, mindless of anything but the push and pull of physical pleasure. Did she think he was going to stick around and hang his towel next to hers, sit beside her in church, shovel the walk? Didn't she know it would only be about sex? Didn't she care? He was trying to protect her from himself, from his worthless lechery.

She reached out and touched his cheek. "Underneath all of this, there is a good man. I see it."

*Jesus!* He grabbed her hand, thrust it away. "What the hell's wrong with you? I'm not a 'good man.' Would a good man be thinking about bending you over that table right now, with your kids asleep in the next room?" He saw the tears starting. "No, don't start. Please." He backed away. "*You* are the good person, Greta. You. And the best thing I can do, the one decent thing, is to *not* touch you."

She stood watching him, face wet with tears, eyes bright, and, for the first time in years, he wished his life had been different, wished he had been different.

"Goodbye, Greta." He took another step toward the door. "I think it would be best if I didn't come here anymore." And with that, he opened the door and walked away from the one true friend in his life.

SHE WAS PACKED TO go, and if she left right this minute, she'd still make the flight. Christine tossed her overnight bag into the trunk of the Saab. The past several hours were still a blur: Nate standing in the middle of the living room learning the truth about his father, Lily crying because "Nate had acted scary," and Miriam sitting beside Christine on the couch, sipping tea and talking into the early-morning hours about losing her baby girl and her husband in the same day, learning to move on, and finally, loving Charlie Blacksworth.

Christine hadn't cringed when she heard this last part; it was easier to understand now, after piecing Miriam's life together. But there was still her father and his duplicity—one man, two lives. Would she ever understand *his* motives?

She'd be back next month for Lily's birthday and the momentous horseback ride. Nothing would keep her from seeing Lily's face the first time she climbed on her mount. Nate would be there, too. Given time and different circumstances, they might have shared something. She took a deep breath and closed the trunk. How was it that she'd dated Connor for almost two years and yet their break up had left her with none of the emptiness she felt right now?

"Christine! Christine!" Lily scrambled toward her, waving a photograph in her right hand. "Here." She held it out. "I almost forgot."

"Oh, Lily." It was a picture of the two of them standing arm in arm in front of Miriam's flowerbed. Their smiles were wide, bodies relaxed, leaning into one another. They both had on red shirts and jean shorts, a seeming coincidence that Christine later learned was no coincidence at all, but merely Lily's eagerness to emulate her sister, which explained her reluctance to dress in the morning before Christine did.

"Take it with you," Lily said, lips parted, waiting.

"Thank you, Lily. Thank you very much." She pulled her sister to her, felt the small arms hug her tight.

"One more month," Lily whispered against her shoulder, "one more month and then I get to ride a horse just like you."

Christine stroked her sister's hair. "One more month. That's it, Lily, one more month."


SHE FOLLOWED THE back road leading out of Magdalena. The picture of her and Lily rested near the gear shift column, and she caught herself glancing at it every few minutes.

How had her father done it all those years? How had he pretended, or maybe he hadn't pretended, maybe he'd really cared, had truly wanted to be with her mother and herself . . . maybe, just not enough. . . .

She didn't hear the truck barreling down the road, horn blaring, engine roaring, until it was almost on top of her. She pulled over, close to a dented guardrail, and waited for the truck to pass, but it didn't; instead it swerved to a stop behind her.

*Dear God, who—Nate!*

He moved toward her, closing the gap between them with long, purposeful strides. "What the hell was that all about?" His large, dark frame filled the window.

"What are you talking about? You're the one who almost ran me off the road."

"After I tried signaling you to stop for two hundred yards."

"I didn't see you."

"Obviously."

"Why were you signaling me?"

He straightened. "I need to talk to you."

"I . . ." She glanced at her watch. "I've got to be at the airport—"

"Screw the airport."

He stared at her, waiting . . . what choice would she make: Chicago or Magdalena . . . him . . . or her other life?

"Okay."

He nodded then, a quick jerk of his head, but she saw the relief that crossed his face. "Follow me back to my place." Then he turned and was gone.

She spent the next fifteen minutes calling herself a fool. Why wasn't she on her way back to Chicago? She'd miss the flight. For what? He'd told her he didn't care about her, that it had been sex, nothing more.

*What was she doing?*

Will pushed her forward, forced her up Nate Desantro's blacktop driveway. As she stepped out of her car she realized she really had no choice; she *had* to do this.

He was already opening the door as she walked up the path, remembering the previous time she was here. "No guests today?"

"What are you talking about?"

"The last time I was here, when you told me I should have called, you were obviously occupied."

"No, I wasn't."

She followed him inside. "Yes, you were," she said to his back.

He turned. "No," he said, in a forceful voice, "I wasn't."

"But—"

"I wasn't. I haven't been . . . not since you."

"But why—"

"Jesus, you ask a lot of questions." He moved toward her. "Haven't you ever heard of a ruse?"

"Of course. But why—"

"Isn't it obvious?" He reached out, stroked her shoulders, eased her toward him. "If a small-town country boy like me can finally figure it out, not that I haven't done my share of denying, then surely a sophisticated city girl like you knows why."

"You've confused me since the day I met you. Why don't you tell me?"

"You're in my blood, Christine Blacksworth. You've been in my blood since before I ever met you, probably the first time I saw those blue eyes staring back at me from one of Lily's pictures."

"But why—"

"Why not just come clean, admit it?"

She nodded.

"Hard to do when you're fighting it like hell, even harder when you're bent on hating the woman's father." His fingers worked their way down her neck. "But the most god-awful part is feeling like a hypocrite, berating my mother for waiting four goddamned days a month for him and then finding myself doing the same thing. How the hell is that for fucking irony?"

She reached up, stroked his hair. "I wasn't even out of Magdalena, and I was already thinking about next month."

"Christ, what a mess."

"We'll figure it out."

He trailed a finger along the inside of her shirt. "Do you think that's what they said when they first met?"

"I don't know." She shivered, leaned into his touch.

"You feel wonderful." His fingers cupped her breast, slid inside to rest on her bare skin. "Like silk," he murmured, brushing his lips against hers.

"Nate," she breathed. "I missed you."

"I missed you, too." He eased her onto the couch, his hands working her body, his lips and tongue covering her as he removed her clothing. She pulled at his belt buckle, grabbed the snap on his jeans, took hold of the zipper, yanked it down.

"Nate ... please ..."

He entered her, still half-clothed. "I can't wait any longer," he said, burying himself deep inside her, his hands cupping her buttocks. "It's been too long ... too damn long."

She pulled him closer, wrapped her legs around his hips, and moaned as his tongue filled her mouth, stroking, pleasing, possessing. It wasn't enough ... it was too much.... She fell apart, shreds of blistering heat filling her seconds before Nate stiffened and spilled himself into her.

She didn't know how long they slept, his body sprawled over hers, his face tucked against her neck, his breathing even, peaceful. This was how it should be, this overwhelming feeling of oneness. She stroked his hair, lifted it to her lips.

She missed him already.

"Warm enough?"

"Hmmhmm. I thought you were asleep."

"I was . . . until you started touching me."

"Was that a complaint?"

"Hardly. Let's go to bed."

"I'm not the least bit tired."

She felt him growing hard inside her. "Good. Neither am I."

# 26

THE PHONE WOKE HER. She reached for it, not wanting to wake Nate. "Hello?"

"Christine?"

"Miriam. Hi."

"You're," there was a short pause, "you didn't leave today?"

"Uh, no."

"Oh."

"Nate wanted to talk to me. He kind of tracked me down."

"Oh." The tone changed from question to understanding. "I see."

Did she "see" Christine lying naked in bed next to her son? "We—" What could she say? "We had a lot to talk about."

"I'm very happy for both of you, Christine."

"Thank you."

"Well, I was calling to invite Nate to dinner, but I'm sure he won't be interested."

"I can ask him when he—" she caught herself, before she said "wakes up."

"Don't give it another thought, dear. You and Nate spend as much time together as you need."

"Thank you. Miriam?"

"Yes?"

"In all the years my Dad came here, he was never late getting home. I mean, maybe by an hour or so, but he never stayed longer than the four days."

"No, he didn't."

"I know, and well, my mother's expecting me; she always has this dinner thing, I'm sure Dad told you about it. It's a really big deal for her. So, what am I going to tell her?"

There was a quietness to Miriam's voice when she spoke. "I wouldn't worry about it, Christine."

"But Miriam, my mother thinks I'm at the cabin. God, this would kill her. What should I do?"

"Do you really want to know what I think?"

"Yes, I do."

"Your mother already knows."

"What?"

"She knows, Christine. She's always known."

A sharp pain shot to her right temple. "You mean since I've been coming here?"

"I'm sure she knows you've been coming here, but no, that's not what I'm talking about. Your mother knows about me . . . and Lily."

"No. She can't."
"Christine, she's known for years."

GLORIA SAT ON THE edge of her bed and sipped her Crown Royal as she re-read the report Lester Conroy had delivered an hour ago. Then she slipped the photos out of the manila envelope and studied them. Christine and that mountain man; good Lord, what had gotten into her? No wonder she wasn't paying attention to Connor; she'd taken up with a lumberjack.

*Another Desantro.*

She probably sympathized with them, the mother, the son, the retarded daughter. And then, to have the audacity to call last night, at six-fifteen, no less, when the lamb was ready to come out of the oven, and tell her she wouldn't be home that evening. That was it, no excuses, no apologies.

She finished her drink, poured another.

*Miriam Desantro.* She hated the name, hated the face, the hair, the long legs. God had punished her for her sins, punished both of them for their unholy acts; he'd given them a retarded child. The girl's name was Lily, and she wasn't smart and beautiful like Christine. There'd be no scholarships, no academia for her. The best she could hope for would be a job as a bagger at the local Stop-n-Shop.

She reached for her bottle of Vicodin. Life was much better lived through a calm haze. She tapped a pill into her palm, lifted it with her fingernails, and popped it in her mouth. Then she slid back onto the peach and blue floral comforter and reached for her drink. Christine would be here soon, filled with apologies and excuses, no doubt. Harry would be coming, too, pain in the ass that he was. He was the most worthless piece of human flesh she'd ever seen, and he didn't have to think she wasn't watching him and that little German piece making goo-goo eyes at each other.

If it weren't so difficult to find someone who could make a decent pork roast and not pocket the silverware, she'd have fired Greta already, just to annoy Harry. She reached for her pack of Salem Lights, slid out a cigarette. Things were going to change; Christine was about to learn that her mother was a fighter who was not going to sit by and watch her daughter ruin her life.

Gloria was halfway through her third cigarette when they arrived. She stamped out her cigarette and eased off the bed. She'd listen to Christine's apologies, and, when the guilt was riding high, she'd mention Connor's name. A smile slipped across her face. By God, there'd be a wedding yet.

She smoothed her hair, ran both hands over her Chanel pantsuit, and opened the bedroom door.

Their voices reached her as she descended the staircase, Christine's quiet, Harry's a few octaves below his usual bellow.

"Well, well, the proverbial sheep has returned."

They turned, faces unsmiling. Why were they looking at her like that, as though she were the accused?

"What's wrong with the two of you? Why are you looking at me like that?"

Harry lifted his glass, took a drink, his eyes still on her. Christine cleared her throat, once, twice, opened her mouth to speak, but nothing came out.

"What? For God's sake what is it?"

"Did you know, Mother? All these years, did you know?"

She stiffened, her daughter's words yanking the air from her lungs. *Breathe, in and out, breathe.*

"Did you?"

"I don't know what you're talking about." She waved a hand in the air, headed for the bar. "I need a drink."

"Mother?"

She poured a double, took a healthy swallow. "Harry, are you ready for a refill yet?"

"Actually, no."

She poured another splash into her glass. "Well, then, why do the two of you look like you've just come from a funeral?" She forced a smile. "I wasn't happy you didn't come yesterday, but I'm not going to disown you over it."

Christine took a step forward. "Did you know about Miriam Desantro, Mother?"

In fourteen years, that name had never been uttered in her presence. "Who?"

"Miriam Desantro, the woman Dad went to see every month for the past fourteen years."

Gloria sank into a chair, splayed a hand across her throat. "Dear God," she whispered, lowering her head. "I never wanted you to find out."

"You knew all this time, and yet you never said anything?"

"No. We loved each other. It was just ... sometimes couples have to compromise ..."

"How could you live like this?"

"*I was his wife.*"

"He loved another woman."

"He loved *me.*"

"It was all a lie."

Gloria looked up, swiped at a tear. "It was necessary. That lie gave you this house, those summer trips to Italy and France, that fancy education you're so proud of."

"How could you?"

"How could I not? Your father owed me, owed us, and I was not going to let that woman take it all away."

"Miriam didn't take anything from you. It was you and Dad—"

"Do not defend that woman in front of me, and do not say her name again."

"Why? Does not saying her name make her disappear? Does it make the whole situation go away, almost as if it had never happened? Is that how you did it all these years? Pretending?"

"I don't like your tone of voice."

"I don't like finding out I've been trying to protect my mother from something she's known about for years."

"We all have to compromise at one time or another."

"But you compromised yourself, Mother."

"I did what I had to do."

"Did you ever confront him, even once?"

"It wouldn't have mattered. By the time I found out, it was too late. There was a child."

"Lily."

"Yes, Lily." The name stuck on her lips, but she forced it out. "The retarded girl. I thanked God for delivering that one small piece of justice."

"She's a wonderful girl."

"Wonderful? Of course she's wonderful, as long as she's petting a dog or participating in the Special Olympics. But what about college, or even trade school? Is she ever going to have a career? A family of her own? Will she ever be able to function independently in *any* capacity? Of course not. She'll be a burden to society her entire life, and the best she can hope for is to bag groceries at Stop-n-Shop."

"That's a horrible thing to say."

"The truth isn't always pretty, Christine."

"You should've divorced him, given both of you a second chance."

"A second chance? For what? A two-bedroom condo and child support? I don't think so."

"Did you really love him?"

"That's a ridiculous question."

"Did you?"

"Yes, I loved him," and then the rest of the truth slipped through her lips, "but I hated him, too."

"You did this all for yourself."

"*He owed me.* He owed us. Can't you see that? Who do you think was taking you to the orthodontist and your piano lessons when he was with her? It was me, *me*."

She jabbed a finger against her chest. "I've got pictures of them together. Would you like to see them? See what I saw? I've got pictures of you, too. Surprised?" Her lips curved into a bloodless smile. "Yes, I know all about you and your mountain man, Christine. Nathan Desantro, isn't it?" Her smile faded. "Connor's the one for you, not this Jeremiah Johnson you've been seeing."

"That's enough, Gloria." Harry stepped away from the liquor cabinet and moved toward her.

"Enough? Spoken from the king of excess? You have no idea what's enough."

"Stop bullying her. She's tired of it, and I'm sure as hell tired of hearing your bellyaching. It's nothing but a damn pity party."

"Shut up, Harry."

"I mean it, Gloria. Leave her alone."

She was so tired of him and his arrogance, making demands, *as though he had a right*. Harry Blacksworth was nothing but an alcoholic degenerate with a fat bank account and a well-known last name. Take the latter two away and he was nothing but a drunk, bedding women half his age. "You," she didn't try to mask the loathing in her voice, "you have no right. She's my daughter, Harry, mine."

"You're trying to run her life, just like you tried to run Charlie's, with guilt." He moved closer. "I can't let you do that anymore, Gloria. I'm going to tell her the truth."

"No!" *No*, he wouldn't. She sucked in a breath through half-closed lips, let the oxygen fill her lungs, her brain, block out Harry's words.

"I never meant to hurt you, Chrissie. God, I'd cut off my right arm to protect you . . ." His voice was fading, blotted out by her breathing, *in and out, in and out.* . . . "Your mother and I . . ." Gloria breathed harder, faster, but the words seeped through, spiraled to her brain. "Your father was in London at the time; he'd been traveling quite a bit . . . your mother was angry and lonely . . . and I, hell, I was resentful of Charlie. He had everything; I was just a trouble-maker, a nuisance. I wanted to take something that was his, prove to myself that I could do it . . ."

Her body shrank into the chair, pulling away, growing smaller, smaller as Harry's words filled her. "We had an affair. Jesus, I am so fucking sorry. It was over before Charlie got back. We realized what a mistake we'd made, and all we wanted was to forget it, get on with our lives, pretend it never happened. But . . ." That one word gouged her heart, ripped it open, still beating, and tore it into tiny shreds. "We couldn't forget it." Piece by piece, she shriveled: hair, nails, skin, the weight of her body dissipating, only her breathing remained forceful, loud, but not loud enough to block out Harry's confession. ". . . six weeks after your father returned, your mother was pregnant. Jesus, God, to this day, I don't know, I just fucking don't know if Charlie was your real father or if it was me."

# 27

THE BITCH WAS BACK, and it had taken her less than forty-eight hours to strike. Harry should have known she wouldn't fade quietly into that goddamned floral chair of hers. Hell, he'd almost felt sorry for her the other day, sitting there looking old and defeated. She hadn't said a word after he confessed their affair, nothing. As for Chrissie, she wasn't willing to talk about it yet.

Life was such a goddamn mess sometimes. You tried, you screwed up, you exercised damage control, tried again, screwed up again, and on and on it went until you died. Maybe Charlie had felt the same way; maybe he'd been as screwed up as Harry. The more he learned about his older brother, the more he understood that the person everyone saw, the CEO, the husband, the father, the brother, wasn't really Charlie Blacksworth at all. The real Charlie was the poor bastard who died on the road that night, the one who tolerated Chicago but lived in

Magdalena . . . the one who was too much a coward to fight for his own happiness.

Harry knew about cowardice; he'd been a coward most of his life, giving up on himself and the rest of the world when he was a mere seventeen and the love of his life had killed their baby with his father's money. Nothing mattered after that except disappointing the old man and screwing himself up on a grand scale. Numb, that's what he'd been after, no feeling, nothing. Except for Chrissie, her he cared about.

*Shit*, he guessed he cared about Greta, too, not as a piece of ass, but as a person. No matter how much he wanted to bang her, he couldn't, much different than *wouldn't*, which implied reasoning on a higher moral ground, a quality he knew he lacked. He wished to hell Greta would realize it, too, stop telling him shit like what a good man he was and looking at him as if he were fucking superman. He was a sleaze bag, a worthless human being, a no-good womanizer. Couldn't she see that? Greta was too good for him. Her kids knew, so did her old lady; that's why they scurried away to the corners when he came, kept their eyes on him, mouths clamped shut. But they watched, and they saw. And they knew.

He'd told Greta he wouldn't be back, that there was nothing he could offer her; he was a taker, a user. But when he heard her voice on the other end of the line tonight, the promises fell away, leaving nothing but a friend in need.

Gloria had fired her, of course, not until after the last dish from the veal scallopini dinner was dried and put away. He knew she'd gotten rid of Greta to punish him for telling Chrissie the truth. Why the hell did everybody always want to shut him up the few times he decided to tell the truth?

He'd be at Greta's soon. The kids and the old lady would be waiting for him, lurking in the corners. Elizabeth, Arnold, and Helene. What the hell kind of name was Arnold for a seven-year-old? Thank God the kid was big for his age; he'd have to learn to throw a mean right hook to defend a name like that. Elizabeth was a smaller version of her mother, fair, blond, blue-eyed. And the old lady, Helene—she reminded Harry of a Clydesdale.

He pulled his Jag into the driveway behind Greta's Toyota. Last week he'd had one of the mechanics from the dealership replace the carburetor and the fuel pump. The car was a piece of shit but it got her around—most of the time.

"Harry!" Greta flew out the door as he eased out of the car. She ran up to him, feet bare, blonde hair flying, and threw her arms around his waist.

"Easy, Greta. You'll make me heave the pork chops and potato I had for dinner."

"I'm sorry, Harry." She pulled away, arms falling

to her side. Her eyes were wet, tears slipping down her pale skin. "I . . ." she looked away, ". . . I don't know what to do."

"You're going to get another job, girl; that's what you're going to do."

"I've already looked in the papers, but there is nothing, only cooks at McDonald's and Bob Evans. I even asked Mrs. Blacksworth if she'd write a letter for me, but she said only that she would think about it."

*Bitch*. "So? Who needs her anyway? We'll find you something."

"I need to find a job, Harry. Fast." She hugged her arms around her waist, blinked hard. She looked so young and vulnerable in her pale pink T-shirt and jean shorts, so incapable of supporting an entire family.

"Calm down, Greta. Let's go inside." He put his arm around her shoulder, careful not to pull her too close, and guided her to the front door. "Where the hell is the kids' father? Doesn't he send you money?"

"When the courts can find him, but that's only once, twice a year, maybe."

"Jesus, that's ridiculous."

She opened the door. "That's real life, Harry."

*Shit*, the world really was fucked up.

"Would you like something to drink? Coffee? Tea?"

She never offered him anything stronger, though

he hadn't missed the bottle of Zinfandel on top of the refrigerator.

"Coffee's fine," he said. There were sounds in the next room, scampering feet, whispers; the spies were readying in position.

She fixed his coffee, black, two sugars, and set it down in front of him. "I knew she wasn't crazy about me, but I thought it was just her way of separating herself from the hired help."

"It wasn't your fault." He took a sip of coffee. "It was mine."

"Yours?"

"I told the truth, and she got pissed."

"But what did that have to do with me?"

"She's trying to get me where it hurts." He looked away. "She knows I," he almost said "care about you," changed it to, "don't want to see anything happen to you." He kept his gaze fixed on a pen mark on the wall, about three inches long, eye level.

"That's a horrible thing to do."

"Yeah, well, that's Gloria." It was safe to look at her now; the topic of him and his feelings had shifted back to Gloria.

"Maybe since Mr. Blacksworth died—"

"Hell, this has nothing to do with Charlie's death. Did you really not know she was like that two seconds after she hired you? You've been with her almost a year."

"I don't know. She's not much different than most of the other employers I've had."

"What do you mean?"

"They don't like hired help to forget their place."

"That's bullshit."

Her lips pulled into a sad smile. "Harry, you are so worldly, and yet, in some ways, you are so naive. I go into other people's homes, cook their filet mignon and veal in their fancy ovens, wash dishes that cost more than a month's rent, and then I come home," she waved a hand in front of her, "to this."

"So?" He shifted in his chair, not wanting to notice the chipped paint on the walls, the cracked linoleum, the old stove. "So?"

"So, this is life, Harry, my life, and I accept it. I cook other people's food and wash their dishes so I can feed my own family. I keep my mouth closed, and I do not gossip. I believe I do a good job." Her voice dipped. "That is why it's so hard to believe Mrs. Blacksworth has fired me."

"I told you, Greta, this has nothing to do with you. It's me. She's getting back at me."

"I have to find a job, Harry."

"I know." Hell, he could float her a loan, even give her the damn money; that wasn't the problem. But how could he do it and not make it look like a pathetic gesture or payment as an expectation for services to be rendered, namely, Greta Servensen's delicious body? She might see it that way, might actually consider it, but in the end, honor would force her to turn away. Wouldn't it? *God*, he hoped it would. She was one of the last decent people he knew, and he didn't want to think she could be corrupted, especially by a no-good bastard like himself.

He was responsible for her predicament, whether she saw it that way or not, and he'd figure a way out of it, whether she liked it or not. He leaned back in his chair, crossed his arms over his chest, and tried to come up with a solution.

"It's not your fault, Harry."

He didn't answer. Maybe she could work for him, cook his food, clean his house . . . naked . . .

"It's God's will, I know this."

. . . naked and moving over him . . .

"God will provide, somehow. I must stay strong, continue praying."

. . . his hand in her hair . . . that beautiful, fucking hair . . .

"Do you believe in God?"

. . . her tits dangling in his face . . .

"Harry? *Harry?*"

"Huh? What?"

"I asked if you believed in God."

"What?"

Her face turned a dull red. "I was telling you

how I think everything that happens is God's will," she paused, flushed a deeper red, "and then I asked if you believed in God."

"Oh. Sure, sure I do."

She let out a sigh of relief. Maybe she'd half-expected him to say he didn't believe in God, that he didn't believe in anything. Well, he'd surprised her, and himself.

"Do you know anyone who needs a cook, Harry? Your friends, maybe? I could clean, too."

She wasn't getting within a football field of any of his friends. They'd all be after her, single and married. "No, sorry, I don't."

She sighed. "I understand."

"We'll find you something; just relax."

They sat together in the tiny kitchen with the chipped paint and cracked linoleum, Harry staring at the pen mark on the wall, Greta staring at Harry. Despite the pain-in-the-ass indecision looming over them, he felt needed. And it was a damn good feeling.

The answer hit him as he studied the smudged end of the pen mark trailing over the off-white wall. It was a perfect solution, brilliant, actually. "I've got it."

"Did you think of someone?"

"Hell, yeah, I thought of someone." He jabbed his chest. "Me."

"What? I thought you didn't want—"

"I love to eat, right? So, I go to The Presidio four, five times a week, and Mi Hermana's Restaurante the rest. Sometimes, I don't like the crowd, sometimes the sauces are a little off, but still, I go. So, why don't I open my own restaurant? Huh?"

"You want to open a restaurant?"

"Hell, yeah, why not? There's this little dive on Monroe Street, been for sale forever. We could gut it, remodel it, the whole works."

"We?"

"You'd help me run it; actually, you'd probably run it, hire a few cooks, whatever. Me, I'd be the front man." He smiled, excitement rippling through his body, a sensation he hadn't been able to generate without the help of booze or a woman in a long time. "I've got a shitload of money, Greta. Maybe I'll start buying up properties that everybody else has given up on, kind of like me, and restore them, turn them into something worthwhile."

Greta whispered, "I think that's a wonderful idea. You'll give those places a second chance."

"Yeah, I guess that's what I'd be doing." He'd be giving himself a second chance, too.

She reached out, covered his hand with her own. "You're a good man, Harry Blacksworth."

"No, I'm not," he said, easing his hand from beneath hers. "I'm just a drowning man trying to catch a few breaths." He opened his wallet, pulled out three hundred-dollar bills. "Get some groceries. I'll send more to tide you over, just a loan, until we can get things up and running."

"Thank you, Harry."

It was there in her eyes, the invitation, calling him, offering. "I'll be in touch." And then he turned and left, not because he didn't care, but because he did.

# 28

SHE GLANCED AT THE packages stacked four-high in the passenger seat. They were Lily's gifts wrapped in orange and pink foil: a pair of riding boots, tan jodhpurs, a black jacket, and a riding hat. Nate had already called the stable and lined up a seven-year-old white mare named Jenny's Promise. Christine thought of her own fourteenth birthday party, the itchy taffeta dress, the too-tight black patent leather shoes, the faceless men and women wishing her happy birthday.

Lily's birthday was different. Hers was small and intimate, with homemade cake and ice cream, pink lemonade, and fourteen balloons dangling from the kitchen light.

Christine turned off the exit leading to Magdalena. She knew this trip by heart, the tiny airport, the rental car counter, the road stops, even the billboards. They were all part of her life now, this stretch of road leading from the airport to her other life, her other home. She understood now how her father had felt, this pull from one commitment to another, one family to another. One month had passed since Uncle Harry revealed the truth about himself and her mother, one month of her mother's solicitous phone calls, bouquets of flowers, dinner invitations, theater tickets, everything but a mention of that night. Uncle Harry had been oddly quiet.

Her whole world had shifted, and there was nothing anyone could say or do that would right it. Perhaps time would ease the shock, but right now it was all too much, so Christine shut it down and concentrated on Lily and the gifts in the passenger seat.

When she pulled onto Artisdale Street, she spotted Lily sitting on the front steps, head tipped to the sky, lips pursed as she blew bubbles. When Lily heard the car, she jumped up and bolted down the steps, yelling, "Christine! Christine!" The second Christine set foot on the sidewalk, Lily hurled herself at her. "I missed you!"

Christine buried her face in her sister's hair, inhaled the clean scent of Johnson & Johnson's. "I missed you, too."

"I've got some presents for you." She eased out of Lily's embrace and reached into the front passenger seat to grab the gifts. "Happy birthday, Lily."

"These are all mine?" Her eyes grew wide as she opened her arms to accept the stack of gifts.

"All yours. Where's your mom?"

"Inside. Making peanut butter cookies with the kisses for you to take back."

Miriam was the kind of mother who took care of children, period, whether they were her own or not. Had her own mother ever baked cookies for her, not by instruction to others because she'd done that her whole life, but actually measured the flour, beaten the eggs, used her own hands, her own *time*?

"Smell them?" Lily smiled up at her as they headed for the kitchen. "She made them so they'd be done when you got here."

"Oh." For some insane reason she wanted to cry.

"You want some milk with yours?"

"Sure." Once, she remembered her mother making instant pudding for her when she had her wisdom teeth out.

"She's the best mom in the whole world, isn't she, Christine?"

"Uh-huh." It was chocolate pudding, kind of chunky from undermixing, but she'd eaten every last bite.

"Yup. She's the best."

Rows of peanut butter blossom cookies lined the kitchen counters, covering every available space.

The kitchen sweltered from the afternoon sun, oven heat, and no air conditioning.

"Mom? Where are you, Mom?" Lily set the presents down on the kitchen table, peeked out the back door. "Mom?"

"Down here. I'll be right up." The sound of footsteps filled the air until Miriam emerged from the basement, arms filled with bags of flour and sugar. "Whew." She set them down on the table and wiped a hand over her forehead. "I almost thought about staying down there a while to cool off. How are you, dear?"

"Fine." Christine walked over and kissed her cheek, started to back away. Their eyes met, and she felt the tears starting again. She threw her arms around Miriam and hugged her. "It's good to see you."

"Tough month?"

"Very."

"I'm sorry."

"I know." She eased away, forced a smile. "I'm really looking forward to this weekend."

"We're *all* looking forward to this weekend," Miriam said, smiling at Lily, who stood by the kitchen table watching them.

"Christine? You okay?"

"I'm fine." She swiped a hand over her eyes. "Just fine, birthday girl."

That made Lily smile. "Can I open my presents now?"

"If your mom doesn't mind."

"She's been counting the minutes, no seconds, until you came," Miriam laughed, scooping peanut butter blossom dough onto a cookie sheet. "Heavens, I wouldn't dream of making her wait a second longer. Go ahead, Lily."

She ripped through the presents, first the hat, then the jacket, the jodhpurs, and finally, the boots, squealing higher with each gift. "Can I try these on?" She held the jacket in one hand, the boots in the other.

"Sure. I'll help you."

"Thank you, thank you so much!" She ran to Christine, threw her arms around her middle, and squeezed tight.

"You're welcome, so much. Come on; let's get this on you so I can take your picture."

Lily talked and giggled as she worked her way out of the red and white short set and into the riding outfit. Christine wouldn't let her look in the mirror until she was completely dressed with her boots on and her hair tucked underneath the black hat.

She led Lily to the full-length mirror behind the door. "There. Now look."

Lily opened her eyes and stared at herself. She inched closer, eyes narrowing behind her thick glasses. Gently, as though afraid the clothes might tear, she reached up and fingered the hat, then the jacket, working her way down to the boots, all the while watching herself in the mirror. She straightened and turned to the right, then left, tilting her head forward, backward, to the side.

"Happy birthday, Lily. You look beautiful."

Lily sniffed, wiped a tear away with her finger. "Daddy's girls, that's us."

Tears clogged Christine's throat, making speech impossible, so she merely nodded and pulled Lily into her arms.

"We miss you, Daddy," Lily murmured into Christine's hair, "we miss you."


"IT'S LATE, NATE. I'D better go."

He stroked her back. "It's," he squinted at the alarm clock on the nightstand, "two o'clock. That's early; stay a while."

"I can't."

"I missed you." Hard to admit, but the truth.

"I was here last night."

"So? I can't want you more than once a month?"

"What about Lily?"

"What about Lily?"

"What will we say when she comes looking for me in the morning and I'm not there?"

"Maybe you got up early and went for a drive."

"For five months, she's had to drag me out of bed; do you think she'll buy that?"

"Hell, I don't know." He lifted her hair, let the weight of it fall through his fingers. "I want you in my bed."

"I'll be in your bed." Her voice spilled over him.

"Not the bed I slept in as a kid, this bed, the one with me in it."

Her laugh made him hard all over again. Would he ever get used to the feel of her on him, the smell of her, the taste? *God*, he hoped not.

"Lily can't wait until Saturday."

He eased his fingers along her hip. "I don't want to talk about Lily right now."

"But she's—"

He flipped her over, spread her legs. "She's my kid sister and I love her, but right now she's cramping my style." He buried himself deep inside her, moved slowly. Christine let out a soft, low moan and clutched his shoulders. He laughed, nuzzling her neck. "Now, what did you say about leaving?"

She did leave at three-thirty with a promise to work on a plausible excuse to stay overnight the next time, which would be tonight if he had his way.

He'd missed her this past month, had found himself watching the calendar, mentally crossing off the days until she'd be back. Lily became his companion in the waiting game. She never tired of sharing little snippets of conversation she'd had with Christine—how Christine was afraid of spiders, how Christine once ate a whole box of Thin Mint Girl Scout cookies, how Christine loved the way the sky lit up during a thunderstorm, and even how Christine missed her father. He was eager, almost desperate to learn all he could about her. And each day he watched Lily mark a big, red X on the calendar, narrowing the days until she'd come back to them.

How in God's name had his mother done it all those years? Four days on, twenty-seven off, some months maybe twenty-six and the big bonus in February when the gap lessened to twenty-four days in between. He couldn't see himself settling for four lousy days a month, even if they were great days. Okay, they were incredible days, but still . . . he wanted more.

What if she couldn't give any more? Would he tell her to go away; it was all or nothing? Did he really want to go back to the nothingness of his prior existence? People walked away all the time, telling themselves they'd be giving up a huge piece of self if they compromised, but in the end, the uncompromised individual ended up with a whole piece of nothing. Go figure.

Maybe that was the way his mother had felt fourteen years ago when she'd had to choose. What would he do in that situation? Hell, sometimes life was just too damned complicated.

He dozed off and on, his brain filled with images of Christine. She was standing beside the bed, watching him, her dark hair framing her face, her naked body cast in perfect shadow. He reached for her, eager to pull her to him, touch her—

The phone rang, splitting his dream in half. *Christ.* He grabbed the receiver. "Hullo?"

"Nate?"

"Lily."

"Today's the day, Nate." She giggled into the receiver. "I'm going riding today."

"What time is it?"

"Seven-oh-two."

"Lily, it's seven o'clock in the morning; you aren't riding until one."

Silence. "Are you mad at me, Nate?"

"No, honey." He yawned. "I was just asleep, that's all."

"Christine said it was okay to call."

"Christine's awake?"

"Uh-huh, since six-thirty."

He smiled. "What'd you do, wake up the whole neighborhood to tell them you're going riding today?"

She giggled again. "No, just you and Christine, and Mom."

"Mom doesn't count; she gets up at five."

"Yup. When are you coming over?"

"Is Mom making breakfast?"

"Pancakes."

"I'll be there in fifteen minutes."

"Okay."

"Okay. Lily?"

"Huh?"

"Today's your day, girl; it's going to be the best one ever."

# 29

JENNY'S PROMISE WAS BIG and white like one of those horses with a horn in the middle of its head. She wanted to touch her, feel the soft fur under her fingers. Christine had told her not to make any quick moves; horses didn't like that, and they didn't like it if a person was scared. She said they could tell if somebody was scared from the way they smelled. Lily wasn't scared; she was excited. Jenny's Promise was watching her. She smiled, waved at the white horse.

The man said she was next, just five more minutes. She straightened her hat, looked behind her. Mom, Christine, and Nate were right there, waiting, too. Mom had the camera ready for when she got on Jenny's Promise. She was going to take Lily's picture, and it would be just like the one of Christine and Lady Annabelle.

*Happy, happy, happy!* She looked up at the sky, smiled. *Watch me, Daddy. Watch me ride just like*

*Christine did. Me and Christine, we're your girls, Daddy.*

"Should we go over everything one more time?"

Lily turned to Christine, shook her head. "I'm ready." She giggled, straightened her hat again. "How do I look?"

"Like a rider," Nate said, "a real rider."

"Press your knees against the horse's belly, toes up in the stirrups, remember?"

"Yup. And don't make any loud noises."

"That's right. And what do you do if she starts to go faster than you want her to?"

"Pull back on the reins."

"Very good."

Lily beamed. "What do I do if she takes off for that fence and tries to jump like Lady Annabelle used to?"

"She won't, and besides, Lady Annabelle was trained to jump."

"But what do I do?"

"Well, if she heads for the fence, you lower your head, grab her neck, and hold on tight."

"Okay." Lily smiled, pushed up her glasses. "Maybe we can learn how to jump like you and Lady Annabelle."

"How about one thing at a time?" Nate said. "Right now, why don't you get on so Mom can take a picture of you?"

"Okay."

The trainer, a man everyone called Mr. Lipton, came up to her. "Lily, we're ready."

"Okay." She rubbed her hands together, let out a tiny squeal. "It's time. I love you, Mom. I love you, Nate. I love you, Christine."

"We love you, too, sweetheart," Mom said.

She turned to go, remembered one more thing. "Christine, you got my watch, right?"

Her sister held up the gold pocket watch. "Right here, waiting for you."

Jenny's Promise was furry, not soft like a bunny, but kind of woolly like the neighbor's dog, Jasper, in the winter. She thought she'd like to press her face to the animal's side, feel the woolliness on her skin. Mr. Lipton helped her into the saddle and took hold of the reins.

She was so tall now, taller than Nate! Lily grinned at them, wanting to wave but not wanting to let go of the knob on the saddle. Her mother snapped her picture as she smiled down at them, happy and excited to finally, *finally*, be on a real horse. Mr. Lipton gave her the rules, but she knew them already. Christine had been teaching her for three days. It was hard to listen, hard to think about anything but riding the beautiful white horse.

"I'll walk twice around the ring holding the reins, and then I'll let you try by yourself." Mr.

Lipton patted the horse's shoulder and they were off, walking and then bumpity-bumping along in what he called a trot. Jenny's Promise was so big, her ears so pointy. Once, twice around with Lily holding the knob on the saddle, toes pointed up, knees pressed into the horse's sides. She looked up at the sky, grinned. *Are you watching me, Daddy? Can you see me now?*

"Okay, Lily," Mr. Lipton handed her the reins. "Now you go twice around by yourself, and I'll watch. Just remember what we went over. Okay?"

"Okay."

"Good luck. You can do it."

She eased the horse into the ring, talking to her as they walked. "Isn't this so much fun, Jenny? What do you think? Huh? I think it's fun." They moved along the path, the sun beating down on them. "Do you like the sun, Jenny? Do you get too hot?" She giggled. "Do you ever get a bath?" They made the first round and started on the second. "Does that thing hurt your mouth? I won't pull too hard, okay? Is that better?" She leaned forward a little, whispered, "You know, my sister, Christine, had a horse that looked like you. Her name was Lady Annabelle, and she won ribbons. Lots of them. Did you ever win a ribbon, Jenny? Huh?" She patted a patch of fur. "We could win ribbons, I bet, me and you. What do you think?" *Pat, pat, pat.* She glanced at the white fence in front of her. "Maybe if Mr. Lipton saw you jump he'd let you be my horse, and we could win ribbons together. Blue's first place." They were almost halfway around; the stretch of field past the white fence was green and soft-looking. "We could win lots of ribbons. Do you want to win a ribbon, Jenny? Do you want to be my horse?"

They *could* win lots of ribbons just like Christine and Lady Annabelle. They could be just like them. Mr. Lipton just had to see that Jenny could jump.

"Let's jump, Jenny. Let's jump!" Lily kicked the animal's sides hard like she'd seen cowboys do in the movies when they wanted to get their horses to run. Jenny's Promise let out a yelp and took off, straight for the fence, fast, faster. "Go, girl!" Lily leaned in low, clutched her arms around the horse's neck, just like Christine had told her to do.

She didn't hear the screams behind her; there was nothing but the sound of hooves beating against the ground, the feel of the wind on her face, the rhythmic speed of Jenny's Promise's body, moving and rising, high, higher, lifting them over the fence in one perfect jump.

*We did it! We did it!*

Lily's eyes were squeezed shut, a smile on her face, when the horse stumbled and threw her to the ground. Jenny's Promise recovered, tore across the field, stopping several hundred feet away, where she lowered her head and began grazing. Mr. Lipton was the first to reach Lily, the first to notice the unnatural bend to her leg as she lay face down in the moss-green pasture, the riding hat several feet in front of her. He swore under his breath and made the sign of the cross, then knelt down and gently eased her onto her back. Lily's eyes fluttered open, and she whispered, "I did it. Just like Christine."

HARRY FLIPPED THROUGH a client file and made a few notes. He'd done a little preventive maintenance, that was it. It was Christine's client, but she hadn't been around much lately, so he'd handled it.

He could see why she liked Magdalena so much. He'd made the trip after Christine called him, half-hysterical about the girl. It was just a broken leg; the kid was smiling and digging into a box of cherry cordials when he visited her at the hospital. She even called him "Uncle Harry." What the hell, why not?

The instant he looked into Miriam Desantro's hazel eyes, heard her soft voice, he knew why Charlie had fallen for her. She was a genuine piece of humanity, sincere, gracious, kind of like Greta in a way, and not bad to look at, either. The son wasn't the son of a bitch Harry thought he'd be. Chrissie hardly left his side, and he was glued pretty tightly to her, too. If Harry's mother had been shacking up with a married man for fourteen years, *and* had a kid with her, he doubted he'd be rolling out the red carpet when the guy died. Either way, Harry liked the guy. He wasn't a Connor Pendleton, thank God. Actually, he was quite civilized, quiet, but that was better than running at the mouth all night. Chrissie said he'd had a full beard but shaved it the morning after the girl broke her leg because she'd never liked it, said it was "too scratchy."

The knock on the door yanked him from his thoughts. "Come in."

It was Chrissie, arms loaded with a stack of files. She looked pale, thinner. In the two weeks since they'd been back, he'd hardly seen her; she'd been holed up at home doing paperwork or God knew what, or buried in her office. "Hi, Uncle Harry, can I come in?"

"Hey, Chrissie girl. You and the cleaning lady are the only ones brave enough to step foot in here. Come on in."

She closed the door behind her, set the files on one of the chairs next to his desk, and sat in the other.

"What's this?" He pointed to the files.

"Client files." She fidgeted in her chair. "Some things I need to go over with you."

"Oh?"

"It just isn't working, Uncle Harry. I just can't do this anymore."

He didn't have to ask what; he knew. She couldn't live the life anymore, not since she'd found another one, a real one. "I know."

"You do?"

"Give me a little credit for having at least a tiny bit of gray matter up here," he said, pointing to his head. "And I'm not talking about the hair, either."

"I do give you credit, Uncle Harry. You don't give yourself enough."

"You're probably right, but you didn't come here to talk about me, did you?"

"No."

"You're coming to dump these files on me, hoping that because I've been sneaking around helping you out, that maybe now I'll start taking an interest in the company and handle some of your clients?"

"Well, kind of."

He held up a hand. "I'm not finished yet. You're doing all of this so you can clear your conscience and head back to that damn boyfriend of yours."

"I thought you liked Nate."

"I do, but that doesn't mean I want him stealing you away."

"He isn't—"

"He already has; that whole damn town has. His mother, him, the girl, even that old geezer, Jack what's his name, they're all in love with you."

She smiled. "Finnegan, Jack Finnegan."

"Whatever."

"I have to give something back, Uncle Harry. I'm going to teach the people of Magdalena how to protect their money, make it grow, through investment strategies, savings, debt reduction, maybe I'll even show them how to apply for a small business loan, analyze mortgage rates—"

"Okay, okay, I get it."

"Those people need me, and I need them."

"Yeah, I guess." She was slipping away; he could feel it.

"Nate said he might even consider starting a custom furniture-making business. I could help him with that, get all the financing in order, maybe even make a small investment, if he'd let me. And Miriam and Lily need me. I want to be there for them."

"Okay, enough. I get the picture."

"I'll be back to see you, and you'll come see me; it's not that far."

"Sure." He twirled his pen between his fingers. "You tell your mother yet?"

"No."

"Are you just going to let her find out when you don't show up for Christmas dinner?"

"I don't know. It's not something you slip into casual conversation."

"Are you ever going to forgive her?" *Are you ever going to forgive me?*

"Some day. I can't deal with that whole issue right now. Uncle Harry?"

"Hmmm?"

"I love you."

"I love you, too, kiddo."

"And whether or not you're my biological father, you did more for me these last months than any father would do for his daughter."

"I don't know about that—"

"Thank you, Uncle Harry, for being a father to me when I really needed one."

He opened his mouth to speak but, *damn it*, he couldn't get the words out. He coughed, cleared his throat, once, twice. "Charlie—"

"Was a good father, too." She reached across the desk and squeezed his hand. "I don't want to know which one of you is my biological father. I've been lucky enough to have two fathers in my life, and that's how I want to leave it."

He nodded. "If I'd known you'd be looking at me like a father, hell, I would've watched my mouth around you."

She laughed. "If you did, Uncle Harry, you wouldn't be you."

"You've got a point there."

"I've got something for you." She reached into her pocket, pulled out a shiny gold object. It was his father's pocket watch.

"What the hell? Where'd you get that?"

"Lily gave it to me." She laid it on the desk, eased it toward him. "She said since you were the baby in the family you should have it, at least until she graduates."

"No." He gripped the armrests on his chair, pushed himself away. He'd spent half his life hating that goddamn fucking watch, secretly wishing his father would consider giving it to him, knowing he wouldn't. "I don't want it."

"Listen to me, please. Dad gave this watch to Lily because he wanted to break the horrible significance associated with owning it. When Lily looks at it, she sees beauty and she sees Dad. She wants you to have it now. Take it."

"I . . ." He eyed the watch, still keeping a respectable distance from it.

"Take it, Uncle Harry. Don't let your father have that hold over you. Take it; think of Lily, the little girl who changed all of our lives."

He reached out, touched the watch's face.

"It's yours now, Uncle Harry."

He covered his hand over the watch, felt its smooth surface mold into his palm. "I'll have to thank her." It was all he could manage.

She stood and walked to his side of the desk. "She'd like hearing from you."

He let out a long sigh. "Guess you're getting ready to head out?"

"My suitcase is already in the car."

"Does Nate know you're coming?"

"No, I didn't know myself until two hours ago."

"Good. Keep him guessing." He eased out of his chair and pulled her into his arms. "You take care, girl. And you better damn well not forget where I live."

"Never." She hugged him tight, buried her face in his jacket. "Thank you." He swore she whispered something else. *Dad?* It sure as hell sounded like it, but he didn't have the guts to find out.

"You better get going, Chrissie, before I change my mind and try to force you to stay here."

She kissed his cheek and smiled up at him. "You're a good man, Uncle Harry."

"Yeah, good for nothing."

"I love you."

"I love you too; now go already. Jesus, I really am going to change my mind. I mean it, damn straight I do."

Her laughter filled the room. When she reached the door, she turned and raised a hand in silent goodbye. Then she was gone.

How could parents raise children and then watch them walk out of their lives? Were they all masochists? Why would they do that to themselves? He knew the answer, deep down; he'd felt it when Chrissie told him she loved him. They did it because for all the pain and heartache children brought, they gave back equal amounts of pure, limitless joy.

The phone rang, and he thought it might be Greta calling about menu selections for the restaurant. *Harry's Folly.* He'd thought of the name himself. He didn't care what the hell she served as long as it wasn't that goddamn radicchio. He wondered sometimes if she fabricated reasons to call him. *Damn*, but the woman didn't give up. He'd told her they were no good together, that he wasn't the settling-down type, and didn't she go and invite him to Sunday dinner? And didn't he go and accept? She was wearing him down, he could feel it, with that little German accent of hers and that damn smile, but truth was, he wasn't fighting as hard as he used to; maybe he wasn't fighting much at all anymore.

What the hell. He picked up the phone, "Harry Blacksworth."

"Excuse me, Mr. Blacksworth, this is Belinda. I'm looking for Ms. Blacksworth."

"You're the new girl, aren't you?"

"I've been here six months, sir."

"Like I said, the new girl. Ten years will make you the old girl." He laughed.

"I'm sorry to bother you, sir, but is Ms. Blacksworth available?"

"No, she's not. She went home." *Home.* Hell, yes, there was truth in those words. "What did you need?"

"One of her clients is on the line." Pause. "It's fine, Mr. Blacksworth. I'll just take a message. I'm so sorry to bother you."

"Slow down. Belinda, right? Maybe I can help."

"Excuse me, sir?"

"Novel idea, I know. Tell you what, why don't you take a message and tell her client I'll get back to him in fifteen minutes or so. Then bring me the file and I'll see what I can do."

Silence.

"Belinda?"

"Thank you, Mr. Blacksworth, thank you so much."

"You're welcome." He hung up the receiver and settled back in his chair. The gold pocket watch lay in the middle of his desk, its power diminishing under the memory of the young girl who'd changed all of their lives. Harry reached for the watch, pressed it into his palm, and laughed.

# Epilogue

HE WOULDN'T BE expecting her for another sixteen days. Christine fit the key he'd given her last month into the lock and opened the door. Streams of late afternoon sun escaped through the half-drawn blinds, casting shadows in the darkened rooms. She walked quietly toward the bedroom, half-hoping he'd be asleep so she could enjoy the luxurious thrill of waking him. Just the thought of touching his hard body again made her breath quicken.

But the bedroom was empty, the bed unmade. She glanced out the back window at the twenty acres of wooded backyard Nate loved. And there he was, dark and glistening, naked to the waist, as he lifted wood into the bed of his truck. Heat pooled low in her belly as she watched him move with the graceful fluidity of a jaguar coupled with the overpowering strength of a mountain lion. She slipped through the double glass door and onto the deck.

Nate must've heard the sound because he looked up, shielding his eyes from the sun, then slowly stripped off his gloves and moved toward her. Without his beard, he looked more vulnerable, yet somehow more untouchable. He stopped a few feet from her, his face dark and unreadable.

"Surprise," Christine whispered, suddenly unsure of the wisdom of her unplanned visit. Maybe he really did only want to see her four days a month. Maybe he wasn't ready for a long-term commitment. Maybe—

Nate pulled her against him, ground his mouth over hers in a fierce kiss. When the kiss ended, she looked up at him and said in a breathless whisper, "I thought I'd surprise you."

Still, he didn't smile, merely stared at her, his dark eyes burrowing deep into her. "You surprised me, all right." He kissed her again, his tongue searching the depths of her mouth, his hands kneading her buttocks, pressing her against his erection.

"Is that good or bad?"

In answer, he lifted up her skirt and eased her panties off. When he straightened, he opened his fist and gazed at the satin thong. "Peach," he murmured, "my favorite."

Christine felt weak and breathless as she watched him unbuckle his belt and yank down his jeans and boxers. Anticipation thrummed through every inch of her body as he lifted her, wrapped her legs around his waist, and entered her in one powerful stroke. The mindless, needful mating began as Nate pumped into her, hard and fierce, his hands molding her buttocks, forcing her closer. She rode him in frantic pleasure, whimpers of ecstasy escaping her lips until he threw back his head, groaned, and exploded with her in a burst of white heat.

Nate eased her off him and pulled his boxers and jeans up. "I need to sit down," he said, falling into a deck chair a few feet away. Christine followed and slipped into the chair beside him.

For several minutes his gaze remained on the woods in front of them. She desperately wanted to reach over and touch him, but something in his expression stopped her.

"Nate?"

"I don't know why you're here, but I'll take whatever I can get. Hell, I'll take one day a month if that's all you're offering." He ran both hands over his face and said, "Guess that makes me nothing but a goddamn hypocrite."

"Look at me, Nate."

He turned to her, torment straining his face.

"I'm here. Now. I'm not leaving."

"What are you talking about?"

"Lily's fall opened my eyes. My suitcase is in your bedroom. I'm not going back to Chicago."

He hesitated, clearly confused. "You want to move in here with me?"

Heat crept up her neck to her cheeks. "I was hoping to," she said in a small voice.

The muscles in his face relaxed, and the smallest smile inched across his face. "A woman usually waits to be asked."

She trailed her fingers up his thigh and murmured, "I'm waiting."

"Come closer." His words poured over her, rich, velvety, sexual.

She inched forward, her fingers settling near his crotch.

"Closer." He pulled her onto his lap and kissed her lightly on the mouth. "This is where you belong. I love you, Christine Blacksworth. I want you by my side, every day, for the rest of our lives."

"Until death do us part?" She leaned in and kissed him again.

"Damn straight."

"If that's a proposal, I accept."

His smile faded. "I never thought I'd thank God for sending Charles Blacksworth to Magdalena, but you're here because of it, and for that, I will always be grateful."

"I love you, Nate." She looked into his dark

eyes, saw the love there. "From this day forward," she murmured, stroking his jaw, "I'm yours—three hundred sixty-five days a year."

He brushed his mouth over hers and whispered, "And all the nights that go with them."

# About the Author

WHETHER AWARD-WINNING author Mary Campisi's romances are contemporary or historical, one thing is certain: they will pull you apart and put you back together but never in quite the same way. *A Family Affair* is Mary's fifth romance novel.

When she's not writing or following the lives of five very active children ages fifteen to twenty-two, she can be found digging in the dirt with her flowers and herbs, cooking, reading, or, on the perfect day, riding off into the sunset with her husband on the back of his Honda Shadow.

Mary would love to hear from her readers. Please visit her website at www.marycampisi.com. Reach her by e-mail at mary@marycampisi.com or by snail mail at Premium Press America, Attn: Mary Campisi, P.O. Box 159015, Nashville TN 37215-9015.